UNCOVERED LOVE

ALINA LANE

VON RIPS PUBLISHING

ISBN: 978-1-7368977-4-4 (ebook)

ISBN: 978-1-7368977-5-1 (paperback)

Cover Design by: Y'All That Graphic

Edited by: Jessica Snyder Edits and Happily Editing Anns

Printed in United States of America

https://alinalane.com

Created with Vellum

❀ Created with Vellum

JOIN ALINA LANE'S NEWSLETTER

Want to receive exclusive news, content, specials and giveaways!

Subscribers are always the first to hear about Alina's new books and projects.

See the back of the book for details on how to sign up.

Gram
I miss you everyday.

ALLY

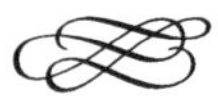

WHO DOESN'T LOVE A PARTY?

Music, dancing, food, and cake on a warm August night in a lovely backyard. Really, what more could a girl want?

And the fact that we're celebrating a double wedding? Even better! The joy is practically fizzing in my veins.

Also, it's possible I'm a wee bit tipsy and there's more than just joy in my bloodstream right now.

The four newlyweds have captured everyone's attention—Arik's twirling Kate around the temporary dance floor while Gram and Ben are receiving hugs and handshakes from friends and family. They all look gorgeous, decked out in beautiful clothes and with cartoon hearts circling their heads.

I love tonight!

Maybe it's the alcohol, or maybe it's the rose-colored glasses and candy hearts of romance, but I don't care.

If there was ever a time…

I turn to look for my girls. Emma and Elle are sitting with Ma at a nearby table, and love for them swamps me. The perpetual juice stain surrounding Emma's lips is spread in a wide grin, and Elle is chowing down on her second slice of cake. They're occupied for a few minutes.

Standing, I skirt around the table and move toward the corner where Connor and Rob are avoiding the festivities.

Tall, built, and so fucking handsome he's hard to look at sometimes, Connor Murtry is laughing at something Rob's saying. Getting the man to smile is a task for God himself, but Rob managed it. I can count the number of times I've seen it over the years.

And if I thought he was devastating in his normal uniform or flannel shirts, the coordinated suits the groomsmen are wearing are enough to make me drool on myself. The way Connor's shoulders fill out his jacket should be illegal. Or mandatory.

"Come on, grumpasaurus," I tease as I step close and grab his beer bottle then pass it to Rob. "You're gonna dance with me."

The first notes of the chicken dance song blare through the speakers.

Perfect.

Maybe the silly song will get him to loosen up a little bit.

"Als, no." A pained wince accompanies his reply, and glee crackles inside me.

"Yes. You've danced with everyone else here"—something I'm trying hard to ignore – "so you can dance with me once."

I tug on his sleeve. Resignation slides through his chocolaty brown gaze before his body gets the memo and he follows me onto the dance floor.

We're stopped four times by friends before we make it out to the center of the backyard, and just as we're getting ready to boogie, the song changes to "Adore" by Dean Lewis.

Thank you, universe.

Connor starts to back away from me, but I snag his jacket.

"One dance. Please?"

Wordlessly, he pulls me into his arms and keeps a solid six inches of space between us. This isn't exactly what I had in mind, but I'll take it.

We sway side to side, and every chance I get, I scoot a little closer until I'm tucked into his solid chest.

Tipping my chin up, I stare into his dark gaze, shooting him a smile. Some of the tension leaves his arms, and a sigh gusts out of him as he pulls me in tighter. Inches—tiny, insignificant inches—separate us, and if I rose to my toes, our lips would line up perfectly.

Connor's a mountain of a man, but my heels line us up in the most delicious way.

"Having fun?" I ask quietly. If my people are happy, I'm happy, so I want to know.

"With the dance or the wedding?" His chest rumbles against me when he speaks.

"Either. Both."

He squeezes my hand. "Yeah, it's a good party."

Nice evasion. Even so, the hand that rests at the base of my spine like a fiery brand tightens almost imperceptibly. My nipples pebble against the industrial strength padding of my bra, and the familiar rush of desire flows through me.

I want to taste that plump lower lip. Gently sink my teeth into it. Hear his growls and sighs of pleasure.

None of that is going to happen though. I've been stuck on Connor Murtry for years, and it's become second nature to stuff down my feelings for him. He acts like a brother to me and has never shown any romantic interest in this divorcée with two little girls.

All the signs have always told me to run in the other

direction, but no matter how hard I try, I've never been able to kick my attraction to him.

Shoot your shot.

The inner voice I can never shut up is right there at the forefront, teasing me, tempting me with the what ifs.

What if I rose to my toes and laid my lips on his? What if I had the kiss I've thought about for years?

What if I crossed that self-imposed line and it didn't blow up in my face?

"What about you?" Connor asks.

"What about me what?"

His lips curve in a slight smirk. "Are you having fun?"

Oh, that's right. We were talking about the wedding.

"Yep. Don't get me wrong, the ceremony was beautiful, but this? Watching my friends drink, dance, and have a great time is even more awesome."

His head cocks to the side. "But what about you—are *you* having fun?"

"I am." My gaze finds his mouth again, and I can't help but think that I'd have a lot more *fun* doing something else with him.

Fuck it. I'm going for it.

I start to rise, my eyes locked on his, the heat of him brushing along my chest.

Connor's swift intake of air is the only thing separating our mouths as I lean in.

"Hey, guys." Arik appears beside us. "It's about time for the bouquet toss. They want us to clear the dance floor for setup."

My heels fall to the ground as Connor yanks his hands away from my body, his features shuttering as he wipes his hands on his pants.

Like he's wiping away the feel of me.

That's a pretty clear rejection. I brush past him and make my way to the cake table for the umpteenth time tonight.

Cake never lets me down.

Taking a bouquet of flowers to the face and chest should be the least of my problems, but the fast-flying foliage is the straw that broke the camel's back.

After I caught the bouquet, I did my best to stay busy, because it was either that or hit up the cash bar and drink my feelings away.

What the hell was I thinking?

"Ally! Get over here and bring the flowers." My brother's voice booms out over the music, and he's waving me over. All the guys are crowded around Connor, slapping him on the back and laughing, but I can't tell what's going on.

I make my way back to the center of the yard where they're setting up a chair, and when the realization of what's happening hits, I want the ground to open up and swallow me whole.

Connor caught the freaking garter, and since the heat-seeking missile of bridal flowers plowed into me like a runaway train, that means I have to sit in a chair and let him put the garter on me.

No, surely, they won't make me—

"Do we really have to do this?" Every ounce of me doesn't want to sit in that damned chair, and the one dance I managed to browbeat out of Connor earlier in the evening is coming back to haunt me right now.

"Sure do. It's tradition." Jackson takes way too much pleasure in ushering me over and shoving my ass down into the chair. There's a gleam in my brother's eye that I can't decipher, and frankly I don't want to.

"Hey, uh, you okay?" Connor asks gruffly from my right.

I clutch the flowers tighter to my chest. He is staring at me in concern, so I loosen my hold on the beautifully crafted cottage bouquet and let it fall to my lap. "I'm fine."

The laughter and cheers of everyone around me was so welcome earlier, but now I'm just exhausted, tired, and nursing a sore heart.

Flashes spark around us as the photographer and our friends capture the moment with their cameras and phones, and I'd give up cupcakes for a year if I could get out of this.

One of my most fervent fantasies is about to come to life —Connor's hands are going to be *up my dress*—but surrounded by fifty of our closest family members and friends while it happens makes it both mortifying and scandalizing.

You know what? I'm gonna enjoy this while I can.

You'd think that Connor being one of Jackson's best friends means I'd be able to squash my attraction to the man because if there's anything that kills attraction to the opposite sex, it's proximity over time. But my desire for him has only gotten stronger over the years, which bodes ill for me considering his response to the tiny almost-kiss.

I can't trust my instincts with men. My track record is horrendous. And I know better than to pine for a man who wants less than nothing to do with me romantically. But sometimes a woman wants an orgasm that isn't self-administered, dammit.

Connor takes a knee and looks up at me. Not one for words, he cocks one of those dense brown brows in silent question.

Not trusting my voice, I just nod for him to get on with it. The sooner this is over, the sooner I can get back to taking care of all the things that still need to be done.

In the background, the photographer is clicking away,

and I try to arrange my features into something that won't translate to constipated-pooping face.

I'm sure my smile looks more like a grimace, but worry about that disappears when Connor's fingers drag the hem of my dress up far enough to slide the silk and elastic band around my calf.

Tingles and sweet chemical electricity arc between the pads of those fingers and my bare skin. Heat creeps into my cheeks, and now I'm worrying about a blushing constipated-pooping face in pictures that will be passed down for generations and *holy fuck* the man has the most amazing, callused fingers in the world.

Those digits leave behind a trail of goosebumps, and I barely suppress the shiver that wants to overtake my body, even as my belly jumps in excited glee at the prospect of him touching me—everywhere.

I'm about to shift forward so he can slide the garter over my knee and to my thigh—a woman needs fantasy fodder—when the elastic band snaps softly around my calf and he pulls back, letting my dress fall back down.

You've got to be fucking kidding me.

Sure enough, the blasted man stands and offers me his hand. I stare at it in resentful silence for a full beat. I know he's trying to be a gentleman, but you'd think with his apparent distaste for touching me, he'd forgo the offer to help me up.

I stand, ignoring his hand, and brush past him and go back to my list of things to be done.

Kate's been harping on me for months to try out a dating app. Swiping left and right based off a simplified version of someone sounds like the seventh circle of hell to me. Maybe she has a point though. I can't remember the last time I went on a date, let alone had sex, and that's just pitiful.

If I can't have the person I want, then maybe it's time for

me to move on. Even if I don't find my forever person, finding *someone* has to be better than this pining. And who knows…maybe I will swipe my way to true love.

Resolving myself to the idea, I'm gonna do it. *Tomorrow. Maybe.*

Time to kick this crush once and for all.

ALLY

Once the party starts to wind down, I survey the backyard for last minute details to attend to. I'm exhausted, but Arik and Kate are still floating around here somewhere since they opted to not take a honeymoon right now. Gram and Ben left a few minutes ago to well wishes and a sea of bubbles.

Their flight to the island resort with an eighties hit songs theme leaves bright and early, so instead of getting up at dawn to head to the airport in Idaho Falls, they opted to drive out tonight and stay in a hotel before flying tomorrow.

My romantic heart sighed at the kiss they shared before getting into the car service and departing. Their kind of love is the best kind—one that spans generations instead of years.

Is it so bad that I want that?

I thought I had that once. I thought I'd met the person I'd spend the rest of my life with, but in all my naive enthusiasm, I overlooked the signs of a man on the prowl.

But *live and learn,* right? I'm happier here at home with my girls, my mom, and my shop than I ever was in San Francisco.

"Hey, you need a hand with anything?" Liv bumps her shoulder to mine, and I glance over at her. The russet tea-length dress looks fantastic on her, and I have a moment to appreciate the settled look she's been wearing lately. I'm glad she and my brother worked through their recent difficulties.

Kate, Taylor, and I knew from the start that if they could both just get out of their own ways they could have something special, and we were right.

Another point for Gram and her matchmaking abilities. If Hedy "Gram" Palicki sticks you with someone romantically, you can bet your behind it's special and something that'll last for the long haul.

Being surrounded by couples has a funny way of working on the brain. I've heard that a single person catches more couples around them, while a person in a relationship focuses more on the single people around them. There's accuracy in the statement.

I'm so happy for my friends and family as they find love. It not only gets me a sister of sorts in Liv, but Jackson's so happy he's practically shooting sunbeams out of his ass. They both deserve this happiness.

Between them and this wedding for Kate and Arik, and Gram and Ben, I'm on the periphery of relationship bliss, and there's a growing part that wonders when it's going to be my turn.

Occasionally over the years I've wondered why Gram never tried to fix me up with anyone, but then something inevitably happened that made me grateful I didn't have to worry about a relationship while dealing with calamities.

Relationships take time, commitment, and energy—three things I have in short supply between the girls and the bakery, so it's probably for the best that I've been stuck in singledom.

But that changes now.

Time to take a chance.

I smile at Liv and ask, "Can you just watch everything? I'm going to go grab a couple of trash bags and start picking up."

"Sure can. Are you still coming over for brunch in the morning?"

"Yeah, Jem's taking the morning shift, so I'll be there."

"Awesome. Do you think you could show me how to make those cinnamon rolls you do?"

For as long as I've been baking, Jackson's always had a soft spot for cinnamon rolls, so I know exactly why she wants the recipe.

On my way inside I call back, "Sure, I'll bring the supplies and come over early."

Walking through the kitchen and into the pantry, I locate the trash bags and, thinking better of it, cart the whole roll out with me.

Gotta start picking up stray trash. There are dishes to be carted in, leftovers to box, and lights to deal with.

The more things I think to do the more my thoughts race and my heartbeat picks up.

Oh God. Not again.

My hands go cold and clammy around the trash bags.

Take a breath, Ally. Just breathe.

I don't know what the hell is going on, but for the third time this week my heart is trying to escape my chest pulse by pulse.

I'm not looking where I'm going and miscalculate the distance between the closet and island. I slam into it hard, knocking my hip bone against the corner and stubbing my toe against the bottom.

"Son of a fluffing biscuit." The jarring impact is enough to knock back whatever was happening in my brain, and while my toe stings, I'm grateful.

Jesus. Maybe I should make a doctor's appointment.

I don't have time for a doctor's appointment though.

While I'd love to give in to the urge to drop a couple of F-bombs, the call from Emma's teacher a few months ago informing me that "shit" was my daughter's new favorite word has had me watching my own language.

Nothing screams *great mother* like getting a call from the school about the sailor's mouth on your seven-year-old.

"You okay?"

I yelp in surprise and whirl around. Once again, my heartbeat picks up, but this time for a different reason. Suit jacket and tie abandoned, Connor's shirt sleeves are rolled to his forearms. His hair is rumpled like he's been running his fingers through it, and I can *just* make out the hazy quality to his gaze in the dim interior of the kitchen.

"Jesus Christ, Con. You scared the shit out of me."

"Sorry, but I heard crashing around in here and thought I should check."

Of course, he thinks he needs to check on me. I'm his best friend's little sister, someone who's like family to him. Someone to look out for. Nothing more, nothing less.

I should have accepted that and let go of this stupid crush years ago, but then he does something like dance with my little girls or help out around Ma's house when he shows up for Sunday dinners, and I melt all over again.

Melting for a man who doesn't even recognize your existence outside of a sorta-kinda family member is insanity at its finest.

I step away from the counter, but the hem of my dress catches on my heel and I trip, because of course I trip.

With a squeal, I stumble and start to drop, but strong hands wrap around my forearms and stop my fall.

I have less grace than a foal finding its feet for the first time, and it takes me a second to get my bearings. Surprisingly, Connor doesn't let go once I'm steady. He's holding me almost as close as he did during our dance, and I try hard to ignore the flutter that quivers in the depths of my core.

"You okay?" he asks again.

There's so much concentration on his face, like he's afraid he's going to do whatever he's doing wrong. The muscle in his jaw clenches, nostrils flaring, as his gaze lingers on my lips. His fingers tighten along the length of my shoulders, not painfully so, but enough that I know his grip is steady.

"Yeah, I'm good."

I don't want to release him either. The fabric of his shirt is silky under my fingers, and I tighten my hold for just a second. I'll let go…any minute now.

Cedar. His scent is fresh air and green forest and purely him. The damned man is already sexy as hell, but then he has to go and smell like a freaking wet dream.

Surely, he's going to pull away and we'll return to the same friendship I've come to value and cherish over the years.

Maybe he'll go back outside and dance with my daughters again.

Then everything will be back to normal tomorrow morning at brunch.

But the longer he holds me, the more confused I get. It's not fair that I react this way around him every single time. It's just not.

Even in the dim room, I can make out the dark chocolate of his eyes. Eyes so dark it's nearly impossible to distinguish iris from pupil.

"Why are you so damn beautiful?"

His words take me by surprise, and I swear, for the briefest moment, heat slides into his eyes.

Melt.

His hands cup my cheeks, and I stop breathing. Then he

tugs, forcing me to the balls of my feet, and lays his lips across mine.

His swift intake of air is the only thing I hear before blood rushes to my head so fast I get dizzy. The slight taste of bourbon on him only enhances the spicy flavor of his skin, and when he rubs his mouth over mine, my eyes slide shut in delicious indulgence.

A rumbling groan erupts from his chest, and I have every intention of investigating that sound, but I'm swept away again.

Yes. Growl for me.

This is everything I've dreamed of and nothing close to it all at once. Bourbon and cedar and Connor invade my senses until my head spins.

Holy hell and hold the handbaskets, Connor Murtry is kissing me in Gram's kitchen.

Then he's not.

Between one heartbeat and the next, the kiss is over, and he pulls back, his eyes sliding open, hands falling from my face.

Confusion holds my tongue in a stranglehold. I have no idea what to say, what to do, but whatever this was, I want to do it all over again.

That is, until the shock hits him. His walls come up, his eyes shutter, and I'm on the other side.

"Uh."

One word, one syllable, and my heart sinks.

It wasn't even a long kiss, but it was enough for him to regret it. The hesitant way he's looking at me now has hot curls of nausea and dread dancing in my stomach.

"I'm gonna go." His voice is gruff, abrupt, and the last of the happy high I just got hit with dwindles away.

Before I can stop him, before I can ask him what the hell just happened, he's gone.

I snatch the trash bags off the counter and head out to clean up, but what I really want is to go home, crawl into bed, and hug my pillow to my chest while I giddily relive every second of his mouth on mine.

My heart beats a little faster at the thought.

Like a teenager after her first kiss, I want to shout and jump for joy, but the hasty way he took off dampens my elation at *finally* tasting the man.

Cold, hard reality washes over me as I think about the stunned look on his face once he broke the kiss off.

My feelings for Connor don't make me immune to his faults. Other than our group, he keeps to himself, and while he's close with our friends, I've never seen him in a relationship. Not that I want to, but I know that he stays closed off in that area of his life. I've wondered why, but never got up the gumption to ask him about it.

Yeah, he backed off pretty quickly just now, but what if he was just in shock? What if he meant to kiss me, but didn't expect it to be that *good*?

Maybe, just maybe, this might be more?

No matter how much I hope for the *more,* I don't want to get my hopes up, even though they're steadily climbing with every piece of trash I stuff into the garbage bag.

The tingle in my lips is not helping tamp down my sunshiny optimism, and I halfheartedly fight it back.

It'll be okay. I'll just talk to him, and everything will be fine.

His abrupt departure is calling me a liar, and the more I think about it, the more my stomach sinks.

Falling for my brother's best friend was likely one more mistake in the long line of mess-ups when it comes to my relationship road map from hell.

CONNOR

Abraham Lincoln apparently once said that discipline is choosing between what you want now and what you want most.

Discipline is keeping myself on a tight leash from here on out, despite knowing how tempting the alternative is.

Damned wedding. Damned alcohol. And damn Ally Sawyer for being so fucking appealing that I kicked aside years of caution for a single taste of her.

The sun's been up for hours by the time I pull into Arik's place, and my self-control is reined in.

Shouldn't have done it. No matter how beautiful she looked or how right she felt in your arms, you damn idiot.

If Jackson knew how often his sister starred in some of my X-rated fantasies, he'd knock my ass out, so over the years I've perfected the cloak of indifference I wear around them both.

When I open the front door, breakfast scents assault me and cause my stomach to rumble. Coffee and something sweet. With a deep inhale, I make out the cinnamon rolls before I'm overrun.

"Connor, you're here!"

Hoisting up one of the loves of my life, I drop a smacking kiss on Elle's cheek and then use my beard to tickle her neck.

My other love has attached herself to my leg, and I drop my hand to ruffle Emma's hair.

I've never been a kid person, but from the first time Ally plunked these girls into my arms, they've owned me.

"Hey Peanut, hi Brittle, what's cooking?"

They look just like their mama, with sunny hair, greenish brown eyes, and dimples for days.

Elle threads her fingers in the hair at the base of my neck, and I shift her to my hip.

These two are just one of the million reasons nothing more can happen between their mama and me.

Adjusting for Emma's weight on my ankle, I shift, stomp, and shuffle my way into the kitchen, where there's a bustle of activity. Kate and Taylor are poring over some sort of document at the table, and Liv's standing at the stove. The window in the back door shows the testosterone for this shindig is hanging out in the yard.

The pantry door opens, and Ally pops out with various baking ingredients overflowing in her arms.

Her hair is bundled up into a clip, highlighting the slender slope of her neck. Pants cut off at the calf and a basic T-shirt shouldn't make my cock twitch, but they do. Really, I should be used to it by now—her loveliness constantly catches me off guard—but it's a sucker punch every time.

"Hey, Con." Her tone is brisk.

I cut my eyes away and wince. We need to talk, to address the elephant in the room, but call me a coward because I'm not keen on the conversation.

The good morning greetings from the others fade as her hazel eyes lock onto me, and I fight the urge to fidget.

Southern mamas have "the look," and the women here in

Felt have their own version of a thousand-yard stare. Ally's mastered it.

"The guys made up some Bloody Marys, and there are mimosas."

Straight to the point. The sunny, exuberant Ally I usually get is absent this morning. Still I ask, "Coffee?"

"Just made a fresh pot. You know where everything is." She turns away and walks back to whatever she and Liv are doing, and I can breathe again.

Telling her she looked beautiful last night? That was the first slipup I've had in years, and kissing her just compounded my stupidity.

Parts of me are crumbling under the pressure of her allure. It's only my unwillingness to rock the boat with Jackson that has me clinging to the edge of sanity and self-control.

That went out the fucking window last night too.

I can't think of anyone who'd be worthy of them.

I have no illusions that I'm good enough for her and the girls, but Jackson's offhand comment this summer struck a chord in me and any inklings I had of "maybe someday" disappeared entirely.

Making myself useful, I grab a stack of dishes and carry them out to the deck. Arik's busy frying bacon on the grill's griddle, and Jackson's watering some of the flowerpots sitting on the banister while Liv's brother, Rob, wanders the yard, phone pressed to his ear.

"Hey, man. Glad you could make it." Jackson doesn't turn away from the plants as he speaks, and I return the greeting after setting the dishes on the table.

I almost didn't come this morning—the guilt ate me alive all night. But logic eventually won out. I have no plans to ever leave Felt, Idaho, which makes avoiding her impossible.

It's better for me, for us, to pretend last night never happened.

Ally's clearly of the same opinion.

The smell of sizzling meat wafts over to me and I ask, "Anything I can help with?"

Arik shakes his head. At a loss for what to do because I am not going back into the kitchen, I start to set the table.

Soon we're all seated and digging into piles of food. The twins are covered in syrup in three seconds flat, and the bacon platter is empty moments later. Conversation pings around me, everyone making plans for the day, and the consensus is to head to the lake.

I consider just heading home, but I haven't had a weekend off in so long that a day at the lake sounds relaxing.

Ally's flittering to and from the house, and I have the urge to get up and help her with the clearing, but her refusal to make eye contact with me keeps me in my seat. If she'd just look at me one time, I'd be able to tell what she's feeling.

After a too-loud laugh at one of Kate's sarcastic quips, she disappears into the house.

But she isn't gone long.

The back door flies open, and Ally runs out, exclaiming, "The bakery is on fire!"

Everyone starts to talk at once.

The deck is chaos and panic.

"All of you, shut up!" I yell. In the silence, I take Ally's elbow and call out orders. "Y'all watch the girls. I'm going to drive Ally to the store. I'll call when we know what's going on."

Dazed, she turns to face me. Her distance from earlier is gone, and her face is pale with fear.

The bakery has been her third baby for years. Ever since she came home with two tiny tots in tow, she's put everything she has into growing the business and done a damned good job of it.

I steer her out of the house and to my Tahoe.

"You don't have to drive me. I'm fine."

The quiver in her voice belies those words, so I don't bother responding. Instead, I usher her into the passenger seat and buckle her in before making my way around the hood. Less than thirty seconds later, I'm tearing out of there and heading into town.

There aren't any heavy clouds of smoke on the horizon, which makes me hope the fire isn't too serious.

Tension is etched into every facet of her face, and she's twisting her fingers so tightly in her lap that the tips are white and bloodless. I reach across the console, lacing our fingers together, and ignore how right it feels to hold her hand.

"It'll be okay," I promise quietly. "We'll figure it out."

Tears gather in her eyes, and she lets out a shaky breath before giving my hand a squeeze, but she says nothing in response.

To get her mind off things I say, "About last night. I'm sorry. I shouldn't have overstepped."

Her head turns my direction, but I stare at the empty, straight road in front of us.

"Overstepped," she echoes. "Right."

From the corner of my eye, I can tell that her features are locked down. And maybe I'm an ass for bringing it up right now, but I don't want things to get weird between us.

Aside from not being able to avoid her, I know that we need to sweep whatever last night was under the rug and continue to ignore this attraction. It's for the best all around.

"We good?"

Tugging her hand out of mine, she lets out a mirthless laugh. "Sure. All good here."

I don't have time to analyze her words before I'm pulling onto Main Street. A fire engine sits in front of The Sweet Tooth. The distinct absence of smoke has to be a good sign, right?

I park in front of Readers' Haven and Ally is out and sprinting down the sidewalk. Hustling after her, I manage to catch up as she whips the door open and shoots into her shop, then back to the kitchen.

The acrid smell of burned food hangs heavy in the air, and the haze of smoke in the shop irritates the back of my throat. The county firefighters are standing near Jem, the part-time clerk, who looks frazzled.

"You the owner?" one of the county guys asks.

Ally steps closer. "I am. What happened?"

Before the firefighter can answer, Jem shoves forward and wraps Ally into a hug. "I'm so sorry! I turned around for two seconds, and the grease must have caught."

Patting her back, Ally goes into soothing mode, something I've seen her do a million times. Once Jem is composed enough to pull back, Ally looks at the firefighters, asking, "Bacon grease fire?"

"Yeah, it caught fire and spread up the wall."

I tune out the rest of what he's saying and take in the space around me. I've never been back here before. Industrial mixers and prep tables are set around the area. Everything is lined up in neat little rows down to the measuring spoons that hang along the back wall. The area looks perfect except for dishes in the sink and the charred oven and wall that're now covered in fire suppression foam.

The messy cake batter-covered remains of a phallus-shaped pan are on the counter next to the oven, and the only thing I can think is that the heat warped it into that shape... because surely, no, they don't make them like that.

The firefighters leave not long after that. The damage to

the wall is mostly superficial, and Colby, the local contractor, can probably fix it in no time.

Jem and Ally are bustling around the kitchen cleaning it up, but I'm still stuck staring at the pan sitting on the counter, because…really?

What would you even use it for?

Ally bumps her shoulder against my arm.

"They're for bachelorette parties. It's a dick cake mold."

Lord have mercy.

"A fucking what?"

Snorting lightly, she explains, "It's a cake mold in the shape of a penis. We get orders for them all the time for bachelorette parties and gag gifts."

I have no words. Ally saves me from my sputtering, saying, "Don't look so scandalized, Connor. I've seen penises in my lifetime. Touched a couple of them too."

I'm not touching that damn comment with a ten-foot pole. Tearing my gaze away from the land mine sitting on the counter, I ask, "Colby coming by to take a look?"

"Yeah, he'll be here soon. I need to close up the front because we can't stay open with it like this."

Again, she's got the worried look on her face. That look alone makes me want to knight-in-shining-armor my way into her life and solve all her problems.

I can't, though, and she'd never let me.

Ally walks to the front of the store with her hands clasped hard in front of her and her face pinched in distress. I wish I could take away the concern.

I pull out my phone and dial her brother. Jackson picks up on the first ring, and without any pleasantries I say, "Everyone is fine. The kitchen is in rough shape, but Ally already called Colby to come down. Jem was frying bacon, and that caused the fire."

"Jesus, okay. Thanks for letting us know. Any word on when y'all will be back this way?"

"Not yet, but I'll text when I know."

"Okay, we'll keep the girls, and…" He trails off with a sigh, but before I can respond, he's continuing, "Connor, you'll take care of her, right?"

There's an underlying tone here, but it's one I'm not comprehending. Hedging, I say, "Of course," and disconnect the call.

No point in trying to figure out what cryptic message Jackson was sending. If he wants me to know, he can tell me directly.

I find Ally at the front of the store as she's flipping the sign and locking the door.

"Updated the troop. Jackson's got the girls. Once we figure out what's what, we'll go from there. You doing okay?"

She shakes her head but says, "Yeah, fine. Colby should be here any minute to take a look at things, and I'm hoping it's a quick and easy fix because I don't want to stay closed for too long."

"If you need money…" The words are out before I realize it.

"No." The denial is firm, absolute. "I don't need money. I have savings and insurance, but the sooner we can reopen, the better."

My hands ache to drag her into a hug, offer the support of my body so she can take a minute to just stop and breathe, but that's the last thing she wants right now. I just want to fucking hold her and wipe the anxiety off her face, but just like everything else in my life, that's not for me.

I thrust my hands into my pockets.

Colby knocks on the main door, breaking the awkward tension between us, and he disappears into the back with Ally.

Jem is organizing things up front, and wanting to be out of her way, I take a seat at a nearby table and stare down Main Street. Eventually, she plunks a cardboard coffee cup in front of me.

Looking up, I say, "Thanks."

"No problem, it's the least I could do after this morning."

"Eh, it's things. Things can be fixed."

"I know, but I just feel horrible. If I would have just let the damn phone ring—"

"Hey, now. Shit happens. The important part is that you weren't hurt."

Jem nods at me and goes back behind the counter. With no idea how long Colby and Ally will take, I pull my phone out of my pocket to check my email.

The most recent message confuses me.

Why the hell would Hedy be emailing me from their honeymoon? Don't they know there are more interesting things to do in the tropics than email people back home?

The subject line reads *The Cowboy Courses*.

I recognize the name of the local annual festival, but I haven't attended since my first year or two in town.

Opening the message, I read through it, and each word sends irritation and refusal through every fiber of my being.

Looks like I'll not only be there this year but helping to plan the whole damn thing.

God fucking dammit.

ALLY

It's after dinner by the time I let myself into the house. Jackson dropped my car off and offered to wrangle the twins so I could get the ball rolling on the logistics of the repairs needed in The Sweet Tooth. Relief no one was hurt was the first weight off my chest, and the minimal damage to the interior was the cherry on top of my relief.

My girls are happy, healthy, and whole. My family is all good. My business is a little rough right now, but everything's going to be fine. I've totally got this.

Footsteps pound down the stairs and before I can brace myself, I'm smothered under the loving care of my girls. Wrapping my arms around them, I breathe in the strawberry scent of their shampoo, and the remaining tension within me dissipates.

"Hey, loves. How was dinner?"

Emma pipes up immediately. "Good. Meemaw made spaghetti and meatballs. I ate thirty gallons of it."

Mmm. Spaghetti sounds delicious. I didn't eat a lot this morning—my stomach was upset for some reason—and I forgot lunch altogether. I reach down and give Emma's belly a light poke. "Thirty?! That's crazy! How about you Elle-belle?"

"It was good."

Ruffling her still-damp hair, I glance at my watch. "Okay, how about a story before bed?"

It's not uncommon that I wish I didn't live at home. I mean, what twenty-seven-year-old woman lives in her mother's house with her daughters? But other times, on days like today, I'm grateful for my mother.

How many people have the support group I do? I know that at any time, I can ask Jackson or Ma to take the girls for whatever reason and they will. No matter how much I hate to lean on them, how much I want to stand on my own two feet, I know they are there for me when I need them.

I usher the girls upstairs and answer what questions about the bakery I can before tucking them into bed for story time.

Ma is loading the dishwasher when I make my way back into the kitchen.

"Ma, I'll get that. It's the least I can do after you made the kids dinner and bathed them."

"Psh, you know that I love it. I don't know why you worry about it so much. If you recall, I was a homemaker before I started at the school."

I roll my eyes at her sass while uncorking a bottle of wine and ask, "Did Jackson update you?"

"He did. Fire wasn't too bad. Colby should have it fixed in no time. Still sucks."

"It does. It also sucks that Colby found extensive mold in the wall once he started to tear down the fire-damaged spots."

"What? Mold? How?"

Shrugging, I say, "I don't know. Just that it's there and needs to be dealt with."

"Well, shit. You've certainly had a day, haven't you?"

"Yeah, but nothing I can't handle. It'll be about a week for the mold to be treated and then assuming the permits come in, Colby can get straight to work."

"How's that going to work with the baking?"

"I'm going to do what I can off-site and reduce my menu options until it's all fixed. That's a lot of what I was doing today—reaching out to the inn and checking if they'd let me use their kitchen, on the phone with the insurance company. Lots of stuff to take care of."

"Well, if you need help with any of those things, just let me know. We'll get you squared away and back up and running in no time."

The urge is there to pass off some of the less tedious tasks on my new to-do list, but I brush it aside since she already does so much for the girls. For me. I've got this.

THE SOUND OF A SAW RIPS ME OUT OF DREAMS OF RAINBOW clouds and weiner dogs and right into Monday morning. Stumbling out of bed, I look out the backyard-facing window in my room. I can just barely make out a figure banging around our dad's shop.

Oh, hell, no.

Jackson *knows* the only day I'm not up at three a.m. to bake for the store is Monday. It's the only day I get to sleep until I have to get the girls up, but here he is slamming around the shop at the hour of—I glance at the clock—five fucking a.m. God, why does it feel so much earlier?

After staying up late with Ma and telling her about the store, I didn't get enough sleep to deal with this new level of bullshit.

I haul ass down the stairs and out the back door. If he wakes the girls, I swear to Christ I'll kill him.

Kill. Him. Dead. Then I'll bury the body and plant endangered plants over him so he can never be dug up.

Dew-damp grass pricks my feet as I fly across the backyard. I don't slow down before ripping the door open and hissing, "What the fuck are you doing?"

But it's not Jackson making all this racket in the shop. The brawny figure that turns to me is one I'm all too familiar with, and I could kick myself for not realizing it was him in here.

Connor whirls around and whips off the safety goggles that sit on his nose as he cuts the power on the saw.

"Hey, Als."

His eyes travel down my body before shooting back to my face. If I didn't know better, I'd say there was the briefest flash of heat in that chocolate gaze.

Good thing I do know better after our chat in the car yesterday.

Black Henley, worn Wranglers, sturdy work boots, and his scruffy beard give him the appearance of a lumberjack, and I curse my damn hormones for surging at the masculine deliciousness in front of me.

I'm not short by any means—I got my height from my daddy—but standing next to Connor makes me feel petite and dainty and *why the hell do I love that so much.*

Since he clearly didn't hear me, I repeat, "What the fuck are you doing?"

"My saw broke. Nan said I could use hers to cut some lumber for the cabin."

"At five a.m.?"

How does he not see that the sun isn't even up yet? It's still dark out. Granted, he has every light blazing in here, so it may not register to him that he's disturbing the single day I get to sleep in.

"Yeah, I have to be at the station later, so I want to get this done. What's the big deal?"

It's always like this between us. Either we ignore each other or we're arguing. My patience is officially at zero.

"What's the big deal? How about that today is *the only day* I don't open the bakery? How about that less than fifty feet away are two seven-year-old girls sleeping, and if you wake them up, I'll shove rusty spoons into your eye sockets until you cry mercy, which I will ignore. How about the fact that I'm so sleep-deprived the Geneva Convention would investigate my torture and plead me not guilty for killing you because I lost out on the extra hour of sleep that I *need* before I deal with more of the shitstorm from yesterday? How about that, Connor?"

"Shit. You could hear me?"

Rolling my eyes because boys are stupid, I say, "Yeah, I could freaking hear you. This place has good insulation, but it's not soundproof, and you're using a table saw, which isn't exactly quiet."

Connor tugs the knit cap off his head before roughly scrubbing his hand through the scalp of his closely shorn inky hair.

"I'm sorry, I didn't realize. I'm just trying to finish..."

"Finish when the sun is up so I don't have two cranky minions on my ass all day, mkay?"

I don't wait for him to reply. Turning to leave, I ignore the searing heat I feel from his eyes on my back.

Moms have eyes in the backs of their heads. The tickle between my shoulders tells me Connor's gaze is trained on my ass, and isn't that curious?

When I push through the still-open back door and see

two sleepy, sunny-haired girls sitting at the table in their pajamas, any hope I had for a little bit more sleep evaporates.

Well, shit.

I guess I have to kill the man now.

I'm working at the stove when the back door opens and Connor steps into the kitchen. He sees the twins at the table and doesn't quite bite back a wince.

"Yep, they're up early," I say, "but that's okay, right, girls? We're gonna have an awesome day!"

Somewhere around battering the fourth piece of French toast, I got over the early wake-up call.

Keep calm and carry on, right?

The round of cheers from the table as I'm frying up the next piece of bread makes me smile.

I got lucky with my girls. They are not troublemakers; both embrace positivity and change like champs. I'm so grateful for them.

"Con! Come sit by us."

The girls are wide awake now, both of them clambering up and rushing him. The last of my irritation at him for waking me up early evaporates when he gathers them up in his arms.

"I'm making French toast, but they need to get dressed first if you wanted to take them up. Emma, make sure you brush the back of your hair. Elle, you cannot wear the Elsa dress today because I didn't get around to washing it this weekend."

Connor and the girls abandon me, and I let my mind wander to everything I need to accomplish today. I have to let the mold remediation specialist into the kitchen later this morning, figure out the permits and timeline for the repairs, and then arrange the whole general process for how to have a functioning business again.

I also have a planning committee meeting for Felt's

Cowboy Courses later today. It's one more thing on my plate I should probably hand off to someone else. It's not like anyone would fault me for backing out after the fire, but I promised Gram and Ben that I'd join the committee in their stead this year.

And to be honest, I freaking love the courses. It's a week-long celebration of fun, friends, and entertainment. I look forward to them every year, and participating in the planning this time has been the highlight of my year.

Plus, me helping out means Gram and Ben get a fantastic honeymoon. Win, win.

I probably need to start thinking about a vacation for the girls and me too. They've been begging to go to Disneyland for years. I can take a little time off, right?

The girls come down as I'm plating breakfast, and not only are they dressed, but they both sport matching braids with bows. *When did Connor learn to braid hair?*

He helps the girls take their seats before the yells for breakfast ring out.

Connor asks, "Is Nan home?"

I shake my head. Ma told me yesterday that she was getting up early to drive into Idaho Falls to have breakfast with a friend. The fact that she's not down here and coffee was already made lead me to believe she got a much earlier start than I thought.

It looks like it's just Connor, the girls, and me for breakfast.

Like a family.

As soon as I think it, I try to squash it.

Don't get me wrong, living with Ma is good. Our routine in the mornings is amazing, and the girls love having their Meemaw here, but the fantasy of having a man, having my person to eat breakfast with before we go about our days, is an intoxicating one.

It's stupid and silly to be stuck on the same guy for years.

He doesn't see me that way, and part of me worries I'm still that same naive young girl who fell in love with Daniel. But then Connor goes and does something so sweet—like putting bows in my girls' braids—and I know I'm not.

Connor isn't Daniel. He could never be as callous or as cold as my ex.

Carrying the plates to the table, I deliver breakfast for everyone and get started on the cleanup. Like Ma, I can't stand a dirty kitchen.

"Hey, where's yours?" Connor's watching me bustle around the kitchen. There's a pinched look to his face, one I can't name. I don't want to name.

The girls are inhaling their breakfast, and shit, does that mean they're going to go through another growth spurt? My wallet winces at the money we'll need to spend on clothes if they do.

"I'm going to have some toast. I'm not really hungry."

Connor pushes away from the table and walks to the sink, running the faucet and rinsing the dirty pans.

"Connor, really, I can do it. You should eat while it's hot." It's great that he wants to help clean, but not while the food is still hot.

He looks at me over his shoulder. "Oh, yeah, and what about you?"

"What about me?"

"I'm not going to sit there and eat a meal you made for me while you clean up."

"What? Why?"

He doesn't say anything though, just goes back to scrubbing the pans until they're clean before setting them in the rack to dry. I'm wiping down the counters and still don't know what the hell to say to that when Emma calls from the table, "Mama, what's a dickhead?"

CONNOR

ALLY AND I SPIN TO FACE THE GIRLS IN UNISON.

She asks, "Uh, honey, where did you hear that?"

"Jenny called Dillion a dickhead on the playground yesterday at the park when he took the swing she wanted. Is it a swear?"

Ally smothers a snorting giggle behind her hand, and my lips twitch.

She doesn't quite manage to pull off the straight face as she answers Emma, "Yes, baby, that's a swear. We don't say that."

"Then why did Jenny say it?"

I jump in and ask, "Dillion took her swing?"

Emma's mouth is stuffed full of food so Elle explains, "Yep, she got really mad. Her face was all red and sweaty."

"Well, then, that's why. He took the swing she wanted, and she got mad, so she said the swear at him."

"So we're allowed to use swears when boys make us mad?"

"Uh," I cut a glance at Ally, whose eyes are as wide as saucers even as the dimples bracketing her mouth deepen.

"No, Emmy," she explains. "We don't use swears at people even when they make us mad. Sometimes swears can be used like mean name calling, and we don't do that no matter how mad some people make us."

I pull my fist to my mouth and cough out, "Liar."

The girls miss my dig, but Ally swats at my arm. I don't stop the grin from stretching my cheeks.

The laugh just spills out, and before I know it, Ally joins in and we're both snickering while the girls look at us like we've lost our minds.

I thought it would be weird for a while. That things would be awkward between us, but I'm relieved that's not the case.

"Eat your breakfast, and 'dickhead' is a swear until I say differently." Ally's word is law, so the twins finish up their breakfast before tromping back upstairs to brush their teeth before school.

Ally starts to gather her own things, and I ask, "Why *aren't* you at the bakery on Mondays?"

"I'm there, I just take the morning off. It's like a little indulgence to myself. I'll go in later to deal with some of the stuff from the fire, but Mondays…Mondays I get to sleep in."

Fuck. And here I am waking her up before the sun.

Coming here first thing this morning to cut the lumber I needed was thoughtless. Not everyone is a morning person or gets up before the sun to work. I hadn't realized Ally had Mondays off or I would have done this another time.

Idiot.

I grab my fork and make quick work of the French toast, eggs, and bacon before loading everyone's plates into the dishwasher.

Cleaning the kitchen earlier distracted me from the lithe length of leg Ally is flashing this morning. Her pajamas aren't even that revealing, just some cotton shorts and a tank, but it's sexier than a negligee.

I have to get the fuck out of here before I do something risky like slip my fingers under the hem of those shorts to discover if her skin is as soft as it looks.

This cozy breakfast was just another reminder of all the things I don't get to have in my life. This level of domesticity isn't in the cards for me...with Ally or anyone else.

The girls are giggling and splashing upstairs. I turn to Ally and say, "Look, hey, I'm sorry. I should have considered the time when I came over. It won't happen again. Why don't I drop the girls off at school so you can go back to bed?"

"Can't. I have to be at the bakery in about two hours, and it's just easier if I drop them off on my way. Thanks, though. I appreciate the thought."

"How long are the repairs going to take?" I ask.

"Depends on the mold damage."

"There was mold?"

"Yeah, and a lot of it. I have to figure out the removal schedule before I can focus on repairs. Not to mention the preservation society hoops I'll have to jump through, but that comes with having an old building as my place of business."

"Shit."

She smiles, but there's a tired quality to it. "That about sums it up."

"Is there anything I can do to help?"

Ally rinses out her coffee mug. "Not really, but thank you."

If I had to pinpoint the one thing I both admire and hate about Ally Sawyer, it's her inability to ask for or take help.

She'd struggled her way through culinary school at night when the girls were babies. She was so determined to take over The Sweet Tooth when the couple who owned it retired and moved.

I've been on the sidelines for years as she's made something out of the business and raised the girls. The fact that she thinks she has to do everything herself is the most fucking irritating nonsense.

She won't listen, but I can't bite back the words. "Just because you *can* handle it, doesn't mean that you need to handle it *alone*. You know that, right?"

Her gaze dropped to her fingers, she gets real interested in her nail beds. "I know. I've got it. I promise."

Frustration threatens my normal caution around her. I'm not big on words because I believe actions should always speak louder, so I hold my tongue.

If she won't ask for help, then I'll just have to do what I can to give it, even if she doesn't want it, or me.

After the kiss the other night, the last thing I should be thinking about is spending more time around my personal kryptonite. But she's going to run herself into the ground if she keeps going like this.

I DROP OFF THE LUMBER AT MY CABIN AND GRAB MY GYM BAG, then drive to Arik's for a workout before heading into the station midmorning. This is my last week on midshift before I switch back to mornings, and then I'm due for vacation time.

It's a working vacation since I've officially been voluntold to help with planning the Cowboy Courses this fall. But three weeks of a meeting here or there is still better than three weeks of work, so I'll take it.

You don't say no when Hedy Palicki asks for a favor. The woman knows everyone and has connections everywhere.

I'm just pushing into the station when Jackson's calling my name.

I drop my coffee thermos, an acquisition from Arik's house, at my desk before working my way back to the conference room where Jackson's tapping away on his keyboard.

"What's up?"

"You're with me on back trails today," he says. "Sequoia needs work—there're a couple spots where the path is worn down and we need to gravel it. Then we're on campground duty for the rest of the day. I'll be ready to go in about twenty."

"Okay."

"Ally texted me this morning, something about her killing you, what was that about?"

"I was running the saw early to cut the lumber for the cabin project."

"Why didn't you just use the one at your place?"

"It needs a new blade, and I didn't have time to get to the hardware store this week, so I asked Nan if I could use hers."

"Makes sense, but Ally doesn't open the bakery on Mondays, so it's her only day to sleep in."

Scrubbing a hand through my hair, I say, "I didn't know that. But now I do."

I've been friends with Jackson Sawyer a long-ass time, and the squinty-eyed look he's giving me is weird. Why do I feel like he's measuring me, or trying to read my mind right now?

"Did you get the lumber cut?"

"Some of it, but I'll swing by the hardware on my way home and do the rest at my place so I don't intrude again."

Jackson leans back against the table, saying, "You're not intruding, and I should have mentioned something about Als's schedule, but I thought you knew. Sorry, man."

"It's okay. Not your fault. I managed to cop breakfast out of it, so it all worked out."

If possible, Jackson's eyes get squintier, and he just stares at me. I'm not sure what he's looking for, and I'm not sure I want to know.

I know it's stupid and it probably wasn't intended to be personal, but his claim that he doesn't know anyone worthy of the girls and Ally stung. We were working out in Arik's gym, heckling him about Liv, and I tried to not let it get to me. It's not even like he knows I have a *thing* for them, but the callous way he said that fucking hurt.

Visiting Felt, Idaho, with Jackson over summer break from college was the first freeing moment in my adult life. The quiet little town with its towering mountain ranges calmed the restlessness in me like nothing had before.

Following Jackson home and moving my life fifteen hundred miles away was the best decision that I've ever made, and I refuse to ruin it by wanting something—someone—that's so off-limits it might as well be illegal.

College was the first taste of freedom I'd had in a long time. Choosing a degree in forestry instead of business wasn't the first time I'd defied my dad, and definitely not the last. It also gave me a job that was far away from home and handed me the escape ticket I needed.

Jackson knows that I was a hell-raiser as a kid, how I turned my mom's suicide into a crusade to fuck over my father by doing the opposite of what he wanted for me. He knows everything, including how I've changed and tried to be a better person.

If he still considers me unworthy of his sister, then I have no place harboring these feelings for Ally.

The sun shines brightly on the trail, and we manage to work the repairs in quickly. The campgrounds are the same, and it's nearing afternoon when we pull back to the station.

These are some of my favorite things about being a

ranger—I'm not chained to a desk, I get to work in the outdoors, and it's important work.

Wildlife and forest preservation is needed more than ever, and my job is literally to make sure that generations down the line can enjoy the natural world. Not only do we do mundane things like we did today, but each ranger in this station has a deep understanding of the local ecosystem and how species can be affected by natural and human contact.

I grew up in Houston, and sure, there's plenty of outdoors stuff to do there, but you have to travel outside the city to get to it. Living in Felt, you're pretty much outdoors all the time.

I took my need to not let people down, to be responsible and a good person, and turned it into my career. What started out as a way to get back at my father turned into a passion, and I love my job.

There's never a dull moment either. From the summer programs to the winter sports hosted by the school district, there's always something going on, so we stay busy.

My back aches and I'm exhausted once we pull into the station. Getting older is a pain in the ass. I snap, crackle, and pop every time I get out of bed in the morning.

Thank God for ibuprofen.

"Hey, man," Jackson says as we unload equipment from the truck bed. "Liv's got a roast in the oven if you wanted to swing by for dinner."

As good as that sounds, I'm dreaming of a beer, takeout, and ESPN on my couch. Spending an hour around the two lovebirds isn't my idea of a fun time.

"I'll pass, but y'all have a good time."

Nodding, he makes his way off to file his reports from the day, and I put in an order to pick up a pizza from Louie's, the lone pizza place in town.

I can cook. Our housekeeper taught me the basics when I

was a kid, but it's not like I have a kitchen to do any serious cooking in right now, so pizza it is.

Once I have more time to work on the place, I'll design a killer kitchen, but that's not for a while, and I'll be more than busy in the meantime.

Jackson's a lucky man. He and Liv get to unwind at the end of the day together, eat dinner together, and *be* together.

Just for a second, I let the daydream play out. Me coming home and having a woman to kiss hello. The brush of our bodies as we work to put a good meal together after a good day.

The fantasy gets away from me until it's Ally and me standing in the kitchen and Emma and Elle doing homework, one of us distracting them while the other chops vegetables the girls won't want to eat.

Then it's tucking them into bed before dragging Ally to our bed and kissing every inch of her body until she's a puddle of need under me. Getting lost in her as she gets lost in me.

"Connor, you okay?"

Ripped out of la-la land, I glance over at Boone, one of the part-time rangers, to find him staring at me.

Guess I was spaced out longer than I thought.

I grunt at him instead of answering because explaining where my head was at would only get me in trouble.

Ten minutes later I'm on my way into town to grab a saw blade and my dinner before I go home to soak in a shower.

I need to get my shit together. Fantasizing about getting Ally into my bed is one thing, but imagining us being a family at the end of a day together is too much.

I know better than to let it go that far.

Parking on Main at Duke's Hardware, I glance over to find Ally's SUV *right there*. Of course, she's fucking here. My forehead thumps on the steering wheel. Twice.

Not like she couldn't have gotten whatever she needed while I was on shift, right?

But that damn saw blade is critical, so I force my way out of my truck and into the store. Maybe I can get in and out without her noticing me. I don't think I can take another Ally encounter today.

Dennis Harrison is behind the counter, his eyes trained on something by the paint section. I can just make out the blonde hair attached to the woman who won't get out of my damned head lately.

Ally's ass is indeed a work of art, and her cut-off shorts are practically criminal. Still, I pin him with a hard stare until he acknowledges me, then he winces and looks at the open book on the checkout counter.

On a mission of stealth and speed, I stride down the aisle toward the blades. I snatch the first one that will work with my saw, and I make it to within three feet of the checkout counter when Ally turns with her paint swatches in hand and sees me.

"Hey, Con. How's it going?"

I grunt and drop my purchase on the counter.

Do not engage.

"Are those the colors you're going for in the kitchen?" Dennis asks Ally as I pull my wallet out.

"It's what I'm leaning toward, but not sure. Could you mix up a couple of samples for me so I can test them out?"

"Sure can, and if you'd like, I could come take a look and maybe help you narrow them down."

"No." *Why the fuck am I inserting myself into their conversation?*

They look at me, clearly expecting me to say something else, and the best I can come up with is, "I'll take a look and give you my opinion if you need it, Als."

Her brother uses that nickname. We all know that the

only feelings I'm allowed for her are familial, friendly. She's basically Jackson, just shorter. And prettier.

Nope. Not going there. I can't let myself get caught up in her allure, but I can step in and put a stop to a guy hitting on her.

Maybe Dennis is her type. Maybe she wants his help with picking out paint. What the hell she's painting I have no idea, but I guess I'm gonna find out now.

What the fuck is wrong with me?

ALLY

I'm more excited than a kid on Christmas morning as I head into the community center for a Cowboy Courses planning meeting on Tuesday afternoon.

A weeklong celebration at the anniversary of our town's creation, the event runs a full week and includes all the fun you'd find on the rodeo circuit with games, activities, fun, and food. Most of the local businesses shut down or reduce their hours to participate.

When I was a kid, it was the best week. As an adult involved in the planning and implementation now? It's even better because I get to help create those memories for kids and families.

Mayor Davis meets me at the door to the conference room and offers a hearty handshake. "Thank you for offering to help out in Hedy and Ben's absence. We appreciate all the support we can get."

"I'm happy to help."

"You go ahead and take a seat and I'll get things started here."

The entire planning committee is settled into their chairs already, and I try to slip into the last open seat unobtrusively.

One person I don't expect to see? Connor, sitting at the back of the room, wearing his customary poker face.

Did he sign up to help too?

"Okay, everyone. As you know, we're here to start the planning for this year's Cowboy Courses. We have six weeks to get the planning and setup done before we're scheduled to start. We have a couple of new faces here taking the place of Hedy and Ben. Let's all give a good planning committee welcome to Ally Sawyer and Connor Murtry. Thank you for stepping in and helping. We're happy to have you here."

I glance at Connor, but his eyes are trained on the front of the room. He doesn't say anything, just offers a head nod.

The group jumps right into planning. The list of events we're doing grows until I know that what little sleep I manage right now is going to be whittled down to nothing in the coming weeks. It'll be worth it though. I'm honored and excited to be part of this group.

Mayor Davis continues, "Looking at early weather reports, it looks like we're all clear going into the first week of October, but we'll keep a close eye on that."

Weeks. We have six weeks to get this done.

The committee has been meeting for a while now, but it wasn't until Hedy and Ben's honeymoon schedule conflicted that I needed to step in. What about Connor? Did Ben ask him to step in? Or was it Hedy?

Pulling out my phone, I fire off a hasty text to Kate.

Did you know that Connor is helping to plan the courses this year?

Yeah. Gram told me she was going to ask him to help.

But why? He's never been interested in these before.

I don't know other than her saying something about needing another strong back to help lift some of the heavy stuff.

That's understandable. Most of the committee members are older women, and some of the setup equipment is heavy, but that's never stopped them from getting it done in the past.

What makes this time different? *Me.*

Hedy knows damned well I've had a crush on Connor for years. You can't hide anything from that woman. Is she finally doing something about it? Is this a matchmaking attempt?

If so, then she miscalculated, based off the way Connor blew off the teeny tiny kiss we shared after the wedding.

My palms get clammy at the thought of her scheming to put us together.

Don't think about that right now. Focus on the courses. You can worry about sneaky grandmas later.

I shake off the nerves and tune back in to the mayor and the planning agenda.

Shortly after we get the setup stages planned, the meeting adjourns, and I'm gathering my things with a hasty exit in mind when Connor starts to approach me. I don't want to talk to him right now, not with matchmaking suspicions at the forefront of my brain.

Bail!

I jump up, but my purse is hooked on the chair.

Shit. My heartbeat does that hamster on a wheel thing and I need to get out of here.

I yank, but it doesn't come loose.

Like a gunshot, the sound of the chair smacking the floor echoes through the room.

Pain explodes in my left foot, and as I reach down, my right slips on the chair back and I go down like a ton of bricks.

Ow.

My elbow crashes against the floor as my legs get tangled in the metal contraption. I'm trying to shove the skirt of my dress down, intent on not flashing the masses, when two hands hook under my armpits and hoist me to my feet.

My face is hotter than Hades right now, and of course my graceful ass would fall right in front of the guy I'm trying to avoid.

My face is sweaty. Why is my face sweaty?

Better yet, why am I panicking? I've known this guy for years and am fully capable of working with him as a professional adult regardless of all the weirdness from this weekend's kiss. This is dumb. I can handle this.

Dusting my skirt off I say, "Thanks."

"You all right?"

No, no I am definitely not all right.

I can't remember eating anything this morning, I've had a nagging headache for days, and I just want a nap.

"Yep, I'm fine."

"I didn't know you were helping out this year."

"Yeah, and by the sound of it, we'll be hosting and announcing the events."

"Fun." Connor couldn't sound less enthusiastic, and this is the best exit invitation I'm going to get.

"Well, I have to get the girls from school, so I'll just be going now."

Grabbing my bag from the floor, I flash him a smile and then get the hell out of there.

Being in close proximity to Connor Murtry is going to test the little sanity I have left, I know it.

~

WHY IS THE SCHOOL PICKUP AND DROP-OFF LINE ALWAYS BUSY? I try to time it so I'm close to the front of the line, but lingering at the committee meeting for the little bit of time I did today did me no favors. I'm in the way, way back, and I'm going to be stuck here for the next thirty minutes.

But that's okay. I can use the time to work through the mountain of emails sitting in my inbox. There's the estimate from the mold specialist, and it frickin' stings. The repair estimate is going to be right behind it. Time to see if I can afford those upgrades for the kitchen.

The stove is completely out of date and needs to be replaced. I'd also like a larger workstation for cake decorating. The wedding cake for Kate and Hedy took up every inch of space and almost overflowed the worktable.

Plus, who doesn't like shopping for new shiny things?

Some girls love jewelry...but for this girl right here? She has her eye on a new Wolf range.

Kate and Gram's wedding cake was massive and only one more reason to have a larger, more accessible workstation.

I didn't expect my cake to be such a hit, but based on the pictures people were taking and requests for the cake designer, I can bet that I'm going to be creating a large number of formal-event cakes in the near future.

Might as well update the space while I have to be closed anyway.

There's a sharp pinch in my temples by the time the back door opens and the kids scramble into their captain's chairs.

"Hey, ladies. How was school?"

Emma launches into a recounting of every minute of her

day, and I'm listening, but my attention is on Elle. Her quietness isn't unusual, but the look on her face is. As soon as Emma takes a breath, I ask, "How about you, Ellie? How was your day?"

I'm pulling away from the curb when I hear the first sniff. Glancing in the rearview mirror, I watch as her little face crumples.

Shit.

"Alex said I was stupid."

Pulling over, I park the SUV.

I climb out of the car, pull the back door open, and unbuckle my daughter so I can hold her while she cries.

Time for a meeting with the principal and Alex's parents because I'll be damned if he gets away with bullying my daughter.

"Honey, you are not stupid, no matter what Alex says."

"But I don't talk. What if I am stupid?"

"Oh Elle, do you think Connor is stupid?"

Why is he always the first person who comes to mind?

At least the girls look up to him.

"No, Connor's the best."

Smiling, I can't help but agree. He is. Except when he's not.

"He doesn't talk a lot either, so just because you don't talk a lot doesn't mean you're stupid or that you're not smart. If anything, it means you're wise because you choose your words before speaking."

Emma's hand plays with the ends of my hair as she asks, "What about me, Mama? I talk a lot."

"That's because you're just like Uncle Jackson. He talks a lot but is still super smart. Talking or not talking doesn't determine how smart someone is, no matter what anyone says otherwise."

Elle wipes her eyes and huffs out a deep breath before hugging me.

Crisis averted.

I buckle the girls back in, but before driving again, I send an email requesting a meeting to the school administration.

Time to deal with this once and for all.

The rest of the drive is uneventful aside from Emma chattering away, but I've learned to listen out of one ear while working through the mental list of things that still need to be done. When we arrive home, the girls race into the kitchen for a snack. Following them, I see Ma standing at the entry to the kitchen.

"Good day, girls?"

I shoot her a look, one that says we'll talk about it later.

The girls spread their homework around the table, and we go through the routine of math questions and reading homework while I start on early prep for dinner. After they go to bed, I'll work on some accounting and try to wrangle the never-ending laundry.

I'm flipping through the endless papers the girls seem to come home with every day when Ma asks, "Hey, did Connor swing by yesterday?"

"Yeah, he was here."

"Did he run into any problems?"

Snorting, I say, "Oh, no. Not unless you count him running the table saw at the ripe hour of five a.m."

Ma winces. "I'm sorry. When I gave him permission to use it, I didn't think about how early he'd be here."

"It's all good."

Ma comes to stand by me, grabbing an apple to slice. "How'd the committee meeting go?"

One of my earliest memories is standing at this counter cooking with Ma, talking about our days. It's as effortless as ever.

"Yeah, that's another thing. Did you know Connor agreed to help this year?"

"No. Did he really? That's not like him."

You're telling me.

Watching Ma's expression closely, I ask, "Do you think Hedy asked him to help out?"

Ma and Hedy are thick as thieves, so if Hedy has some sort of harebrained idea to match us up, Ma likely knows about it.

Her expression gives nothing away. "I don't know. Hedy didn't mention anything to me about it."

If my gut instinct wasn't pinging so wildly around the topic, I'd be inclined to believe her. Still, I'm more than suspicious of the timing of it all.

Once dinner and dishes are done, I take the girls upstairs for bath time. My email dings with a new notification while they are playing in the tub.

Well, snap. Looks like Connor and I are going to be working closer than I thought.

I text Connor.

Did you see the email from Mayor Davis?

Probably not, idiot. You just got it like two seconds ago.

When I don't see the read notification immediately, I set the phone down and focus on getting the girls out of the bath and into pajamas.

Just as I'm drying Emma's hair, my phone chimes.

Yeah. Looks like we're partners?

Looks like. Want to meet up at the fairgrounds tomorrow morning and we can go over everything?

Sure. Is 6 okay?

The baking will be done, and I guess I could let Jem handle the morning rush.

Yep.

Oh boy.

Short responses tonight aside, I guess I'll get a good idea of how he feels about it tomorrow.

I'm just closing the bedtime story for the girls when Emma sleepily says, "Princes are dumb. I'd rather be friends with the dragon, then I could fly him to the moon."

I chuckle—sometimes my kids' brains astonish me—and say, "Me too, baby. Good night."

My eyes are so heavy. I'm so tired after today, and tomorrow's going to be as busy, if not more so.

It's okay. I only have to get through some accounting and paperwork and then after I look at new stoves and do the laundry, I can head to bed myself.

Ma's already sitting on the small sofa in the study with a glass of wine and a book when I get downstairs. The space used to be shared between her and Dad, but after he passed away and she retired, she let me make it a home office.

"So what happened at school today?" she asks.

"Alex called her stupid."

Eyebrows pinched, she says, "That's starting to get out of hand."

I turn on the computer. "I know, I emailed Principal Phillips for a meeting."

"Let me know how it goes. Anything I can help with?"

"Nah, I've got it. Thank you."

Using her wineglass as a pointer, she asks, "What are you looking at there?"

"Trying to see if I can afford some of the changes I've got in mind for the bakery."

"About time. I don't know how you've been functioning with that ancient stove as long as you have."

"Yeah, well, it got pretty toasted with the fire, so I might as well replace it instead of trying to fix it."

"Makes sense."

Ma takes a sip of her wine, and I'm a little jealous of it because I know that even half a glass would put me right to sleep.

"I need a penis cake for a book club party."

Thank God I'm not drinking anything, otherwise I'd be choking right now.

"For book club?" There's no way I heard that right.

"Yeah. We just started reading those fairy porn books, and we want to start the series off with a bang, so to speak."

Oh my God.

We have a pretty open relationship. She was with me when I gave birth. Hell, we've compared notes on our favorite romance novels for years, but there's just something about her asking me for a dick cake to read erotica that makes my shoulders hunch and gut clench.

"Oka-a-ay." I draw the word out before blowing out a laugh. "Let me know what flavors you want, and I'll get Jem on it."

I've been training Jem in addition to her taking culinary courses to be more active in the day-to-day baking, so it doesn't all fall to me. Dick cakes are easy enough to make and decorate so those fall to her right now unless we get a special request.

It's also less weird if she's the one doing it.

"Wanna look at new ranges with me?"

From business to dick cakes. Sometimes my life is fucking weird.

CONNOR

SUNRISE IN FELT IS ONE OF MY FAVORITE TIMES. EVERYTHING IS quiet and peaceful, as if there's a lull over the town. Oranges, pinks, and purples outline the Tetons, and if you look at the range just right, it looks like a sleeping man.

The air is crisp and cool, which is just one sign that we're on the cusp of transitioning into fall. A breeze flitters among the trees that line the area like a makeshift fence, and the only sound in the still morning is the chirp of crickets.

Working with Ally in the coming weeks is going to test me. It's not like I don't see her very often otherwise, but there's always the buffer of other people around.

The kiss was a fluke. Chalk it up to too much alcohol or something.

It *won't* happen again.

I'd be lying if I said I wasn't nervous about it.

However, thinking back to her swift departure after the committee meeting yesterday, I can only assume she's not looking forward to being stuck with me either.

I hadn't known she was going to be in on the planning for

this damn thing. If I had? I wouldn't have agreed to being voluntold.

There's a difference in having discipline and willingly signing up to have it tested over and over again.

I'm a creature of habit. I learned at a very young age that the less you rock the boat in your life, the less other people rocking it will get to you. Knowing that I have to spend a large part of the coming weeks with the first woman to make me wonder *what if* in a long time? I'd be stupid not to be cautious. Especially considering that anything with her would ruin a decades-long friendship, and I'm not rash enough to risk that.

The rumble of a vehicle draws my attention to the road, Ally's SUV leaving a dust trail behind her. I pull down the iron fist of my control.

She's probably been up for hours, between baking for The Sweet Tooth and getting the girls up and ready for school. Her schedule is more packed than mine.

The brief little slice into their morning routine earlier this week? Spending that little bit of time with her and the girls stoked the held-back *want* that's plagued me since Jackson introduced me to her the first time.

She climbs out of her car, juggling a notebook, her purse, and a coffee thermos. As much as I'd like to offer to help her, I stay where I am.

Agreeing to help is what got me into this nightmare in the first place.

I was perfectly content to stay in my lane, work on the addition to my cabin in the woods, and avoid people as much or as little as it suited me.

"Good morning," she says.

Ally with the early morning light playing over all that clipped-up sunny hair? From her luminous eyes down to the confident way she strides toward me has lust spiraling through me until I have to breathe through my nose to get a grip on it.

Sipping from my own thermos, I let the hot tea clear my throat for me.

Yeah, I've got it bad for Ally. Nothing new there.

I might as well try to be cordial, so I call out, "Morning."

Smiling brighter than the sun, she replies, "Thanks for coming out so early. I know it's a pain in the ass, but I appreciate it."

"You're good. I'm usually up this early."

She reaches up and tucks a strand of hair behind her ear, shifting her feet and looking away.

Her fidgeting leads me to believe she's as nervous to be out here with me as I am with her.

"How did you want to work this?" She's already setting her drink down to flip to an open page in her notebook, pen poised and at the ready.

"We were assigned to the cow chip and frying pan tosses, right?"

I've been to a couple of the events at the Cowboy Courses over the years. Jackson works the schedule so that each of us has some time off during the week even though we're flooded with the end of our summer tourist season.

"Yep, but I was thinking we might be able to work them a little differently this year."

"What'd you have in mind?"

The damn breeze is playing havoc with her hair, whipping the single loose strand around her face, and my hands itch to tuck it behind her ear for her.

"Well, they have our events at the far back because they run the same day the whip-cracking contest does. Because the whip-cracking is fancier with Sylvie's fire whip, the tosses don't always get a lot of attention, even though they're fun and a lot of people like to participate in them. I was thinking if we could set her up in the middle of the two events, we'd draw a bigger crowd."

The fairgrounds are huge and host events throughout the year, like a midway carnival over the Fourth of July and the annual winter holiday festivities. Food and kids' games are usually stationed near the main entrance, where most people congregate after they funnel through the entrance ticket booths. The farther away other events are located, the less they are visited.

Ally's got a good point. While I've heard of the frying pan toss and the cow chip contest, I've never bothered to walk far enough back to actually watch either of them.

Her pen flies across her notebook page, and after a second, she turns it to me. Roughly sketched, she's outlined where each of the vendor and local business booths will sit.

I had no idea she could draw or that she had this level of skill with it.

In less than two minutes, she has a comprehensive visual that mirrors the layout of previous years.

Then I remember the cake from the wedding. Five whole tiers of delicious, detailed design. My mouth watered at the sight of it being carted out to the table.

I never considered it before now, but those cakes should have given me some idea that she's experienced in design.

"What if we had the whip-cracking set up with the frying pan toss to the left and the cow chip to the right? That would ensure there's some crowd carryover for both." She's staring at the page, using the pen as a pointer.

"That'd be fine." She knows what she's doing here more than I do.

Ally eyes me for a second before looking down again, saying, "You know, we have to announce our events. You're going to have to say more than four words in a matter of weeks."

Well, that's fucking news to me. Public speaking doesn't scare me as much as skydiving without a parachute, but it's a close second. I didn't see anything that mentioned public speaking in the email from Mayor Davis, and Hedy never said a damn thing either.

"What?"

"Yeah, whoever is in charge of the event announces it to the crowd. It's always been like that. You've never noticed?"

I shake my head. It's weeks in the future, yet sweat gathers on my forehead, my hands are suddenly clammy, and my heart races in my chest.

I fucking hate public speaking.

I should have done my damned research before signing up for this madness.

"I can't do it."

It ain't happening.

Thinking about it has nausea curling in the pit of my stomach until I'm not sure I'm going to keep down my breakfast. I've been known to toss my cookies more than once when it comes to being verbose in front of a crowd.

Most people assume I'm quiet by nature, that I'm just a grumpy motherfucker, but it's more of a lifelong habit born of necessity than anything else.

Get reprimanded over and over again by an unsympathetic father for a stutter you can't control and you learn to be quiet, to think before you speak. I grew out of the stutter, but not the impact it had on my ability to talk in front of large crowds.

"What do you mean you can't do it?"

"I mean I can't. You'll have to announce both of ours because I can't."

Her mouth falls open and just as quickly snaps shut. After a beat she says, "Con, I don't know that I can. The two events run at the same time. I can't be in two places at once."

"Then someone else has to announce mine."

"Why?"

How the hell do I explain a hang-up about public speaking without sounding like a ninny? "I had a bad experience in school. I used to have a stutter—a bad one. I was on the debate team. It was the first mock event that we had, and I froze when I got up there. My team was prompting me to talk, but I knew that if I opened my mouth I'd end up embarrassing myself. In the end, I lost my lunch all over the podium. I haven't been a fan of public speaking since then."

Sympathy covers her features. "Oh, Jesus. I'm sorry, Con. I didn't know."

"It's okay. Not many people know that about me, but public speaking isn't my friend."

"But you give presentations at the nature center all the time."

"There aren't as many people in those crowds, and it's something I've done so many times. It's less about who's listening and more about what I'm teaching them. I don't know why, but that helps."

"Okay. I'll try to get it switched around so you don't have to speak. We'll figure it out."

I don't know if it's my relief at not having to address a crowd of hundreds or the way the wind is still fluttering that strand of hair around her face.

Maybe it's the way she's softly smiling at me like we're a team, but I do the one thing I know I shouldn't.

I kiss her.

Hands around her waist, I haul her into me. Her breasts are pressed to my chest and her notebook falls to the ground as her hands grip my shoulders even as her lips rub against mine.

Shock and surprise cross her face right before I close my eyes, and time slows down to near standstill. I hitch her closer, and her arms circle my neck in reward. If I'm doing this, then I'm gonna fucking *do this.*

The soft cushion of her mouth, the feel of her lips under mine, that snapping fire that roars through me at the taste of her? That's enough to tear my tattered discipline to bits.

My head swims as I sip at the cherry-flavored stuff that slicks her mouth. *My new favorite flavor.*

A tiny taste, that's all I allow myself before reining in the need to plunder deeper. Her sigh of pleasure has need raging through me. The same need to dip into the heat of her mouth for a full taste tugs at me until I'm sure I'm going insane.

I pull back and her eyes open sleepily, as if she's coming awake for the first time today, and the gut punch of lust that flays me also kicks my cock to life behind the fly of my jeans.

As quickly as the urge came over me, it's gone, leaving behind the realization of what I just did.

Goddammit.

ALLY

What the fuck just happened?

After our conversation in the car, I did not expect Connor to kiss me this morning. Hell, I barely expected him to show up, considering how weird things have been between us.

But another lip lock? Where the hell did that come from? Not that I'm complaining, mind you, but I'd like a better idea of what's going on than what I'm picking up from the jittery, fidgeting man in front of me.

Yeah, he's hiding behind his implacable resolve, but I've known him for years. I look down, and sure enough, his thumb dances against his ring finger in an irritated flick.

The only tell he has.

He's nervous.

I stare into those chocolaty eyes and try to understand what's going on, but I'm at a loss. There's nothing behind them…at least nothing that I can decipher.

We can be adults about this, right? I can just ask him what happened, and maybe he'll have an explanation that doesn't leave me baffled.

I open my mouth and start to respond when Connor says, "I've gotta go."

I stand there, stunned speechless as he swipes up his thermos and hauls ass out of the picnic area like the hounds of hell are nipping at his heels. Between one inhalation and the next, he's roaring down the dirt road to get the fuck out of Dodge.

Connor kissed me.

And then he ran away.

Again.

~

WE'VE TURNED AVOIDANCE INTO AN ART FORM. FOR DAYS NOW, the only communication we've shared has been cordial, professional emails. Stilted conversations about an event that I'm strangely less enthusiastic about than I was earlier this week.

Because Connor and Jackson are besties, I haven't seen my brother in days either. Which means I haven't been able to finagle details about Connor's reaction out of him or even confirm if he knows that Connor kissed me in the first place. Either time.

Gram's pristine matchmaking record is about to be broken if Connor and I have anything to say about it.

Despite our tacit refusal to work together in person, we've completed the tasks we were assigned this week. I hate my alarm because she's a loud bitch, but I'm getting it done. Everything is under control.

And the planning committee approved my request to change the event schedule so the competitions are on different days. That way, I can announce everything and Connor won't have to.

Sunday afternoon, I'm hauling the girls in from a last-minute playdate with friends when I see the big-ass truck parked in my driveway. I know my unspoken agreement with Connor to evade each other has ended.

Looks like Connor decided to join us for dinner.

Sunday night dinners are a staple in our house, something that isn't missed unless you're dead or dying.

They're not new. I'd known I'd see my big bro today, but I still haven't come up with a way to rationalize Connor's behavior or what to even make of the short stint of insanity that must have come over us last week. So him being here for dinner throws me off.

Maybe Jackson doesn't know about it.

I'm lugging the girls' things inside when they both let out excited shrieks and scamper through the living room, shouting, "Uncle Jackson!"

"Hey there, tater tots! Did you have fun at the park?"

At the door, I unload the millions of pounds of mom accoutrements that plague me before kicking off my shoes. "Hey, J. How's it going?"

I refuse to meet his eyes, scared of what I'll see there. I need some liquid courage before I deal with this crap, y'all.

Does he know and disapprove? Does he not know and is clueless?

Either way, I don't want to know.

"Good, good. Ma said she wouldn't be here for dinner, so I got chicken noodle soup ready to reheat on the stove, and I was hoping you could make some of your dinner rolls. Hey, you want a drink?"

"Hmm. Yeah, I'll grab it though."

My eyes are still trained on my feet as I move past him for the kitchen. I have one objective in mind, and it's the largest glass of wine I can find and consume.

Hell, I might even just drink straight from the bottle at this point.

I whip around the corner of the kitchen and come face-first with the object of my avoidance's chest.

My luck is great today.

All I wanted was some alcoholic salvation.

But no.

I had to bump into the solid wall of man on my way to eluding a mental breakdown.

"Shit. Sorry, Con."

"I'm sorry. I didn't hear you coming."

And you never will.

We both speak at the same time, but the inner twelve-year-old boy thought makes me want to snicker. I shut it down.

Emma rounds the corner. "Mama, that's a bad word. How come you get to say them and we don't?"

After Emma's love for the word *shit* became apparent, I've worked on curbing my swearing, but if I know my daughter, she's going to be dropping F-bombs at every opportunity. Maybe it's time for a swear jar.

"That is a bad word, and I shouldn't have said it. Sorry, baby."

Connor avoids my gaze.

Who the hell does he think he is to kiss me until my brain is a scrambled mess, bail on me *twice,* and then show up at my mother's fucking house like nothing ever happened?

The instant and obvious regret on his face after both kisses stung, and I've barely coaxed my flagging pride back into place. And now he's in *my* kitchen, expecting to eat food that *I'm* cooking, as though everything about our seven-year friendship hasn't been flipped on its head.

Anger burns in my chest as I stride toward the pantry. Connor hops out of my way when he realizes I'm planning to walk right through him if he doesn't move.

I can ignore him and stay silent just as easily as he does.

Let's see how he likes that.

Maybe I set the bottle of wine down more forcefully than I mean to. Maybe the drawer holding the corkscrew closes harder than I intend. But I don't give a shit right now.

"Did Ma say why she wasn't going to be home?" I ask.

Jackson's playing slap hands with Elle and looks up, giving her the perfect opportunity to slam her hands down across the backs of his. "She said she had a thing in Idaho Falls and that she'd probably be late."

Well, shit. That's okay. I can use the dinner rolls to knead the aggression right out of my soul and then all will be right in the world.

I'm grabbing flour and yeast from the pantry when Jackson's voice comes from behind me.

"Hey, Als. You okay?"

Through the kitchen sink window, I see Connor and the girls playing in the backyard.

Nerf guns for Emma and bubble paraphernalia for Elle.

Connor's bobbing and weaving among the darts Emma shoots his way and the bubbles Elle blows as if they're bullets flying at him. Like always, the sight of Connor playing with them melts my heart and sucks the wind out of my angry sails. Guess I won't need the dough to fix that.

I don't want to tear my eyes away from them playing, but I force myself to.

No matter how bad I wish, no matter how bad I want, I have to do what's best for me and the girls. He doesn't want that type of relationship, and if I push, then that'll just end in disaster for me.

It's better if things go back to the way they were before.

Glancing back at Jackson, I say, "Yeah, I'm fine. Why don't you go out there and even the odds a little bit?"

He glances out the window behind me. "You remember when you first handed Elle off to him? He was so worried he was going to do something wrong, that something that precious couldn't possibly be in his hands. Watching him go from that shutdown quiet guy to chasing those same girls around the backyard does my heart good. He's a good guy."

He's the best guy—just not the best guy *for me.*

I do remember the first time I put Elle in his arms. His big hands cradling her when she was less than a month old at the time.

Home from California on a rare trip to visit, I was nursing Emma at the table. She managed to kick one of her tiny little feet out and knock over a cup of water. I unlatched Emma right as Elle started to cry, which then set Emma off.

Jackson was busy at the stove, so I did the first thing I could think of, swooping up Elle and passing her off to Connor while Ma cleaned up the mess and we soothed babies.

He panicked at first and stood stiff as a tree, but as Elle settled—the quieter baby, even then—he relaxed and cuddled her closer.

It's not the first memory I have of him, but it's one of the strongest.

Jackson rummages around in the umbrella stand at the back door then pulls out a Nerf gun the size of a German Shepherd and equipped with a Rambo-style bullet belt. He races into the backyard with a yell.

I watch them all play for a little bit before turning back to the rolls Jackson requested.

Baking is my passion, and feeding the people I care about is my love language. I'm grateful every day for a career I can enjoy while it supports my family.

Once I have the bread on its second rise, I start to warm up the soup. It's a pretty easy process to add more seasonings to bring out the flavor over a longer simmer.

"Hey, lady. Whatever you're cooking smells like I'm starving."

I squeak and drop the spoon with a clatter at Olivia's voice. I'd assumed that because she wasn't here with Jackson earlier that she wasn't joining us tonight.

She's hit or miss on Sunday dinners, though she's gotten a lot better about making them. Still, she has deadlines of her own and books to write. I didn't think she was going to make it here tonight.

"Hi. Just chicken noodle that Jackson made. I'm doing the bread."

"Sounds delicious. But I have a surprise for you."

Liv pulls out a paperback from the enormous handbag she carries, and the sight of it is almost better than a spontaneous orgasm.

If I can't have a real-life man, then I can have all the fictional book boyfriends I need.

"Is that what I think it is?" I squeal.

"Sure is. Hot off the press. I just got some advanced copies in and figured you could use the conclusion to Cassius's duet."

Giddy excitement makes me break out in a happy dance. I've been waiting for this book for months, so I'm more than ready to dive right in.

Tonight's plans of work and more work just upgraded to a little bit of work before a bath and some reading time.

Setting aside the book, I clean up what dishes I can before grabbing the bottle of wine to top off my glass. I gesture with it toward Liv and ask, "You want?"

"Yes, please. What are the guys up to?"

"Nerf war out back. They're keeping the girls occupied for me."

We both turn fully to watch the action. Jackson is pinned

behind the trunk of a tree, and Connor is laid out in the grass like he's been shot.

I grin.

Good job, girls. Took out the biggest threat first.

"Why don't you just ask him out on a date?"

I gape at her. *Erm, what?*

"Oh, come on, Ally. We all see it. You've got the hots for the man—you should ask him out."

I start to shake my head before she even finishes, dismissing the notion. I can't ask him out on a fucking date.

One rejection I could handle.

Two was a little too much.

But three? Setting myself up for that kind of hurt doesn't sound like a good time for me.

Pass.

"No, we're just friends."

"I don't believe that for a fucking second. Give me some credit. It is my job to look for romance, and the way his face lights up when you walk into a room is enough to have me calling bullshit on the 'just friends' crap."

"He doesn't want to want me like that, Liv."

"And how do you know?"

"Because when he kissed..." I could smack myself.

"He kissed you! When? Where? What happened?"

I hold up a hand to stop her onslaught of questions. So much for keeping it to myself. At least one of my concerns is addressed though.

Connor didn't tell Jackson anything. Because if he did, then Liv wouldn't be so surprised.

"You *cannot* tell Jackson. Promise you won't say anything."

Liv's slim blonde brow climbs and she takes a second before responding. "I won't say anything unless he asks me, but I'm not going to lie to him."

A lie of omission caused them some serious trouble not

too long ago, so I wouldn't ever expect her to lie to him for me. He won't ask a specific enough question for Liv to spill the beans, so that's good.

"The first time—"

"First time?"

"Would you hush? The first time was after the wedding. He did it again earlier this week when we were at the fairgrounds going over the plans for the Cowboy Courses."

A grin creases her cheeks and her left dimple winks.

"And? How was it?"

Like calorie-free cake and fireworks on a hot summer night, but I can't tell her that.

"It was okay."

"Just okay? That's it? That's all you're going to give me, the writer of romance? I need more than that, Ally."

I wave a hand at her to keep it down. The guys are on the back patio now, and I do *not* need them to hear us talking.

Whispering, I say, "Fine. It was amazing and hot, but he bailed right after both times and tried to brush off the first one like nothing happened."

They were the best basic kisses of my life, and although I want more, I know that's never going to happen again. I'll make sure of it. I have to.

I don't think my heart could handle it.

CONNOR

A SOFT DART PINGS OFF MY MIDSECTION, AND I CATCH IT before it falls to the ground.

Jackson and I just spent the better part of an hour waging war against the girls, and we did not come out the victors.

How two waist-high pipsqueaks were able to beat me with dart guns, I'll never know.

Maybe I'm getting slow in my old age.

I send the dart sailing back into the yard, where the girls are chasing each other, and lean back in my deck chair with a fresh beer.

Ally's excited shouting a few minutes ago told me Liv is here, likely with a new book for her.

You'd think I would've learned my lesson and kept my distance until I got my head on straight, and I did.

For about two metaphorical seconds.

Maybe my discipline isn't as robust as I thought.

But curiosity got the better of me, and I wanted to see Ally outside of the stiff-necked emails she's been sending me.

I know better than to go down this path, better than to get involved with someone who's the closest thing to family, but I apparently haven't learned that lesson either. Which is why I submitted an application for a lead ranger position at another station early this morning.

If I can't get a handle on myself, then I need an escape hatch.

"Hey, man. You okay?" Jackson asks.

I have to tell him, but I don't fucking want to. Best-case scenario is that a metric ton of tension is about to be dropped into our friendship. Worst case is that I lose him *and* Ally and the rest of this little community I've built in Felt due to my own selfishness.

"Yeah, actually, there's something I wanted to talk to you about."

"Sure. What's up?"

Time to rip the bandage off.

"I kissed Ally. Twice."

I pick at the label on my beer bottle. I don't want to see disappointment or anger right now.

"You kissed Ally?"

A quick look shows his face is unreadable. All the signs of his brand of anger that I'm familiar with are absent.

Clearing my throat, I say, "Yeah. I'm sorry, man."

I am sorry. As soon as my brain reengaged with reality, I'd regretted it. One poor decision, acted on twice, was all it took for me to jeopardize a friendship and challenge the status quo.

Jackson's silent, and I'm waiting for his rage or a bare-knuckled punch to the face. But nothing happens. My thumb starts to tick against my ring finger. Seconds tick by as my shoulders hike higher and higher to my ears, until I can't take it anymore and look at my best friend.

There's zero reaction, zero emotion on his face.

"Hmm. How about that?" he says.

How about that? What the hell is that supposed to mean?

Jackson's never been one to hold back when he has opinions on something—he's the most outspoken guy I know—but there is nothing for me to go off.

He takes a long drink of his beer and looks across the backyard.

The early afternoon sun shines brightly; the girls shout and laugh as they play. I just confessed to one of the cardinal sins of best friends to him, and his reaction is *how about that?*

Panic floods my system, begging to be let loose. I don't want to lose my best friend over this, but I wasn't thinking of Jackson when I kissed Ally.

I definitely wasn't thinking about consequences. Hell, I don't even know what I was thinking of other than getting my mouth on hers.

"What did Ally have to say about you kissing her?"

His question takes me off guard because he's made his feelings on his sister's relationships clear in the past.

"Which time?"

"Either."

"Well, after the first, I talked to her, and we chalked it up to a moment. I didn't stick around after the second one long enough to find out."

I brace for the worst. With a slight shake of his head—finally a fucking reaction—he says, "Con, man, we aren't gossiping chicks. Lay out the situation for me."

I must be in an alternate dimension, some twisted take on reality, because I never considered that he'd want *details.*

"Uh, the first time was after the wedding. We were in the kitchen and she tripped on her dress. The second time was when we were planning the toss portion of the Cowboy Courses, and she wanted to make some changes. She was telling me how each planner has to announce the event they were assigned."

"Which would be a no-go for you."

We've been friends since college. This man knows me better than literally anyone. And yet I shit all over that by making a move on his sister.

"Yeah, I shut that down and told her why I couldn't do it."

"What happened after that?"

"She smiled at me. The damn wind was whipping her bangs around her face, and I don't know what the hell came over me."

"So you kissed her as, what? A thank you?"

My answer could go one of two ways here. I could say yes and likely get hit for it, or I could lie and make up some excuse, plead temporary insanity or some such shit—and get hit for it.

It's the years of friendship that have me telling the truth. It's the memory of an excited Jackson dragging me home with him for that first summer break that has me opting for the truth. Fuck, please don't let me screw this up.

"You could say that, but it's more complicated on my end of things."

Scratching a hand through his beard, Jackson asks, "And you think I'd disapprove, which is why you look like you're facing the gallows right now?"

Of course I think he'd disapprove. He flat-out said that. Jackson's always made it plain he's the protective older brother. This one-eighty is throwing me off balance.

"You haven't exactly been quiet about how protective you are of her and the girls," I reply.

Holding up a finger, he takes another draw from his beer before saying, "I'm gonna stop you right there. I'm protective of those girls because"—he drops his voice to a near whisper—"their father is a piece of shit and because Ally has had shit luck in relationships. Anyone would be protective of their sister and her kids because of that. But I don't know where you get the idea that I wouldn't be okay with *you* dating her if that was something you both wanted."

"At Arik's earlier this summer, you said you didn't know anybody who'd be worthy of them. That's where I got that idea, Jackson."

"Really? One sentence? That's where you got the idea I'd end a decade-long friendship with you over kissing my sister?"

"Well, yeah. You were pretty clear."

"Connor, I'm gonna level with you. I don't dictate who Ally dates—never have, never will. I trust my sister to make those decisions for herself."

I start to interrupt, but he holds his finger up again.

"Now that's not to say I won't keep an eye on her and the girls or have an opinion on who she decides to see. But I trust Ally. She's a grown-ass woman, more than capable of making her own decisions."

I don't know how we went from me confessing to kissing his sister to her dating life, but the relief that loosens the tight feeling I've had in my chest for the last week is more than welcome.

I could have mentioned it to Jackson at any time, but I was scared to mar our relationship, considering I work with him and can't go a week without seeing both him and Ally.

"And," he continues, "if you wanted to date Ally, then I have no say in it. I would also like to add, why the hell would I be friends with someone I don't approve of, let alone let them around my family if I weren't one hundred percent convinced they're a good person? I'd like to think I'm a better judge of character than that. I trust you, man."

Did Jackson just give me his blessing? I don't know, and frankly I don't want to ask. His point is logical. I wouldn't be friends with anyone I didn't want around my family or whom I didn't trust implicitly.

"Thanks, I guess?"

We both sip our beers and watch the girls fire up the bubble machine. The soapy orbs fly around the backyard, and the girls screech as they chase them.

"You kissed her and then took off? Twice?"

Familiar regret slides through me, but lighter somehow. Without digging into that I say, "Yeah, I panicked and left."

"Well, I guess you two are due for a conversation then?"

Fearful shame has me scrubbing a hand through my beard because he's right. I do have to talk to her.

"Yeah, I guess so."

"I know it's not my place to say, but she deserves to know why you panicked and bailed." Jackson stands and drops his beer into the trash. "And I'm not talking about you being a scaredy-cat about me either. Tell her about April and Del."

Rip open a wound that scarred over years ago? That sounds like volunteering for a prostate exam and a root canal in one day.

"Based on the look on your face, you're coming up with reasons not to. But she deserves the truth of why you're hesitant to date her."

"Why would I want to put all that out for her to hear?"

"Look, man, I'm not going to demand you marry my sister over one kiss. You want to date her, go for it. I have no say in the matter. You want to chalk up a couple of kisses to a few moments, that's fine too. But if you do go the dating route, then you should tell her. That's all I'm saying."

Jackson walks back into the house with that parting shot.

Tell her about the worst day of my life? Hard pass.

But I can at least be honest with her and clear the air about taking off yet again.

Maybe it'll get us back to normal.

What normal is anymore? I have no idea.

~

THERE'S NOTHING THE SAWYERS CAN'T DO IN THE KITCHEN. IS it still too warm for soup for dinner? Yeah, but I'm not going to decline a free home-cooked meal, not when my best efforts come from firing up the grill.

Nan showed up right before we all sat down and kept the conversation around the table lively when there was a lull. That didn't stop me from watching the silent communication between Liv and Jackson though.

The sneaky way they slid their eyes first to Ally and then to me didn't go unnoticed by anyone, though nobody addressed that elephant in the room. He's right—she and I need to talk.

He and Liv left a few minutes ago, after he gave me an obvious *get on with it* look.

"Well, I'm going to take this glass of wine up and get my grandbabies into bed." Ally starts to object, but Nan continues, "You're not going to try to deprive me of time with my girls, are you?"

Her mouth shuts and she looks around the kitchen. If I had to guess, she's assessing her exit strategy and looking for a polite way to kick me out. The way she slammed shit around before I took the girls outside to play earlier made it abundantly clear she was pissed at me. She doesn't want to have this conversation any more than I do, and that gives me a second of pause.

She's never been one to beat around the bush or to hold back when it doesn't suit her, but I threw us off-kilter with those kisses. We're both wobbly, trying to get back to normal.

Better to just get this over with.

Tone neutral, I say, "I'm gonna go clean up the backyard. Want to give me a hand?"

For the first time in hours, she meets my gaze. Like Jackson, however, she has her features locked down tight. This is why I never play poker with the two of them.

Her stare is intent on the dishtowel she's wrapping around the handle of the stove. Her voice is quiet when she says, "Sure."

We both make our way into the backyard, and I try to give her space. Despite the later hour, the sun is still up, weakly shining, so we have plenty of light to see the neon darts and guns scattered on the grass.

She starts to gather the darts and load them into the basket they keep on the deck for toys and random kid gear.

Her shoulders are stiff, and she's moving with purpose. Probably to get this done and then escape.

"Hey, so we should talk," I say.

Her hands flex on a dart, the soft foam compressing, before she loosens her grip. Her expression remains placid even as her hands form fists.

"What's there to talk about?"

I put my hand on her elbow; that small touch is enough to drag her gaze up to mine.

"About the other day, I'm sorry. I stepped out of line again."

"Why did you?" she asks.

It's my turn to look away now because I don't want her to see the conflict on my face. I have a couple of options. I could tell her the truth, something sure to lead to more questions, or I could hedge my bets and just brush the whole thing off.

Like Jackson, she deserves honesty from me, but this is harder for me to get out.

"I wanted to. I've wanted to kiss you for a long time."

Her mouth opens slightly, as if she's surprised at my honesty, before she asks, "Really? But after the first time you said..."

"Jackson's my best friend, and it wasn't right for me to look at you as anything other than a surrogate sister. You're someone I admire, and I'm here for you if you need me, but more recently it's been harder to put you in that *safe* category. After the wedding, I'd had a little bit too much to drink and I overstepped, then I did it again at the fairgrounds. I'm sorry for it. I told Jackson about it, and he suggested we talk, so I just wanted to clear the air."

She's quiet and seems curious at first...until I tell her I'm sorry for the second kiss. Then she shuts down, and I understand that wasn't what she wanted to hear.

"Okay," she says finally.

I should be relieved by her simple acceptance. Instead, I feel like I just damned myself to the far reaches of hell.

ALLY

HE'S SORRY FOR IT.

Gah. Why does that *hurt* so much?

Why do I keep getting my hopes up with Connor? I should have known. And this is the last nail in the coffin on that pointless crush I have for the man.

It has to be. I can't keep doing this.

I assumed his request to talk was going to be something along these lines, but I didn't anticipate how badly hearing him say that he's sorry it happened was going to hurt.

But oh boy, it does.

Only by sheer will do I keep the pain from showing. I refuse to let him see how much his rejection affects me. I have more dignity than that.

My earlier affirmation that I didn't have time for a relationship—or the inclination for one—stands.

Connor regrets kissing me. Fine. We'll chalk it up to a mistake and move on. I still have to work with him for the next month and a half at a minimum. After that? I'll go back to doing what I do best—staying busy.

"Well, okay then. I'm going to go in." Sheer force of will keeps my chin from wobbling.

I don't know why I feel like crying right now, but I do.

This sucks.

Those dark eyes watch me, trying to see past the armor I'm fiercely guarding myself with, but after a second, he lets out a defeated sigh. Was he expecting me to push back, to demand something more from him?

I won't do it. I won't ask for anything he doesn't want to give me.

The simple admission that he tries *not* to look at me as anything other than a sister explains it all.

"Wait, Als."

That stupid nickname. It's one thing when Jackson uses it. It's completely different when Connor does, although I assume it serves the purpose of putting me into the sister category for him.

I twist to face him, hiking a brow up, waiting for him to say something—anything—to take the ache out of the snub he so effortlessly delivered.

"Yes?"

"We're okay, right? You and me?"

You and me.

"Can I ask you a question?"

"Yeah."

"Why are you sorry it happened? I mean, if you've *tried* not to look at me like that, which I'm taking to mean you have looked at me like *that*, why are you sorry?"

I shouldn't drill down on this, but I need to know.

His thumb starts ticking against that ring finger, and I just *know* that whatever he says now isn't going to be the answer I'm looking for.

"Let's just say I've been down this road before, and it never ends well."

Typical Connor deflection. "What does that mean? You've been down this road before?"

Connor's been a constant presence in my life for so long, it's hard to reconcile that there are important things I may not be aware of. Sure, he's quiet, but over the years you pick up little things about people. And I'm realizing at this very moment how little I truly know about his past.

Something like resignation passes over his face.

"I guess I should start at the beginning. Me and my ma moved around a lot. That is, until my father found out about me.

"I had a friend—Delaney. He was my best friend. Both of our fathers put us in a new school around the same time, so we went through the new-kid routine together."

The school system is small here in Felt, and I stayed with the same classmates from the first day of kindergarten through graduation. Changing schools wasn't something I had to deal with, but I can imagine it's tough for kids.

"Delaney and I were buds. We grew up together in that damn school, both of us just trying to keep our heads down. When we got pulled back home to start high school, I met April, Delaney's sister."

I have a feeling I know where this is going, but I don't want to interrupt.

"April and I started dating my sophomore year of high school. Delaney knew about it and approved—said it was like having a real brother—and for the next two years we were all pretty much inseparable. Senior year rolls around and we planned this epic summer road trip. We were going to try to visit fifteen states and tour the state parks and monuments. Delaney ended up having to cancel because he was scheduled to start working with his dad before he went to college."

Connor's voice is telling the story by rote—no inflection, no emotion, just stating the facts—and the sinking sensation in my stomach gets deeper. I bet this story isn't going to have a good ending.

"April and I set off the next morning. By the time we made our first stop, she was begging me to let her drive. She'd just gotten her license and wanted to test it out on the trip. I waited until we were well enough on the way that she couldn't get us lost before I handed over the driving reins. It was just starting to get dark when a deer darted into the road in front of us. April swerved to miss it, but we went off the road and into a tree. She died on impact."

Jesus. "Connor, I'm so sorry."

As if I hadn't spoken, he starts to peel the label on his beer while continuing, "About two weeks later, they held the funeral for her. Right there at her graveside, Delaney blamed me for her dying."

Voice thick, he's not looking at me now. He's staring out over the yard as he says, "How could I have let her drive when her license was so new? It should have been me that died…and things like that. The shitty part was that I believed him. I believed him for a long time. Instead of just recognizing that he was grieving and hurt, letting him vent his rage at me, I took a swing at him.

"We fought. Right there at April's fucking grave. I fought with her brother, my best friend. There was so much helpless rage in me at the time that I didn't know what the hell to do. It should have been me driving, it should have been me to get hurt—" His voice breaks on the word, and I can feel the burn of my own tears in the back of my eyes. "At least, that's what I thought at the time. I didn't realize then it was just a shitty outcome to a shitty situation. But that day, I said goodbye to a girl I loved and the years-long friendship with her brother."

"Does Jackson know about this?"

His lips roll in. "Jackson knows. I told him a long time ago."

Connor's hesitance toward me and regret over the kiss make sense now. I'd be leery of starting something up with a friend's sister after that nightmare.

I don't say that to him though, because as much as it's in the past, bringing it up still has to hurt. Explaining it all to someone has to reopen that hurt, and I don't want to make it worse for him.

Brows pinched, he looks at me. Sometime during his recounting, I took his hand. The pain in his voice made me reach out, either as a reminder that I'm here, that I'm listening, or that I just needed to help him through it.

Either way, his hand is in mine, and his thumb coasts along the back of my knuckles, sending a shiver across my shoulders.

"I'm sorry you had to go through that. That you lost her, and you lost a friend. It wasn't fair. But you know it's not your fault, right?"

"I do know. It took me a long time to get there, to understand it was just an accident. Actually, coming up here helped a lot."

"How so?"

"My third year in college, I was still pissed at the world and pretty shut down, dealing with my father and everything else, when I met Jackson."

"Oh, boy."

Finally, a small smile plays across his face, and I feel like I just placed gold in the Olympics. Connor's not much of a smiler. I've managed to drag a few of them out of him over the years, but this might be the best yet because of the circumstances.

"Yeah. I was less than interested in making a friend that year. But we had to find a volunteer forestry position over the summer as part of our junior-year degree requirements.

He told me I should come up here, and I did. One of the best decisions I've ever made."

"Why?"

"Because of your dad."

Thinking back, I vaguely remember that summer. It was just after I had graduated from high school and had started a job at a local hotel resort. I had a little studio apartment, and between that, long hours, and a decent commute, I wasn't home very often. When Daniel and I began dating that fall, my schedule got even more hectic.

"My dad?"

"Yeah. James saw all the anger behind the surly exterior, and over the course of the summer, he pulled me out of the dark place I was in. He helped me come to the realization that sometimes shitty things happen to good people, but that it wasn't my fault."

Sounds like Dad. He was always the calm in the storm, he and Ma handling with ease whatever life threw at them.

"He was great like that."

"He was. When Jackson got the call that he'd had the heart attack, I was just as devastated as y'all were. I really looked up to him."

Me too.

A lot more makes sense now, a lot of why Connor would fit me into the role of surrogate sister even if he was attracted to me. I understand now if he did have feelings for me they would be conflicted.

The sun's slide toward the horizon is more apparent now; the crickets came out sometime in the last half hour. As much as I'd like to sit out here for the rest of the night, talking to Connor, learning more about him, I can't.

If I picked up anything from his story, it's that no matter how much I might want it to be different, how much I'd love to show him we could be different, he needs to be on board first.

That realization leaves behind a mild ache, but one I'm more than familiar with by now when it comes to Connor.

His rejection and regret around our kisses are less about me and more about his own past. I won't browbeat him into seeing me in a different light or even into considering something more with me.

Pulling my hand from his, I say, "Thank you for telling me and being honest with me. Bygones?"

His hands rub down the length of his jeans before he eventually says, "Bygones."

"Okay, well, I'm going to head in, but I'll get in touch with you next week sometime about finalizing the courses and the changes that Mayor Davis put into place for the events. You can come by the bakery, and we'll talk it out."

"How's the bakery going?" he asks as he follows me back into the kitchen.

"It's good. The mold specialist finished up this week. Now I'm just waiting for Colby to get in and get everything squared away for me. We're making some basic changes to the layout."

"Y'all need anything?"

The slight Southern drawl I hear in his voice never fails to make me smile. "Nah, we're good. It's just a matter of juggling everything. Thanks, though."

By the time we reach the front door, the nerves I felt when I first realized he was here at the start of the afternoon surface again. Twisting my hands at my waist, I don't know what the best thing to do would be.

Do I hug him, kiss his cheek? What's the protocol when your friend shares something tragic with you in the name of rejecting you as a woman?

In the end, I just go with it, wrapping my arms around him. His cedar scent goes right to my head.

After the shortest hug in the history of the world concludes, he's out the door and gone.

Shutting off the lights, I carry the remainder of my wine upstairs. With a quick glance at the clock, I figure I can stand to be a little tired tomorrow. Self-care this evening is calling for wine, a bath, and a good book.

But submerged in steamy water with my book ready, my mind doesn't get lost between the pages of the vampire romcom. It circles back to Connor and his admission.

History has a funny way of coming back to haunt us, especially when we've done our best to bury it.

I can't think about that, not right now. I need to get my bakery put back together and get through planning the festival event with him.

Better to not throw a wrench in that, for now at least.

CONNOR

The Sweet Tooth is the last place I want to be on a Friday morning when I should be sorting out the inspector issue that has stopped all progress on my house, but here I am.

I'm in the homestretch with the cabin. Soon I'll have a fully finished house, if I could just get the cocksucking inspector to clear my electrical, plumbing, and HVAC.

Instead, he was a no-show yesterday, and I haven't been able to schedule another inspection for sooner than two more weeks out.

Irritation buzzes at the back of my mind until I'm not fit for company.

The two-room cabin wasn't the draw on the land I purchased when I got the first shot of my inheritance. It was the uncleared land.

The twenty acres sits adjacent to Liv and Jackson's place but is still secluded enough to suit my hermit tendencies while being close enough to town that I can come and go easily.

The small cabin that was out there is what I'm living in

now, and that took some time to get into good enough shape until I could focus on the addition.

The inspector is the first hitch in my plans.

I yank open the door, letting my irritation carry me into the corner building.

Ally's sitting in the back of the dining room, papers spread out around her, and I can make out the sounds of a construction site coming from the kitchen.

The morning rush is done, and Jem is restocking behind the counter, switching things over for the lunch crowd, but other than that?

It's empty in here.

Like always, looking at Ally, I'm hit with how *lovely* she is, and it goes a long way toward knocking some of the surliness out of my attitude.

I want all of that loveliness under me, sweat slick and panting for more of my touch, even if it's only the fantasies I'll allow myself.

After telling her about April and receiving the acceptance Ally offered, a small weight I didn't even know I was carrying had fallen off my shoulders.

Her understanding why a relationship isn't a good idea should have alleviated the never-ending craving I have for the woman, but, if anything, it's gotten worse.

Ally senses me watching her, and her head lifts, eyes meeting mine, before her customary smile covers her face.

Eyebrow hitched, she asks, "You letting all the bought air out?"

I'm holding the door open, standing here like an idiot.

Get a hold of yourself, man.

I close the door and wind through the bistro tables and chairs to reach her. Plopping myself down into the chair across from her, I ask, "What's all this?"

It looks like a bunch of plans, and it isn't until she flips the blueprint paper around that I can make out the building.

"I'm renovating the kitchen and the upper floor of the building. With Jackson moving in with Liv, I'm thinking that I might remodel the floor to make it into a place for me and the girls." She looks at me like she wants my opinion, her lower lip caught between her teeth.

"For you and the girls? You're moving out of Nan's place?"

"I've been thinking about it. It was supposed to be temporary—moving home—something to hold me until I could find my own place. Then I bought the bakery but couldn't exactly move us into a small two-bedroom apartment upstairs. They needed a lot of work back then, and I needed a lot of help. But now that the girls are older and I have the means to renovate the space into one big apartment, we'd have more than enough space. I'm trying to decide whether I want to do it."

The schematics show the floor above us transformed into three bedrooms, two bathrooms and more than enough kitchen space for a baker like Ally.

The whole idea sits wrong with me, though I can't put my finger on why.

It might just be my hesitation with change, but I like knowing she's at her ma's, that she has help with the girls if she needs it.

This move wouldn't put her that far away from Nan, and it's not like the support she gets from Nan and Jackson would just disappear, but still, I don't like it.

I must not keep the distaste off my face because she asks, "Not a fan, huh?"

"Are you unhappy there?"

"At Ma's house? No. Nothing like that. It's just…"

"Just what?"

"I'm almost thirty, and I'm still living at home with Ma.

I'm a successful business owner. It's about time I moved out on my own."

She's twenty-seven, so "almost thirty" is a stretch, but I can't argue with the rest of her explanation. I never would have made it that long living with my father.

Then again, Nan isn't an abusive asshole with a list of sins a mile long.

"Well, you're having more luck in the housing department than I am."

Reaching up to tuck a strand of hair behind her ear, she asks, "Cabin addition not going according to plan?"

"You could say that."

All her attention is focused on me, and the laser pinpoint of her hazel eyes makes me want to squirm.

"What's going on?" she asks.

In for a penny, in for a pound. Some part of me must want to unload this shit. "The insulation and drywall were supposed to go in Monday, but the inspector to clear my electrical, HVAC, and plumbing was a no-show yesterday, so I've got materials coming this afternoon, but no go-ahead on moving forward."

"Did you call the Division of Building Safety?"

"I did, but got the runaround. The best they could do was reschedule me for two weeks out."

"Who was your inspector?"

"Matthew Hayward."

"No shit? He's the one who did the inspection for the permits on my renovation when I first took over the bakery. Give me ten minutes."

She whips her phone out of her pocket before I can stop her and dials.

"Matt? Hey, it's Ally Sawyer. How're you doing?"

I listen as she sweet-talks the person on the other line.

"Can you do that for me? I've got a dozen doughnuts with

your name on them if we can make this work. Mm-hmm. Okay, yeah, that's perfect. Thank you so much. You're a literal lifesaver! We'll see you soon."

She disconnects the call and stacks her papers into neat piles. "He'll be at your place in twenty minutes. Come on, let's go."

That fucking easy. She made a single phone call and managed to get an inspector to agree to come out there on a dime to do a walk-through of my house.

She's already threading her way toward the counter when I think to ask, "You're coming with?"

Laughing lightly, she says, "Of course. I can't deliver doughnuts if I'm not there. Plus, I know Matt; we went to school together. And I wanted to talk to you about splitting up the contacts for the participant list, which is why I asked you to come down here in the first place. Can't exactly do that if you're there and I'm here."

Well, shit. I guess we're going on a field trip. She boxes up the doughnuts, and I point her toward my truck.

Eyes squinted, she looks me over, and I try not to fidget.

This should be interesting.

We're both buckling in when she speaks again. "Matt and Joe are the only inspectors for our region, so I'm not surprised you got Matt, but it is surprising that he no-showed on you. That's not like him."

An invisible tension gathers in the cab of the truck, and the skin on my arms forms bumps in the proximity to Ally.

She reaches over and pats the back of my hand. "We'll get you squared away today, then you can get cooking on the rest of the house."

Before she can pull back, I capture her hand in mine.

I shouldn't be doing this. I shouldn't be holding her hand. I shouldn't be thinking about her coming undone under me. I shouldn't be having any of these thoughts, but I fucking am.

The smooth skin of her hand is warm against mine, and I force the logical part of my brain to shut off and just enjoy this for as long as I can.

"So." Her voice has a slight waver to it before solidifying. "The courses. I spoke with Mayor Davis, and he's fine with the changes to the schedule I suggested."

"Changes?" I recognize the rough texture in my own tone, but I can't do anything about it. I'm surprised she hasn't pulled her hand back yet; the air-clearing we had the other night gives her more than enough reason to, but I guess we're both just living in the moment.

"Yeah, I proposed that we hold the cow chip toss on Monday and the fry pan toss on Friday, with the whip-cracking on Wednesday, to spread them out and make it so I can announce them for you."

"Thank you. I appreciate it."

The rest of the ride goes by with Ally and me discussing the plans for splitting up our to-do list for the event. Her hand is still in mine, and she's doing something on her phone when we pull into my makeshift driveway.

"Holy shit!"

I whip around and see her eyes locked on the cabin and relax.

"It's so different from the last time I was out here. You've made a lot of progress, Con. It looks like it's almost done."

"It is."

I have this inspection and then it's drywall and insulation before final connections go into place. And then we just have the punch list.

Working construction every summer through high school gave me the foundation I needed to do a lot of the addition myself, but there are things I can't do, hence my irritation at the delay with the inspector.

There's a blue Silverado parked along the dirt road, and a guy my age is sitting in the cab.

Ally releases my hand to climb out of the cab. The way this fucker swoops her into his arms gets my back up.

That's a little too *friendly* for two people who "went to school together."

Looks like I'll be fighting back the jealousy monster.

I climb out of the truck and make my way over to them.

Ally introduces us, and the guy gives me a solid handshake with no macho posturing in it. There's also zero attraction in his gaze when they chat about the changes she wants to make to the bakery.

This guy's not a threat.

A threat? When did I start worrying about the guys interested in Ally? It's none of my business, and I'd do well to remember that.

"Hey, man. Sorry about yesterday. My wife went into labor, and I don't get reception at the hospital. I tried to get ahold of Joe to come out and do your inspection, but he must not have gotten my message."

His wedding ring shines in the sunlight, and his disinterest in Ally makes more sense.

Makes more sense? What the hell *is wrong with me?*

"Congratulations, and thanks for coming out, considering."

"No worries. It's probably gonna be a pretty quick walk-through because it's residential. Should we get started?"

Ally waves us off saying, "I've gotta make a call, you two go ahead. I'll be out here."

While we walk through the house, he takes notes and measures doorways, checks electrical socket placement, and works his way down the inspection list. Sure enough, less than an hour later, he's tucking his notebook in his messenger bag and saying, "I'll head in and file this now so your tradespeople can come in and get started on Monday."

Getting the go-ahead for the next step is a huge weight off my shoulders. My goal is to have the house done by the beginning of winter because I don't want to be working on the house in the snow. Winters can get brutal, and even after living here almost a decade, I'm still not quite used to the cold.

"Thanks, man. I appreciate it," I tell him.

"Any time." With a wave over his shoulder and his doughnuts in the other hand, he hoofs it out to his truck and is gone.

Because I'm making all sorts of spontaneous decisions today, I ask, "Want a tour?"

She grins. "Duh."

ALLY

THE RUSTIC CABIN THAT HAD ALMOST ROTTED INTO THE WOODS surrounding it has been transformed.

Heavily guarded by a surly park ranger, this place is so off-limits it might as well be the Batcave.

The last time I was out here was last winter, when Connor caught a bad flu and Ma sent me over to take him some chicken soup. Back then it was little more than a single room, but in the last year, he's changed it up.

Connor's hand finds mine, and just like in his truck, my stomach plays tilt-o-whirl while my heart tries to escape my chest.

What am I, in middle school again?

Leading me through the first floor of the house, Connor shows me the place, which is man-tidy. Most of the clutter is put away, but there's still visible dust and the odd sock on the floor, which makes sense since the majority of the living room is set up like a studio apartment.

Kicking at a pair of running shoes, he's all shy awkwardness. "Sorry about the mess. It's been a busy couple of weeks, and I haven't had time to pick up."

"Psh, I'm used to it. The girls are like little hoarders, and their room is always a disaster unless I stay on top of them to clean it up."

Breaking away from him, I ignore his stiff countenance as I start to explore. The addition is still rough, but not the plywood and ripped-down-to-the-studs walls that I was expecting.

After practically living in The Sweet Tooth during the last renovation, I can see what he's doing with the space.

The entirety of the original cabin looks like it'll become the living room, and the first-floor addition has pipes and wires placed to suggest that his new kitchen is going to be massive. The powder room off the living room also looks like it's going through a major overhaul.

He's pretty much taking the cabin and building a new house surrounding it. I'm a fan of the layout he's aiming for.

"What are your plans design-wise?"

"Eh, I didn't really think of that."

Before I think of hectic schedules, volunteering for the town committees, or rebuilding my own damn bakery, I offer, "Oh, please let me do it."

He gapes at me. "You want to design a soon-to-be three-thousand-square-foot house?"

I laugh at the shock playing across his face. I love design, but I guess we don't know a lot about each other if he's questioning me on this.

The more I think about it, the more I like the idea. I've always loved design and DIY projects. Yeah, the timeline will be a little more insane, but insanity is something I'm good at juggling.

"You force me to repeat myself, but duh. I'd love to give you a hand. I did all of the planning and decor at The Sweet Tooth, and if I hadn't gone to culinary school, interior design was my backup."

Indecision covers his expression, and I capitalize on the moment. "You could save some money and let me do it. I've always wanted to design a house from the ground up, so I'd be living vicariously through you…please." I draw out the plea in the hopes that I'm just annoying enough for him to give in.

I may not know everything about him, but I know enough.

"Fine. Go crazy. But don't, like, put in a bunch of girly shit, okay?"

Snapping my fingers, I roll my eyes, saying, "Dammit. And here I was going to paint your walls Pepto Bismol pink."

Ugh, boys.

"Ally." The gruff way he growls my name sets off the needy parts of me, and just like that, my mind is in a dozen different dirty positions with the man.

I have to roll my eyes at him, even if he makes me wanton, because it's just too easy to fuck with him.

"Connor, first off, that's not how this works; we design together. I'm just helping, but you? You have to live here. So you'll get final say. We also need to set up a budget for everything because I need to know the parameters I can work within. But you and I, we're going to be in this together."

There's fear in his eyes now, just a smidge of it, and I take great pride in having scared him.

Before he can get too in his head about it, I ask, "Show me the second floor?"

We head up the roughed-in stairs. The second level is even better than the first. There are four bedrooms up here, and a loft space that would be perfect for a playroom. You know, if he had kids.

Since he doesn't, I'm curious about how he plans on using all this space when it's just him.

"Do you have any idea for the rooms yet? And where's the master bedroom?"

Each pair of bedrooms is connected by a shared bathroom, and I have serious house envy now.

Tugging on his ear, he says, "I'll think about it and let you know. The master is on the first floor."

"Okay. We can't do a lot until the punch list is done, but I can come up with some ideas between now and then. When is this supposed to be finished?"

"The last week of September. So right before the Cowboy Courses kick off."

"Wow. We're going to be busy."

"We?" Connor scoffs and shakes his head. "You already are busy. Why I'm letting you help me with this is beyond me."

He's got a point. But I'm not turning down the opportunity for something *fun.* "Oh, psh. This is fun for me, not work at all. I love getting into a new project. There're only so many changes Ma will let me make to the house, so this? This is exciting and not nearly difficult enough to be considered work."

"Glad you'll be enjoying yourself at least."

"It'll be fun. You'll see. Show me the master downstairs. Is that the only area I haven't seen yet?"

"Yeah, and an office of sorts. What I need a damned office for I have no idea, but it made sense when I was drawing up the plans."

"Hmm, how about a manly study? Let's go take a look, and we can figure something out."

Back downstairs, Connor opens a set of pocket doors, and my heart sighs at the serious envy I have for this house. Once it's done, it's going to be beautiful.

Floor-to-ceiling windows let in the surrounding forest and soft light. The whole room is illuminated, and it's almost as if you can step through the windows directly into the wilderness. I'm adding something like this if I ever get the chance to build my own house.

There's not much in the actual space, just a desk holding some papers and a laptop. The desk chair is ancient and needs to be replaced if the duct tape surrounding the base is an indicator.

A glass fireplace sits in the far corner, and, like magic, the room starts to take shape in my mind.

Narrating as I go, I point out various ideas. "Mahogany mantel over the fireplace. Built-ins along the far wall; maybe some shelving for pictures. On this wall, you must put the vintage globe map you have, the one that Jackson had on the wall in the apartment. You still have it, right?"

"Yeah, it's in storage, but I've got it."

"Perfect. We'll do soft-light sconces on the walls to complement the recessed lighting in here. You need a better desk. Something big and dark. Throw in a warm gold on the walls and a couple of dark leather couches with lighter throw pillows, and you'll have yourself a very nice study."

Connor's head swivels, following my finger and descriptions, and by the time I finish, his eyebrows have climbed higher on his forehead.

Smug smile in place, I ask, "Not bad, huh?"

Shaking his head, he replies, "No, not bad at all. And you can do that for the rest of the house too?"

"Sure can." Glancing down at my watch, I note the time. We're cutting it close to the start of the lunch rush, so I say, "Show me the master and then I need you to take me back so Jem isn't slammed by herself."

"Sure, come on."

Down the hall, I note another bathroom, which brings the total to four—yep, definitely envious—before he throws open a door at the far end of the house.

Like the rest of this place, his room is massive. A giant wooden sleigh bed dominates the space, with mismatched dresser and nightstands taking up the rest of it.

He's got good lighting in here as well. With the flooring done and walls intact, I surmise this is part of the original cabin. Not too shabby. Not too shabby at all.

I'm wandering around the bed trying to get a feel for the space when a frame on his nightstand catches my attention.

Heart sighing at the sight of it, I pick it up. "You have my girls on your nightstand."

Their tiny faces smile broadly at the camera. Emma is holding up a trout, and Elle's nose is covered in thick, white sunscreen. Both of them are in waders, standing in the lake. The gapped teeth tell me this was taken summer before last when the girls were signed up for the fishing and hunting portion of the outdoor summer programs the ranger station hosts each year.

Programs that Connor takes the lead on.

I had no idea he had this picture or that he even took it, but it makes me want to cry happy tears.

"Uh, yeah. I, uh, hope that's okay. It was on the solo fishing day where each of us took a couple of kids out."

"No, it's perfect. I love it. They look so happy."

"They're happy girls. If I remember right, this was right before Elle slipped on a mossy rock and went down in the water, dragging Emma with her. In the scramble, the fish managed to escape, line and hook still in its mouth."

"I remember them telling me about that." They came home that evening soaking wet, excited and hyper from a good day of fishing.

I'd been dog-tired, but their enthusiasm had given me a second wind, so we ended up grilling for dinner and making s'mores that night.

He loves them.

I look up. Connor's attention is on the frame in my hands. I don't question it. I don't stop myself or pause to wonder and think about why I shouldn't. I just pivot, rise on my toes, and press my lips to his in a light kiss.

He stiffens for a second before relaxing into the kiss and, after a beat, moving his lips against mine. This isn't like the kisses before—they were all heat and fireworks. This one is the smooth slide of molasses, slow, deep, and heady.

Connor's hands burrow into my hair. His fingers scrape along my scalp as his tongue dances across the seam of my mouth, asking for permission.

Fuck it. I jump into the deep end, parting my lips. Cedar and heat singe my senses until I'm just as lost in the moment as he is, until I can't tell where my mouth ends and his starts.

My nipples pebble, and goosebumps break out as I realize my fingers are digging into the expanse of Connor's shoulders. The abrasive texture of his beard rubs along my chin and cheeks, careening me into a whirlpool of sensation. Faintly, I hear my cellphone ringing in my bag in the living room.

Breaking the kiss, I pause for a second of stunned silence. Connor's dark gaze shifts across my face. Does he see how much I want him?

The shrill ringtone starts up again and jolts me out of the panty-incinerating kiss and back to reality.

"Shit. That's the girls' school." I sprint to the living room, grabbing the device and swiping to answer.

"Ms. Sawyer?"

"This is she."

"This is Nurse Shelly. I've got Emma here. She threw up, and Elle's complaining of an upset stomach as well."

"Okay, I'll be right there to pick them up."

"Thank you."

Disconnecting the call, I ring Ma's phone, but she doesn't answer. Next, I try Jackson with the same result.

I cannot leave Jem to handle the Friday lunch crowd on her own. Both of my part-time employees are off today; the crowds lately are enough to overwhelm the most seasoned worker, and that's not even considering the repairs going on right now either.

Calling Kate, I get her voice mail too. I'm staring at the contacts in my phone, but I have no idea who to call for backup.

"Can you take me back to my SUV?" I ask Connor. "I've got to go pick up the girls from school."

"Are they okay?"

"Emma threw up, and Elle isn't feeling well. Probably just a stomach bug, but I need to help Jem at the bakery, so I'll take them back there with me."

"I can take them."

I lift my head to peer at Connor. The placid expression that's standard for him is present, and I wonder...

No, I can't ask him to take two sick girls. Taking them fishing or hiking when they're healthy is one thing, but the possibility of projectile vomiting is different.

I open my mouth to decline but he interrupts, "Als, come on, let me help. You aren't going to be able to watch them and work, and them being sick in the office of the bakery won't be fun for anyone. I'm assuming you can't get ahold of anyone, so let me take them. I'll hang out with them at Nan's until you get home or Nan does. I can handle it."

Nervous mom anxiety pings around my head as I consider it.

He has no experience with sick kids, but he's not wrong. I can't exactly watch the girls while I'm working the lunch counter, and they'd be most comfortable at home. Plus, sick kids in a restaurant spells disaster.

Where the hell is Ma?

I can't remember her saying that she had anything to do today, but I could be wrong since it's not like we keep a family calendar.

"Are you sure?" Not that I have many options at this point.

"Yes. I'll drop you at your car and then I'll go grab the girls from school."

"We'll have to swap cars; you need their car seats."

He nods. "Okay. I'll take you back to the bakery, you call the school and give me permission to pick them up, I'll load them up and take them back to Nan's place, and we'll hang out with puke buckets."

Shouldering my purse, I say, "In the main bathroom, there's a thermometer in the medicine cabinet. If they start to run a fever over one hundred one point seven, you'll need to give them Tylenol or ibuprofen. The dosage directions are on the back. Emma will tell you when she's about to be sick, but Elle won't. There are saltines in the pantry and water in the fridge. If they don't want to drink the water you can give them a little bit of juice, but try to keep them hydrated."

His hand slides along my lower back as I hastily give him instructions for taking care of the girls. Every appendage I have is crossed that this works.

From the passenger seat, I fire off text message after text message. First to my friends and family, but they're all unanswered. By the time we get to the store, I've messaged my two part-time clerks to see if either of them can come in and relieve me.

Those go unanswered too, until I'm forced to accept Connor's offer of help.

Still hoping for the best, I call the school and let them know that Connor is going to pick up the girls before switching my phone volume to loud so if I get a call or text, I'll hear the phone go off.

I hand him my keys and hustle inside. The line at the counter is already wrapped around the interior of the store, and Jem is shooting me glances, pleading for help.

Please let this go smoothly.

CONNOR

TWO MISERABLE FACES STARE AT ME FROM THE BACKSEAT OF the car. I don't blame them—stomach bugs suck.

The short trip from the elementary school is luckily made with no fanfare in the vomit department. Still, I made sure they had bags to aim for should they feel sick.

Now I just have to get them inside.

"Okay, Peanut Brittle. Let's go in."

No response, but that's okay. The goal here is to get them comfortable.

Then? No fucking clue.

Carting the girls inside and laying them on the couch, I take a second to look them over. Obviously sick, but as much as I want, I can't take the bug from them. Best to make them as comfortable as I can, I guess.

"C-c-can we have blankets?" Elle's teeth chatter as she hugs her arms to her chest.

Shifting the throw off the couch, I start to tug it around her shoulders when she says, "Not this one. Can I have my unicorn blanket from my room?"

"Sure, sweetie. Here, let's wrap you in this one for now, and I'll be right back."

Uncharacteristically quiet, Emma is just watching me, so I ask, "Do you want anything from your room, honey?"

Emma starts to open her mouth before closing it again, a weird expression crossing her face.

She's gonna throw up.

I don't know where the thought comes from, but I run with instinct and scoop her into my arms. Like The Flash, I dash into the first-floor bathroom and flip up the toilet lid right before Emma loses whatever else she has in her stomach.

Scooping her blonde hair back, I hold it out of the way as she sicks up the rest of her breakfast, lunch, and what I assume are a couple of internal organs.

Poor girl.

I rub lightly at her back while she finishes. Her little hand reaches over for toilet paper to wipe her mouth before I let her hair drop.

"Hang on, honey. Let me get you some water. Just stay right here. I'll be right back."

Moving with purpose, I grab a bottle of water from the fridge and head back into the living room. Elle's still bundled on the couch, and thinking back, I remember that she hasn't thrown up yet.

If she caught the same bug that Emma did, it's only a matter of time.

Dipping back into the bathroom, I offer the water to Emma, who's just sitting on the closed toilet.

"Here you go. Swish it around and then spit it out."

Emma does the swish-and-spit routine as a low whine comes from Elle on the couch.

Scooping up Emma, I drop her at the couch just as Elle starts to gag.

I hoist her up and run for the bathroom.

We make it—just barely, again—and it's worse for her.

In between gags, she starts to push at my arms. "No, Con. This is gross. Don't watch; go away."

Ah. I should have expected my shy girl to have an issue throwing up in front of me. Still, I'm hesitant to leave her.

I keep rubbing her back. "Shh. It's okay, sweetie. I've thrown up myself a fair share of times."

"I want Mama."

The way her voice trembles puts me on alert. If she cries, I'm a goner. I can't handle them crying. I want to fix everything for them and take away all the hurts.

How does their mom deal with the worry, the constant nagging feeling of inadequacy when they're sick or hurt?

She's magic. That's the only way to describe it.

Soothingly, I say, "I know you do, and she'll be here as soon as she can be. But for right now, I'm going to do my best to make you feel better, okay?"

She raises her arms, and I lean down to pick her up. She lays her head on my shoulder and rubs her hand along my chin. I get Elle situated on the couch before double-timing it up the stairs to grab blankets.

After tucking them in, I head back into the bathroom to get the thermometer. Emma calls, "I'm hungry."

I bet. I'd be hungry too after all that. Still, I know better than to give her anything overly heavy.

Running the thermometer between them, I pull my phone out and fire a message off to Ally.

Temps are at 98. We're home and settled on the couch.

OK. I should be there in a couple of hours unless Ma beats me home. Keep me updated?

Of course.

Thank you so much. I can't tell you how much I appreciate your help. Let me know if you need anything.

Another kiss sounds nice right about now.

I shove that thought away and don't respond to the message. Instead I pocket the device and head to the kitchen. With a pack of crackers from the pantry and a couple more bottles of water, I hoof it back to the living room and pop the packet open.

"Here, girls. You can nibble on these if you're hungry, but take it easy, okay?"

"Can I have lovies?" Emma asks.

What the hell is a lovie?

"Uh, sure. What's it look like?"

"My stuffed elephant off my bed."

"Can I have my lion?" Elle pipes up.

"Sure thing, ladies. I'll be right back."

Most of the afternoon passes that way. I'm running up and down the stairs, in and out of the kitchen, and to the bathroom whenever one of the girls starts to lose their stomach. It's approaching midafternoon when I sit down at last.

The opening theme to *The Little Mermaid* starts, and I relax into the couch with a sigh. My body is fucking exhausted. I feel like I just ran a marathon.

How the hell does Ally do this? Not only is she going to come home and take care of these girls, but then she's also got her business to run, the Cowboy Courses to organize and —now—she's helping me finish out my house.

Does she have superpowers?

Honestly, it wouldn't surprise me.

A shark is chasing the mermaid and her fish friend around on TV when I realize the seven-year-olds on each side of me are silent. They're both passed out cold. I lay my hand on their brows. They're still cool enough that I'm not worried about a fever cropping up while they sleep.

I drop kisses to their hair and rest my head against the couch, wrapping my arms around them and tucking them deeper into my sides. If either of them wakes up, I'll feel them move.

Going from kissing Ally in my bedroom to cleaning up puke today couldn't be stranger.

Weirdly, I don't mind. And I'm not talking about just the kiss either. Helping her with the girls, spending time listening to her detail her thoughts on the interior design of my house, just being around Ally…is turning from want to need, and I don't know what to do about it.

I'd do today all over again in a heartbeat, and that's a little scary to consider.

~

"Connor. Connor, hon. Wake up."

A hand is shaking me awake, but I'm warm and I don't want to get up.

There's pressure on my chest. I feel a bony elbow dig into my rib cage, hitting the tickle spot there, and my eyes snap open.

Guess I'm awake now.

Nan is standing over me, a soft smile on her face. Shifting, I roll out from under the girls. How we made it from me snoozing sitting up to me lying down and them sleeping on my chest, I have no idea.

They settle back in together on the couch, and I glance at the clock on the wall. It's only been about an hour, but man, we conked out.

Clearing my throat I ask, "Hey, is Ally home?"

"Not yet. She got stuck at the shop. She told me to send you home. She'll swing by after work and swap cars with you."

"Oh, okay." I scrub my hands down my face. Naps always make my brain sluggish, and I'm not firing on all pistons yet.

Nan tucks the blanket back around the sleeping girls. "You want some tea?"

"Nah, I'm gonna get home, get some dinner, and work on the house for a bit."

"Okay, well, thanks for helping out. Ally and I both appreciate it."

There's an underlying emphasis on Ally's name, but I'm still firmly in the camp of not digging into whatever is going on between us, so I just nod and slip my shoes on at the door before taking off.

It's late afternoon, so I stop at O'Malley's to grab some takeout, detour to the Felt Floral Shop, and figure I can swing by The Sweet Tooth to save Ally the trip.

The rush that was here at lunch is completely gone now, and through the parlor window I can see Jem cleaning the lobby and Ally organizing the stock behind the counter. The displays are empty in preparation for closing.

I bet she's eager to get home to the girls. Sidling up to the door, I note the closed sign is flipped, so I rap my knuckles against the wood trim.

Ally's head comes up, and she hurries around the counter to unlock the door and let me in.

"Hey, how're they?"

She looks so fucking tired. Like if she stopped moving she'd pass out cold. "They were sleeping when I left, but they had a rough afternoon. They snacked on saltines, and I had them sip water as much as I could."

"Okay. Are those for me?"

I forgot I was holding the bouquet of mixed flowers.

Passing her the cellophane-wrapped bundle, I say, "Yeah." Once my hands are free, I scrub a hand against my scalp.

"What's the occasion?"

"Just a thank you."

She slowly blinks a couple of times before smiling softly. "A thank you for passing two sick kids off to you so I could work?"

"Yes, er, I mean no. A thanks for your help today with the house."

"Oh, you didn't have to do that, but you're welcome. I appreciate it and your help today."

"No problem. How long do you think they'll be under for?"

Lips pursed, Ally takes a second to respond. "Usually Elle bounces back quicker than Emma, but if this is the bug that's been going around school, no more than a day or two. Why? What's up?"

"I'm on duty this weekend, and I was going to see if the girls wanted to come out and check trails with me on Sunday."

Head cocked to the side, she asks, "Just the girls?"

Shit. Should I invite her along? Normally when I steal the girls for the day, it's just me and them and they'll tag along at work with me while Ally works or does whatever she needs to.

"Uh."

Laughing, she says, "No, it's okay. I'm sure if they're feeling up to it, they'd love to hang out with you on Sunday. If you're sure it's not an imposition?"

"Not at all. We'll have fun."

"Okay. Sure. Let's see how they make it through tomorrow, and then I'll let you know."

"Sounds good."

Ally watches me for a few seconds, the silence between us

not uncomfortable for once. The pale skin of her face is almost ashen, and I know that she's probably running on fumes. Remembering what she's got on her plate as soon as she gets home makes me wish that I could do more for her than bring her some flowers.

If she were mine, I'd make her sit down while I take on the tasks of cooking dinner and cleaning up as well as watching over the twins.

She needs a break. But the stubborn woman won't ask for help, and getting her to accept it is like leading a horse to water and forcing it to drink.

Maybe there's something we can do about that though.

It'd be tricky, and I'd have to get Nan and Jackson in on the plan, but I'm sure between the three of us, we could make it happen.

"Let me grab your keys and you can head home. You have to be tired," Ally says.

You're one to talk.

Ally disappears behind the kitchen doors to grab her purse, I presume.

"Jem," I say quietly. "Who's working Sunday?"

"Clark is on first thing in the morning with me. Also, nice job with the flowers. You romancing our Ally?"

Ally comes back through the door before I can answer, and I'm relieved at the interruption because I don't know how to answer that question. I had my reasons for shoving Ally into the impossible-to-fit *just friends* box over the years, but maybe I shouldn't have. She deserves better than me, but after that kiss at my place, maybe she doesn't seem to think so?

I don't fucking know, though. I could always take it a day at a time and see what happens.

The thought of someone depending on me for something outside my work makes my shoulders itch. After April, I swore I wouldn't muddy the lines of friendship and romance again.

I can be as dependable as the sun when it comes to myself and my work, but if I move Ally out of the friend category to something more, what happens when I fuck it all up?

That's not a question I'm comfortable thinking about right now.

But first, Ally needs a break, and I'm gonna be the one to ensure she takes it.

ALLY

SUNDAY MORNING, I'M SCRUBBING THE TWINS' ROOM DOWN with Clorox.

Once again I'd been up late, doing paperwork for the shop. Cleaning out and organizing my business files. Dealing with the errant files on my computer that always seem to build up no matter how I try to keep them organized.

After fighting exhaustion for the first coffeepot of the day, I grabbed a refill and shuffled the girls outside so I could attack the germ infestation that is their bedroom. Ma has them weeding the flower beds right now, and I'm grateful for the reprieve.

The worst of the stomach bug passed yesterday afternoon. At dinner last night, they ate as if they were starving, so I'm optimistic about today.

When I brought up the prospect of hanging with Connor for the day, they were more than excited. After taking care of them while they were sick, he's officially cemented in hero status for them.

"Hey, you," Ma calls from the hallway. "We're all done. I'm gonna make the girls a snack."

"That's good. I'm done here myself. I'll come down and pack them a lunch to take with them."

Connor texted this morning, letting me know he'd be here by eleven to grab the girls. I don't know exactly what he's got planned for the day, but I figure it's a good idea to have them take some food with them.

I'm going to have *hours* without the kids around when I can catch up on work. The sign-up form for the Cowboy Courses went out last month and closed earlier this week, so getting those entries categorized is on the to-do list for this evening. I still have to find time to walk the obstacle course route, schedule the logistics for setup, and organize the participants for our events.

Then there's my own accounting that needs to be dealt with.

Never-ending fun over here, y'all.

Focused on my to-do list, I almost run into Kate at the bottom of the stairs. My brain takes a second to process that my friend is in my house. And that Liv is closing the front door behind her. Did we have plans I've forgotten about?

"Hey, guys. What are you doing here?"

A sinister smile slides across Kate's face, and I have a moment to think *uh-oh* before she says, "We're kidnapping you for the day."

What? "Kidnapping?"

Liv says, "Yep, we're under explicit orders. So you need to come with us."

"Um. What orders?" I whine. Really, was it too much to hope for a few uninterrupted hours to get my life together?

A rumble of masculine laughter comes from the kitchen. I didn't expect Connor to get here so early, but I know that laugh. It's accompanied by two more familiar ones. Suspicious, I narrow my eyes at Kate and Liv before skirting around them to head into the kitchen.

Arik and Jackson are standing at the island while Connor rinses strawberries. The girls are sitting on barstools, and their tinkling laughter dominates the space.

Arik looks up, and Kate must be standing behind me because his eyes warm and fill with laughter and love. "Katie, you had one job. You were supposed to get this one out of here."

She walks to him and brushes a kiss across his mouth, and an odd sensation washes over me.

I don't have time for a relationship, so why does the sight of their ease and affection with each other make my chest tighten?

Liv abandons me for Jackson. I was worried about those two for a while this summer, but they managed to pull it together, and seeing her tucked under his arm makes my heart happy for them.

Despite the schemes these four yahoos are planning.

Jackson drops a kiss on Liv's head before saying, "Yeah, Liv, what happened to getting her out of here before she could ask questions?"

"What the heck is going on?" I ask.

Arik throws a thumb over his shoulder in Connor's direction. "This guy arranged for you to have a day up at the resort. Jackson and I capitalized on his plan by sacrificing Sunday with our ladies. Y'all are headed up the mountain for an overnight trip."

I'm already shaking my head before Arik finishes his explanation. "I can't. I have to—"

"Already taken care of," Connor says. "Jem will open tomorrow, and she called Clark in to take your lunch shift. You're off work for the day."

I know that he means well, but I have a *routine.* My teeth clench hard and my hands ache to curl into fists. Him coming in here and rearranging everything is going to mess that all up. I was just fantasizing about the hours I won't have the girls around, but this? This is too much. Too expensive. Too presumptuous. Too fucking much.

Clenching my teeth harder, I try to hold the irritation out of my tone when I say, "Can I talk to you outside?"

Shrugging, he walks through the back door, leaving me to follow him.

I pull the door shut behind me. Sure, it's not much of a noise deterrent, but it's something at least.

"Look, I know you mean well, but—"

"I do," he says.

Ignoring his interruption, I continue, "You can't just rearrange the schedule at *my* bakery."

Connor holds his hands up. "I'm gonna stop you right there. I didn't rearrange the schedule. I asked Jem to do it."

Irritation is quickly morphing into pissed-the-fuck-off, but I hold on to my temper. "And that makes it okay for you to barge in here and make decisions for me, for my girls, for my business?"

"Looks like it." He's all smug, smirking satisfaction, and I want to wipe the impish curl of his lips off his smarmy freaking face.

"Connor, look."

Mouth flattening, eyes narrowing, even the hint of his previous smirk is gone. Looks like someone else's temper is coming out to play.

"No. You look, Ally. Go look in the mirror. You're fucking exhausted. We all see it. The bags under your eyes could fit the luggage for a five-person family. You barely fucking sleep, you keep adding more and more to your bottomless list of responsibilities, but you won't ask for help because you just *have* to do everything yourself. Well, that's not gonna fly anymore."

Oh, no, he didn't.

"Oh, really? And who made you the boss of me?"

"I did. You need a keeper, and lucky for you, I'm up for the task."

This asshat.

It takes a lot for me to lose my temper, but I'm precariously close to exploding. Who the fuck does he think he is to waltz in here and tell me how to live my life?

I bite out, "I'm not going."

I don't realize we're toe to toe until the heat of his breath coasts along my cheekbone as he leans down. "Oh, *honey,* you're going. If I have to hog-tie you and throw you in the car myself, you're going."

"Over my dead body." All that's missing from the vow is a stamping foot, but I hold back—barely.

Eyes flat, his own irritation starts to show. "As appealing as that sounds right now, you'll go. You'll go, and you'll fucking relax for the first time in your life. If not for you, do it for those girls. The ones watching us through the window right now. The ones you're trying to raise right. How do you think they're going to learn to ask for help, to take breaks, to accept help when they need it if the most influential woman in their life won't do it? Not a great example you're setting there, Ally."

His sarcasm inflames my rage.

"You son of a b—"

Body bumping against mine, he backs me out of the range of the kitchen window, where after a quick glance I confirm what he said. Not only were the girls watching, but so was everyone else.

Once we're away from the window, he nudges me back until my shoulders meet the siding of the house.

Then his mouth is on mine again.

His hands fist in the length of my hair as mine clutch at his forearms to keep my balance. My hips line up with his, and our thighs bump when he hauls me into his chest. The heat of his erection sears through the thin yoga pants I'm wearing.

We're four for four on the difference between kisses. There's angry lust attached to the way his tongue dips in to taste, teeth nipping along my lower lip. I bite back the sounds that want to erupt from my throat at such a swift shift from irritation to passion.

Giving as good as I'm getting, I thread my arms around his neck and plaster myself against him. If he thinks he can kiss me quiet, then he's got another think coming.

I scratch and tug at his scalp, and the short strands of his hair slide between my fingers. I let him plunder my mouth, reveling in the rumbling groans he lets out.

Two can play this game. I'll plunder right the heck back.

One of his hands bites into my hip while the other leaves my hair to rest right under my breast, his thumb caressing the underside of it. He softens the kiss before disengaging.

My knees are shaking—from the kiss or the coffee overload of the day, I have no idea. My core thumps in time with my pulse, angry at the neglect. I can't remember the last time I felt this needy, this turned on, or this desperate for a kiss to continue, even being mad at him.

Pulling back, his harsh whisper ghosts across my lips. "Do it for me, Als. Take a day. We'll hold the fort here. Take a day —for me."

Fuck.

"Fine, I'll go. But don't you ever use my daughters against me like that again. I'm a damn good mother, and your opinion on that fact is neither warranted nor solicited, so keep it to yourself."

"That's not what I mean—"

"Trust me, I got what you meant loud and clear, Connor."

"No, you didn't. Maybe it came out rougher than I meant

it to because you *are* a great mom, but when are you going to put down that mantle and take some time for your damn self?"

"I know my limits."

A humorous laugh leaves his lips. "No, you don't. You were sheet-white when I dropped off your car on Friday, and I know for a fact you came home to take care of those girls. Hell, the first thing you did this morning was clean their room. I'm not faulting you for that; I don't have the faintest clue how you do it all. I'm just trying to give you some time to be Ally. Just Ally. Not Mom, not boss, not the business owner, not the baker, not the daughter or the sister. Just Ally."

The sentiment reflects my own recent thoughts and takes me down a peg. Maybe I didn't like the high-handed method, but he has a point—though I'm loath to admit it. I'm starting to get ragged around the edges. I've been nursing a headache for days, and Tylenol barely takes the edge off. Not to mention my memory has more holes than my favorite pair of jeans from high school. Then there's the lack of appetite and fatigue.

I definitely need to make a doctor's appointment.

My anger leaves me in a rush, and I let my head drop back to the wall behind me.

"You're right."

A mile-wide smile creases his cheeks. "How much did that hurt to say?"

The little bit of irritation at the man I have left evaporates as I swat at his arm. "Ass."

His hand comes up and tucks the ever-escaping strand of my bangs behind my ear. "I could have gone about it differently, so I'm sorry for that. I also didn't mean to imply you're anything less than an amazing mom, because those girls are lucky to have you. But you need to remember that you can only be amazing when you take care of yourself too."

"I know."

"Hey, if it makes you feel better, you can consider this as payment for the design help I'm tapping you for."

I let my head thunk to his chest as giggles overtake me. "Sure, we can do that."

"OH, SWEET JESUS. YES. THAT'S THE SPOT."

Firm hands knead into the boulders of stress-knots I'm housing along the length of my shoulders and neck. Every couple of minutes, there's a sharp pinch and a release of pressure so glorious I feel like I've died and gone to heaven.

"Same, girl. Same." Kate's at the table to my left and making some sexy noises all on her own. Liv's passed out cold on the table to my right. Kate and I had a good laugh when not five minutes into her massage, Liv's soft snores whispered through the room.

After a deep tissue, hot stone, ninety-minute massage from the most beautifully talented strong hands, the name of the game for the next twenty-four hours is indulgence. Next up? We have body masks and mud baths.

I can't remember the last time I sprang for a pedicure, let alone something more extravagant, so maybe there's a point to Connor's arrogant confidence in getting me to take a break.

"I can't remember the last time I got a massage," Kate unknowingly echoes.

Whispering back, I say, "I've never done it. No time, ya know? But you can bet your ass I'm going to schedule them more often now because *this*? This is flipping amazing."

She scoffs. "Yeah, you'll schedule them as often as I remember to take a day off from Readers' Haven."

That's a direct hit. How can I expect to prioritize self-care in the future, when I've always been so bad about it in the past?

"Let's be better about it together. We'll schedule a girls' day once a month, come up here and get something done. It doesn't have to be as extravagant as this"—because this deal is probably out of my personal budget, especially as I revamp the second floor of the shop—"but we can do something. Just for us."

The massage therapist hits a particularly tender spot and works the tension from my lower back. There's another painful ping before the pressure releases, and everything in my hips relaxes.

Maybe I can swing a massage a month because I've never felt this good. Even my self-administered orgasms don't make me this loose and boneless, and how sad is that?

"Like an accountability thing? We keep each other on track and force us to put some time aside for ourselves? I like it. Deal."

The scent of lavender is heavy in the air, and the plink of running water from a countertop fountain is the only sound in the room aside from Liv's snores and the occasional wistful sigh from me or Kate.

At first the thought of getting naked for a stranger made me wildly uncomfortable. But five minutes into it, I let my therapist manipulate my body however he needed. And now? I'm a fan for life. I'll strip down for Jake's amazing hands here every single time.

Jake's warm palms leave my back, and he says, "Okay, we're all finished. Please feel free to lie here and rest as long as you need to. Some residual soreness is expected, so be sure to hydrate and stretch this evening."

All three therapists exit the room, and I leave my eyes closed, taking stock of my body. I didn't realize there was so much tension built up in my back, but I no longer feel like a geriatric in a twenty-seven-year-old body.

After a few minutes, I sit up and reach for a robe, careful to keep the sheet tucked around me so I don't flash the girls to the world.

Decadent indulgence. That's the only way to describe the day Connor planned for me.

Facial, massage, mani, pedi, mud bath, dinner tonight—the man sprang for the whole shebang of spa days, and I don't know how I'll pay him back, but I will.

Sure, he went about it in an asshat way, but that doesn't change the result. He's trying to take care of me, and for the first time in a long time, I feel cherished.

And that's not even considering the devastating kisses we're trading like baseball cards.

Liv's just starting to wake up. Like me, she sits up with the sheet wrapped around her. Bright green eyes lock onto me before she asks, "So, Ally. What's going on with you and Connor?"

That's what I'd like to know myself.

CONNOR

WEEKENDS AT THE STATION ARE HIT OR MISS.

I'm either so busy my head spins, or it's so dead that I can't find enough things to do.

It's slower today, but having the twins keeps me on my toes. By midafternoon, we've checked the trails and done what little paperwork was waiting around for us.

Elle and Emma are currently outside in the picnic area, and my shift is about over.

"Hey, Boone, I'm taking off. You good?"

"Yeah, man. Have a good weekend."

"You too."

Pushing out of the station, I call, "Ladies, let's go!"

They scramble over to me, Emma tossing herself dramatically into my arms and Elle waiting until I have her sister situated before tucking her small hand into my much larger one.

I'd racked my brain to come up with stuff for us to do today until Jackson and Arik mentioned going to the lake. We can get some fishing in while the kids wear themselves out playing in the water, though we don't anticipate catching much.

"Y'all ready to go?"

"Where are we going next?" Emma asks.

Shifting her so she sits more firmly on my hip, I answer, "We're going to meet Uncle Jackson and Arik up at the lake."

Elle's hand squeezes mine. "We didn't bring our suits though."

"I had your Meemaw pack them before we left the house. I have them in my car."

"Okay then. Is the water going to be cold?"

The lake is cold, but I brought plenty of towels and figured they can splash around on the bank before I build up a fire to roast some hotdogs.

"A little bit, but you don't have to swim if you don't want to. You can play in the lake, or you can fish with me."

We set off, them bumping around in their booster seats in the back when we hit the rough patches of the trail.

It's a hot day. The sun's shining brightly overhead, and there's a cool breeze blowing through my Jeep's open top. Usually September means that it starts to cool off, but the days are blazing lately.

My phone chimes from my cup holder, but the number calling through is unfamiliar, so I let it roll over to voice mail while we clear the last rise before the descent into the lake.

At the first sight of water, the girls whoop from the back seat.

I know just how they feel. Nothing beats a lake day, even though I should be working on my house.

I'm hoping to just about finish out the big stuff for the house and then that'll roll me right into the Cowboy Courses, which is going to be busy but also hopefully fun.

Maybe I should consider putting in some sort of play set

for the girls at my house. Once it's finished, I'm sure I'll be hosting my fair share of the group's hangouts.

Jackson's and Arik's cars are parked at the shore, and the guys are sprawled in chairs with their lines cast already.

"Con! I want to swim! Can I swim?" Emma squeals.

"Sure can, bug. Let me park and then you guys can change."

I guess now that they've seen the water, the temperature won't matter too much to them.

My plan? To drop the girls off after dinner and have them so exhausted they'll crash out early for Nan.

Ally won't be home until after I show up at the resort and take her to brunch tomorrow.

I'm still unsure. The thought of giving in and taking the woman on a date after a decade of shoving my attraction to her into a box feels weird.

Four kisses and the very fabric of our lives throwing us together? I'm taking it as a sign.

Maybe I can make it work this time. I've been so dead set against trying that I haven't considered anything else. After spending time with Ally and seeing how well our lives could mesh, it kinda gives a man hope that this time can be different. But I guess we'll see.

Once the kids are splashing around the shallow shore of the lake, I drop my chair a little bit farther down and tossed my lure out.

"Everything set for tomorrow?" Arik questions while reeling in his line a couple of clicks.

"Yeah, I'll swing by around checkout and ask Ally out." The thought alone is enough to send my stomach on a free fall.

What if she says no?

What if I fuck it all up?

What if I let her and the girls down?

Stop it. It's gonna be fine.

"So, you're going for it, huh?" Jackson's question is quiet. Both of them turn in my direction, waiting for my answer, which doesn't help the weightless sensation in my gut.

What the fuck am I supposed to say right here? *Yeah, man, I'm falling for your sister, and the most I've done is kiss her a couple of times.*

My feelings for her progressed past simple *like* years ago, but I can't describe exactly what I feel for the woman.

After years of thinking her brother would disapprove and then that boundary being demolished, the allure of her has become impossibly stronger. Years of hiding the traffic-stopping lust I harbor for the woman under the misguided notion that it would be wrong, a betrayal to consider more with her? Years of thinking I'm not good enough, that I'd never be good enough for them?

I can't say that shit to them. They'd laugh me out of town. Even if I'm trying to be done with that line of thinking.

I look at Elle and Emma, who are happily splashing in the water, taking turns trying to get farther than the other on that death-trap diving board someone made out of an old fallen tree.

Those girls mean the world to me, so I really can't mess this up.

I've been so strongly against a relationship with anyone, let alone with her, that it feels weird to be not only considering it but planning for it now.

"Yeah."

Arik's face stretches in a grin. Jackson's eyebrow kicks up his forehead when he says, "That's it? Just 'yeah'?"

I shrug and nod.

Arik jumps in. "Ah, man, give him a break. You've been so adamantly against Ally dating, you're practically in the dad status with all of your 'nobody's good enough for my sister' bullshit. Anybody'd keep it close to the vest after hearing that for years."

Jackson winces. "Yeah, man. I'm sorry about that. I didn't know that you, uh, liked Ally. I was just talking out my ass. I didn't mean it specifically toward you or anything."

I nod because I know. He has a habit of speaking before thinking, and I've gotten used to it over the years. But still I have to ask, "What changed your mind?"

"Well, honestly, Liv."

"Liv? How so?"

Jackson reaches down and slowly starts to reel in his line. "She brought it up as you guys were dancing at the wedding. I'll admit I had some conflicted feelings about it, but then she pointed out a very good fact."

Arik chuckles. "Oh, yeah? What was that?"

"Why would I be best friends with someone I wouldn't approve of dating my sister? That kinda put it into a new light for me and made a weird sort of sense. So I had to think about it, and the more I thought about it, the less it bothered me."

Standing, Jackson walks a short distance away before recasting his line into the water and continuing, "I mean, you definitely don't need my approval—neither does Ally, for that matter—but I'm glad I had a chance to wrap my mind around it before y'all started seeing each other because I likely would have made an ass of myself otherwise. I know I have in the past. For that, I'm sorry."

Arik mimes wiping an imaginary tear. "Our boy is growing up. I'm so proud."

Jackson kicks at his feet as he walks back to his chair. "Fuck off. I'm just sayin'."

I get what he's saying, because if I had a little sister, I likely would be the same way. Still, there's relief at the fact he can be reasonable.

I know I'll have to tread lightly, but the pseudo approval means a lot to me.

Out of the corner of my eye, I watch Emma's foot slip. She plummets to the ground, and my heart jumps into my throat right as she lands on her arm. Hard.

I'm up and running toward her before her scream registers. The guys aren't far behind me, and we all reach her at the same time.

Her face is twisted in a grimace of pain. Eyes are red, and fat tears drip with the lake water down her face.

Like she's a football, I hoist her up before high-stepping us back to the shore.

Elle follows us. Once I get to the bank, I set Emma down, running my eyes over her.

She's bawling, and I can't catch my breath.

"Emmy, honey, where does it hurt?"

Through hiccupping sobs, she cries, "My arm."

She's clutching her left arm tight to her chest. It's bruised and already starting to swell.

Fuck. Did she break it? I don't see the bone, but it's so swollen already.

I've gotta get her to the hospital. It's either a bad sprain or a break with that rate of inflammation.

I dip my head to line my eyes up with hers, making sure to keep my face calm, my breathing steady. "Here's what we're going to do, baby…we're going to get you into my Jeep and then we're going to take you up to the doctor. They're going to take a couple of pictures of your wrist so they can make you feel better, okay?"

She nods, but she's still crying, and a million recriminations fly through my head.

I should have been watching them closer.

I shouldn't have let them play on that tree.

We shouldn't have even come to the lake today.

She got hurt on my fucking watch, and I hate myself for it.

The way her wrist is still swelling tells me it's likely a break. How the fuck could I have let something like this happen?

Guilt at the fact that Ally trusted me with her girls and I put one of them in the hospital is a leaden weight on my heart.

Jackson speaks up. "Hey, I'll call Ally. We'll be right behind you into town."

"No, I'll call her. Go ahead and get Em buckled in. I'll be right there."

It was my fuckup, so I have to call her. I dial, and the call goes to voice mail. A dry laugh wants to escape. Of course I would push her into going to the spa for a day and then send her daughter to the emergency room.

Way to go, dumbass. Everything you touch turns to shit. You should just stop trying.

"Ally." My voice nearly breaks on her name, but I force myself to hold steady. "Emma fell. She hurt her wrist, so we're taking her up to the hospital. Call me when you get this."

For good measure, I fire off a text to Liv and Kate. Kate drove Ally up there, so I'm confident she won't be driving herself to the hospital.

I'm just getting ready to dial the resort when my phone rings in my hand.

"Hello?"

"Con?" Ally's tone is all business. "What happened?"

"The girls were playing on the shore. Emma tried to walk the tree diving board and then she fell. Landed hard on her arm. It's swollen and painful to move, so we're gonna take her to the hospital."

"Okay. I'll meet you there."

I nod before I realize she can't see me, so I say, "Okay."

"Con? It's gonna be all right. You know that, right?"

I make agreeable sounds before she disconnects, but I don't believe it.

Climbing into my Jeep, I see that Jackson transferred Elle's booster seat to Arik's Jeep, and both Jackson and Emma are buckled into my back seat and ready to go.

Wise decision on Jackson's part. He can keep her wrist mostly stabilized during the drive out of here. More self-loathing gathers at the thought of her in even more pain from being jostled by the roughness of the trail.

The trip out is much slower than the trip in, and it's not until an hour later that we're pulling into the parking lot of the county hospital.

Ally jumps out of her car and is pulling on the door handle to the back seat before I can even shut off the engine.

"Mama!" Emma's tear-stained wail stabs my heart because I caused this. This is all my fault.

"Shh, baby. It's okay. Come on, let's get you inside, and the doctors will take a look."

Ally picks Emma up bridal-style before turning to me, saying, "I'll be back. Hang out in the waiting room for me, okay?"

The gentle way she asks makes my shoulders hunch. How is she so calm?

My negligence caused this. If I were her and Emma was my daughter, I'd flay me alive.

She and Jackson disappear through the automatic doors of the hospital, and as much as I want to stay, my feet itch with the need to bail. To get out of the way so I don't make things worse.

Recriminations are tearing me apart, and it's only by sheer force of will that I'm holding on to my calm. My eyes sting against the onslaught of remorse.

What the fuck was I thinking, taking them up to the lake like that?

Sure, I've done it in the past, but it only takes one time to ruin everything, as evidenced by today.

I should have been paying better attention to Emma. I should have been focused on the girls so that I could actually deliver on the promise to give Ally a stress-free day.

Why do I break all the good things in my life?

What started as an offer to reduce some of the load on her shoulders ended up adding to it. Once again, I'm letting down those closest to me and making everything worse.

I don't wait for Ally to tell me everything I already know. I don't wait for someone to come out and collect me or to tell me how bad Emma's arm is.

Coward.

Shutting down the nasty voice yelling at me to stay here, to face the music and take responsibility for my fuckup, I climb into my Jeep, peel out of the hospital parking lot, and drive like a bat out of hell up to my mountain.

I just need to get away from everyone else.

My phone signals from the cup holder, and I see a voice mail waiting in the inbox.

I leave it until I'm pulling into my driveway and then pluck the device up and click to play it.

"Hello. This message is for Mr. Connor Murtry. This is Hal over at Everette Ranger Station. I wanted to have a talk with you about a senior ranger position you applied for recently." He recites a number and ends the message with "Give me a call."

Why does everyone I love end up hurt?

Maybe it's time I protected them from *me.*

ALLY

EMMA'S SMALL FRAME IS CURLED UP ON THE HOSPITAL BED, HER arm plastered into a neon pink cast. Jackson is hanging out in here whispering to her, trying to get her to rest. Arik and Kate took Elle home for a sleepover, and Liv is waiting for us in the waiting room.

Just Liv.

Kate got the text message about the accident, and as I listened to Connor's unsteady voice mail telling me he was taking Emma to the hospital, I knew without a doubt he was going to blame himself for this. The look of guilt on his face as I got Emma out of the car? That look gutted me.

Oh, Connor.

I haven't had a chance to get back out there to talk to him, but Jackson telling me shortly after he came into the triage room that Connor had taken off wasn't surprising.

You can run, but you can't hide, buddy.

Once I get Emma squared away, I have plans to hunt his ass down.

Why the hell would I condemn him for something that

was an accident? What I *do* have a problem with is him taking off without a word to me.

I'm sure he thinks I'm angry at him, but I learned one of the hardest truths about being a parent a long time ago. Sometimes your babies get hurt. No matter how much you try to avoid it, how careful you are, it's inevitable.

"Hey." Jackson's whisper draws my attention to him and Emma. Snoring softly, she's finally sleeping, and I barely hold back my sigh of relief. I'd bet she's going to be out for a bit, and I know the best thing for her right now is rest.

"Yeah?" I whisper back, trying not to wake her.

"So you and Connor, huh?"

Me and Connor.

As much as I don't know what's going on with us, that phrase raises goosebumps down my arms and sends my heart rate careening through the roof as a smile tugs at my lips.

"I don't know."

For all my justifications and arguments that I don't have the time for a relationship, I know I'd jump at the prospect if given the chance.

I'd thought I was getting the chance. Between the kisses and him arranging today for me on the sly, I read too much into it and hoped that maybe, just maybe, this meant more.

Now? I just don't know.

Part of the reason I'm so hell-bent on hunting him down is because I can imagine how much Emma getting hurt tossed him into a tailspin. After him telling me what went down with his girlfriend and friend in Texas? I'm certain of it.

The other part of it? I want some damn answers—any answers—on what the hell is going on with us. I can't keep doing the back and forth, *maybe he likes me, maybe he doesn't* crap. It's got me on pins and needles, and I need to know one way or the other.

Would it be easier if we both ignored our attraction to each other? Just wrote off those kisses and carried on with our lives?

Absolutely.

But the more I see who Connor is, who he really is, the less I want to carry on without him.

I've always known Connor is a great guy. It's part of the reason I fell face-first for him so long ago. I know he's steady and calm when the world is burning down around you—or in my case, a bakery is burning—and he's always had my back.

The rough, grumpy mountain man is only one part of him, and one I'm learning is more defense mechanism than anything else. The way he interacts with my daughters, the way he loves them, convinces me he's holding part of himself back out of fear of letting someone in again.

We could have something if he'd pull his head out of his ass long enough to consider it.

And despite how hard I know it can be, I want to try.

Going out of his way to give me a day where I can set down the responsibilities, a day where I got to actually relax and turn off the overly busy part of my brain?

Those aren't the actions of a guy who doesn't care.

Cocking his head to the side, Jackson looks me over. He's reading me like a book right now, but I don't have the energy to worry about it.

"Well, I hope whatever you decide you know I've got your back. Both of your backs. Okay?"

"I know…but what changed?" I ask before I can stop myself. He's never made it a secret that to so much as glance in my direction is a direct violation of his protectiveness when it comes to me and relationships.

His muffled chuckle shakes his shoulders before he says, "Connor pretty much asked me the same thing. Let's just say I had my eyes opened. I trust you both, so if y'all want to give it a go, I'm not going to stand in your way. Con's a good guy. You're a grown woman. You can both decide what works for you."

"Thanks."

Standing, he wraps an arm around my shoulders. "You got it. But if he hurts you, I reserve the right to knock him on his ass. Same goes if you hurt him."

I start to laugh but get interrupted by the doctor opening the door. He takes in Emma on the bed and quietly asks, "Ready to go home?"

Discharge goes relatively smoothly. Liv catches up with us as we walk toward the exit, and I let Jackson carry Emma to my car. After buckling her in, he reaches into his pocket and tosses me his keys.

"I'll take her home and get her comfortable. You go find our guy and talk some sense into him."

Maybe it makes me a bad mom. Maybe my priorities are skewed, but I don't object. Emma's out, likely for a few hours, so the only thing stopping me from finding Connor and giving him a piece of my mind is my worry for Emma.

I know she's in good hands with Jackson, Liv, and Ma. I know that. But still.

Liv runs a hand down my arm. "Ally, go. We've got Emma. Don't worry."

"Okay, but call me if she needs anything."

"We will. Swing by our place tomorrow. I'll drag Kate over, and we can have lunch," Liv replies.

"Sounds good."

Ready or not, here I come, Connor.

Time to get some answers.

~

I BEAT ON THE DOOR AND WAIT IMPATIENTLY FOR CONNOR TO answer.

Fuck it.

The man is hiding. A six-and-a-half-foot man is hiding from me, and if I weren't seriously determined, I'd laugh at the notion.

The door is unlocked when I twist the handle, and that's too bad for him. I'm not waiting for him to work up the gumption to let me in. The living room is empty, and I spy an open cooler on the floor in the entryway of the kitchen.

Where the hell are you?

"Connor?" I call out, but silence is the only greeting I get in return.

Could he be outside somewhere? But then the faint staticky sound of the shower reaches me.

Perfect.

I'll just plant my ass in his room and wait for him to finish up. It's not like he can avoid me if I'm sitting on his bed when he gets out, right?

The bathroom door is cracked open, and the mental image of mist dotting those broad shoulders before the water droplets run down his abs gives me the absurd urge to peek.

It's been a long time since I saw a naked man in person, but my imagination isn't rusty. I can get inventive in my shower sex fantasies, and Connor being wet, naked, and slippery?

Sign me up.

The shower shuts off before I get lost in those thoughts, which are sure to turn me into a horny mess of a woman and would accomplish nothing.

Fabric rustling against skin carries into the room. Good. He should be done any time now.

I glance down at the picture he has of the girls on his nightstand. He's torn up about Emma, which means I'm likely going to be dealing with the grumpy exterior he hides behind. Cracking my neck, I prepare for battle.

The bathroom door opens the whole way, and my brain shoots me right back into the sexually repressed, lusty woman I am.

I assumed he'd have the towel around his waist.

That he'd wear it until he got some clothes on.

I've never been more pleased to be wrong in my life.

Fully nude, he emerges, and any thought I had of getting to the bottom of whatever the hell is going on in his head evaporates.

Strong, wide shoulders still hold several drops of water. His chest is dusted with a light covering of hair that trails down his washboard stomach until meeting the crisp hair surrounding the most mouthwatering dick I've ever seen.

Wowza!

A water drop trails down his ribcage, and I want to chase it with my tongue.

"Ally?! What the fuck are you doing here?" Two big hands —but not quite big enough—shoot down to cover his junk, and a delicious thrill shivers along my spine.

Sweet baby Jesus.

I should not be ogling the man after I broke into his house, but this is better than anything my imagination came up with.

Averting my eyes—even though I don't want to—I say, "You took off before we could talk, so I had to chase you down."

And would you look at that? Maybe I am still irritated enough to focus on the issue at hand.

Connor ducks back into the bathroom, and the back is just as impressive as the front. Two muscled glutes greet my gaze—the man has some junk in his trunk, and I ain't even mad about it. I watch him disappear into the bathroom, and when he reemerges, he's covered from the waist down.

Pity.

"I'd have figured me leaving would tell you I didn't want to talk, let alone give you a peep show."

I lift my gaze to his. He's shut down, brown eyes flat.

Rolling my eyes, I scoff, "Tough shit."

His mouth drops open, one eyebrow hitching up, as he parrots me. "Tough shit?"

"Yeah, tough shit. We all have to do things we don't want to, and this is one of them." Rising from the bed, I move out of his room. "Get dressed. I'll be in the living room."

My face is hot, and I can feel sweat building at my hair line. I stifle the urge to fan myself, because after that, I could definitely benefit from more airflow to my face. At least if he kicks me out of his house and never talks to me again, I have enough fantasy fodder to last a lifetime.

Powerful.

If I had to come up with one word to describe Connor naked? That would be it.

Thick slabs of muscle all flow together seamlessly to create a physique I want to sink my teeth into.

Down, girl. Get it together, Ally.

Not long after I sit down on his really ugly couch, Connor comes out.

Irritation isn't only present in his expression, but every ounce of his demeanor is a closed door. Good thing I'm a battering ram.

I pat the couch next to me and give him my patented *I'm dealing with a pushy customer* smile.

He chooses the recliner across from me, but at least he sits down.

Softly, I ask, "What happened?"

His close-cropped hair is still damp as he scrubs his hand through it before wiping his moist palm along the leg of his gym shorts.

I hold my silence while trying to avoid the distraction his bare torso on display teases me with.

When the hell did I turn into a lust-filled hormone rocket?

"They were playing on the diving board out at Packsaddle. Emma slipped and went down right off the bank. When she came up, her wrist had already started to swell, so we got her in the car, I called you, and we headed to the hospital." Almost reluctantly, he asks in a quieter tone, "How's she doing?"

Poor Connor. Tone hushed, I answer, "She's okay. They called it a greenstick fracture and said she'll be in a cast for four weeks. She was sleeping when Jackson and Liv took her home."

"You didn't have to come up here. I know you probably want to be home with her."

"She's in good hands, and I figured you're the bigger concern right now. Connor—"

"I'm sorry, Als. I should have been watching her closer, or not let her play on that death trap. I shouldn't have let her get hurt, and that's on me. It won't happen again."

He means it. The finality in his tone is proof. He's pulling back from me, from my girls, and I've had just about enough of that.

"You're wrong. It will happen again." His head pops up, but before he can jump in, I keep going. "It'll happen again because we can't encase them in bubble wrap. Accidents happen, and if you beat yourself up over that, you'll end up perpetually black and blue."

I take a chance and stand before crossing the short distance between us. Sitting gently across his lap, I hold my breath, hoping he doesn't push me away. When his hands come to rest on my hips, I brush my mouth across his in a gentle kiss. That small caress is enough for his shoulders to drop, the tense line of his frame softening.

I pull back slightly, saying, "When Elle first learned to walk, we didn't get the baby gates installed on the stairs fast enough. I didn't hear her wake up on the baby monitor, and I was in the kitchen making us all breakfast. She made it about halfway down before she slipped. Ended up bashing her head on the bottom stair tread. Had a knot the size of an egg on her head for days. I beat myself up about it until Ma gave me some sage advice for kids."

"What advice?" The heat of his breath fans across my face. We're close enough to share secrets.

"That while they're accident-prone, they're remarkably resilient." I laugh because I remember the days of being the nervously insane helicopter mom.

Dark chocolate eyes lock on my mouth, and he murmurs, "Good to know." His eyes find mine before he says, "Still, I can't. I just can't."

He's not talking about the girls getting hurt now. The shifting dance we've been spinning around each other is the reason behind his *can't.* Emma being hurt was the final straw for him, and he's retreating.

"Why?"

"It's a long story."

"I've got time."

His fingers dance along my hips, and his gaze goes far away, like he's remembering something and deciding whether he wants to tell me.

Tell me. It's not a want to know, it's a need to know now.

"I told you I moved around with my ma a lot growing up, right?"

"You did."

"Then I went to live with my dad when he found out

about me. The reason he found out about me? My ma committed suicide when I was eight."

Oh God.

One of his hands comes up to play with a strand of my hair, but his voice is dead when he continues, "See. My dad had an affair with my ma. He didn't know about me, because he broke it off when Ma told him she was pregnant with me. She still put his name on my birth certificate so when I found her body..."

"You found her?"

"After school."

"Jesus, Con..." He was so young. Barely older than my own daughters.

"I came home and she looked like she was sleeping." His voice breaks, but he continues, "She was so cold though, and then I saw the empty bottle of pills. I remember calling nine one one, and the only reason I knew to do that was because we had a safety talk at school that week."

Jesus Christ. My heart fractures in my chest thinking about the little boy coming home from school to discover tragedy.

"I'm so sorry."

"It was a long time ago. She was depressed. I didn't know what it was called at the time, but I found out later she was diagnosed with depression, and I guess it all got to be too much for her to handle."

I don't know what to say.

He continues, "That's how my father found out about me. Can't say living with him was a picnic either. Then you know what happened in high school with April. And now this with Emma. I'm never where I'm supposed to be when it matters most, so I can't, Als."

With that he drops his hand from my hair.

I'm sitting in his lap, but he couldn't be farther from me.

"Can't or won't, Con?"

"Does it matter?" His eyes hold a challenge, a plea. *Let this go. Ignore it.* He wants to forget about the madness that has overcome us lately.

My heart breaks for the little boy. I feel for the teenager who had his first taste of young love before it was ripped away. But I'm not backing down. I've had a taste of him, and I'm not giving in that easily.

Standing, I say, "It does. Because if it's *can't,* then we can work through it—together—until you can. If it's *won't,* then I'd call you a coward."

"That's not fair, and you know it, Ally."

"No. What's not fair? You're letting your past determine your future. You're letting what happened before railroad what *can* happen. You're letting one terrible accident in your past stop whatever *this* is in your present. I deserve better than that."

He shoves to his feet, some of his temper starting to come through, as he harshly says, "Don't you think I know that? Don't you think I'm aware that you and the girls deserve better than me? Don't you think I know we should forget this—forget whatever is going on between us—and go back to normal?"

"What's normal, Connor? Us wanting each other and ignoring it? I've done that; I've ignored it for years. I'm not doing it anymore. I'm sorry for your mom and April. I'm so damned sorry you had to go through that. But all I'm saying is whatever is going on up here"—I lightly touch his forehead—"is stopping what can grow in here." I place my other hand over his heart. The steady beat of it thumps against my palm. "And that's a shame."

His eyes flare, and I think I'm getting through to him.

Before he can reply, I say, "I can't—no, I won't—force

your hand. If you don't want me and the girls—because we're a package deal—that's your choice."

I turn to walk toward the front door.

I deserve a man who'll face life's challenges with me, one who will hold me up when I falter and ground me if I'm flying too high. One who won't live in the past but instead look to the brightness of the future with me.

I'm done playing the back-and-forth game. I *do* deserve better.

CONNOR

WATCHING ALLY TURN AWAY FROM ME?

Urgency grips me, and before I stop myself, before I rationalize that it's for the best that she's leaving, I lunge after her.

My previous resolve to write off the kisses, the affection, and the *feelings* I have for her dies as I lock my hand around her elbow, whipping her around to face me before I crash my mouth down to hers.

Where the urgency came from? I have no idea.

I don't know if it was her point that we can't always protect the ones we love, or that I was letting my past overshadow my life, but something broke through.

If she thinks we can make this work, then I'll do my damnedest to be the man she needs.

Maybe it's stupid. Maybe I'm making a mistake. But when the sweet taste of her lips invades my senses, I couldn't give a shit less.

One thought rings loudly through the blood rushing in my ears.

Mine.

Threading my hand through her hair, I give in to the sultry promise of her lips under mine. I'm done fighting the sheer *need* I have for her.

I want to taste every inch of her. I want her to plead, to writhe, and unravel before my eyes.

I nip at her bottom lip and capitalize on her hitched breath by dipping my tongue into her mouth, gliding and swirling around her own. I let her elbow go and grasp her chin to tilt her head for an even deeper taste.

Her hands lock onto my forearms, and I can feel the tremor in her fingers as she digs her nails into my skin. The slight sting brings me back to my senses and I pull back, gentling the kiss before breaking away.

Being the man she needs doesn't mean mauling her in my half-finished living room.

The silky texture of her hair is sliding against my palms. I need to say something. The best I come up with is, "Okay. I'll try. We'll try."

A small smile curls her lips. "Wow."

My forehead drops to hers and our breaths mingle. My heart is thundering. I was so against *this,* so against being with her that I wasn't prepared for the way she demanded more from me. I didn't know she could demand more from me, but she did.

"Yeah." My voice is gruff, like two rocks scraping together. "You could say that again."

"Say it? Why don't we do it again?" Her hands come up to cradle my face, and she drags my lips back to hers.

Fire singes along my scalp, and my fingers itch to drag her back to my lair like a caveman, but I know she can't stay, no matter how badly I want her to.

She pulls back and squeezes her eyes shut. "Wait. Wait. I don't want to take advantage of you. You're upset and I want you to be sure."

Now she's the one having doubts.

"I'm sure." The declaration is firm. She's everything warm and light. She's what I *need*. If she thinks that I can be what she needs then I'm in.

Her hands dip into the band of my shorts, and my cock rises to the occasion of meeting her fingers. I'm desperate for her touch, even though I know we should take it slower.

Before I can capture her hands to move them into a safer zone, she shoves at my shorts and follows them down until she's on her knees in front of me.

Talk about a fucking fantasy.

One of her hands wraps tightly around my cock as the other digs into my ass cheek to hold me in place. I hiss out a breath even as I try to tug her back to her feet.

"Als, baby…"

"Hush, you. I wouldn't be down here if I didn't want to be, so just let me have my fun."

Fun? Sucking my dick is fun for her?

All rational thought flees as her tongue dips along the crown. If I'm not careful, I'm going to come in three seconds. I'm biting back the need to fist my hands in her hair and savagely fuck her mouth.

Don't look down. Don't look down.

If I see her sucking me, it's all over from there. I can't come back from that image.

With her lips closing over the head, she sucks gently, and my hips shoot forward uncontrollably.

No. This isn't going to work. I'm not going to bust in her mouth after seconds like an untried kid.

I fight back the rising orgasm that's clawing its way through me. Baseball cards, flesh-eating amoebas…I call to mind pretty much every unsexy thing I can to get my focus off the fact that Ally fucking Sawyer is sucking my dick in my living room.

She takes me deep, and I feel the back of her throat close around my length. Her hum of appreciation has me looking down before I can stop myself.

Eyes the most beautiful hazel lock with mine. Her lips stretch around my girth as her fingers trace over me lightly in an almost reverent caress of discovery, and *feelings* erupt in my chest.

Game over.

"Jesus fucking Christ!" I shout.

Waves of pleasure batter me boneless, and I'm seconds from toppling over. That was both the most amazing and embarrassing moment of my life.

Who the hell comes in thirty seconds from a fucking blow job?

This guy right here.

My heart pounds, and I can't catch my breath as she lovingly nuzzles my groin, licking the last drops of my release from me like a cat lapping up the last of its milk. I. Am. Undone.

Chin to my chest, I watch Ally's smug smile dance along her lips, and she should be smug.

I came like a lightning strike, one minute indiscernible and the next *right fucking there.*

Once I get my sea legs back, I'm going to haul her ass all the way to my room and sully the shit out of her. Just as soon as I catch my breath.

Fuck it. Who needs air anyway? Crouching down, I hook my arms under her elbows and lift. "Come here, baby."

I brush her hair off her face and fasten my mouth to hers.

The salty evidence of my release is barely detectable, but there's still enough to send blood rushing to my dick in anticipation of a repeat.

"Can you stay?" The question is quiet, and I hold my breath waiting for her to answer.

"Not all night, but I don't have to be home for a little bit."

Would I love it if I could fuck her, fall asleep next to her, and then wake up with her? Without a doubt, but I'm more than happy to take what I can get right now. As much as I want the former, I know Emma will need her, so I have to be content with the latter.

I step out of the shorts sitting at my ankles and hitch Ally up, carrying her to my room, before dropping her on my bed.

She's tumbled in my sheets, and I get hit with the feeling that this is where she belongs. Here with me. Always with me.

I can think about that later. I reach down and tug at the hem of her shirt, pulling it over her head and tossing it aside. The lacy red of her bra catches my attention for the briefest moment before I give in to my instinct and dip down to suck her nipple into my mouth through the fabric.

"Oh, God."

"Mm," I rumble against the tip of her breast. "You taste fantastic."

I remove her bra, and it joins her shirt on my floor somewhere. The pale mounds of her breasts are on display, and my mouth waters at the sight of her pink nipples, hardening further under my gaze.

She lies back, and a flush of arousal covers her chest. I want to beat my chest and conquer the world for her. I want to lock her to me, never let her go, and cherish her.

Before I can get too caught up in the emotions raging through me, I drag my lips along her collarbone, then run my fingers up to massage and cup her breasts. With a pointed tip pinched between my fingers, I get insane pleasure at the way her hips shoot forward in search of friction.

Soon, baby. Soon.

"Connor, please. I don't need foreplay, I swear. Just fuck me already."

I kiss my way down her sternum to the faint lines that prove she held, grew, and delivered life. These marks are evidence her body can do amazing and wonderful things, evidence of her bringing two of the brightest lights in my life into the world.

The girls might not be *mine* biologically, but ever since she plopped them into my arms, they've owned a part of my heart no one else has.

I can't go by without paying homage to those battle scars, no matter Ally's urging otherwise.

With light kisses along her navel and abdomen, I tug her denim pants down and off. Like her bra, her panties are fire engine red, and I dip a finger along her core over the lace. Sure enough, I can feel the damp pool of arousal gathered behind the fabric.

"You may not need foreplay, baby, but until your legs are shaking and you're praying, begging, to go over that edge, I'm not letting you. So let *me* have my fun."

If someone had told me at the start of the day that I'd have Ally in my bed, I wouldn't have believed it. I'm still fuzzy on how we went from her giving me a piece of her mind to me having a slice of nirvana under my hands and mouth, but here we are.

Damned if I squander the opportunity.

"I love the feel of you under my hands, under my lips. The taste of you on my tongue is fucking addictive. So, no, Ally. I'm not going to 'just fuck you.' I'm going to savor this, savor you, until we can't take it anymore, until we're both going to lose our minds from the need, from the want, and then you can come on my face. Got it?" Dipping my tongue along the lace, I suck her into my mouth through her panties.

A breath gusts out of her as she answers, "Got it. Yep. Oh, fucking Jesus."

"Not Jesus. Say it with me—Connor. If you're going to be calling anything out, it better be that."

I drag her panties down until I'm left with only the quivering, sexy woman who has starred in more of my fantasies than I care to admit.

I spread her legs farther before settling my frame between her legs. The thatch of light blonde curls at the top of her sex beckons me as much as the shadowed crease of her entrance.

My thumbs spread her lips until the hood of her clit comes into view. I can't hold back or slow down. Tongue to clit, I lavish the button with attention and am rewarded with stifled curses falling from Ally's mouth.

Her musky flavor shorts out my brain, and the dirty-talking suave part of me dies as my control dwindles.

I'm not a neat pussy eater. I'm a "get in there and make her beg" sloppy pussy eater, and I'm damned proud of it.

Sucking her labia into my mouth, I tease the swollen flesh with gentle scrapes of my teeth as my thumb dips toward her core.

She twitches against the pad of my finger, and with the slightest bit of pressure, her hips thrust against my face in search of more.

Restlessly, I piston my hips against my sheets in search of my own friction, but it's not enough. I need the snug heat of her wrapped around me. I need to feel her in my arms as I fuck us both over the cliff that's been years in the making.

I can't get carried away though. I don't have any condoms, and I won't push her for more right now.

Swiping my tongue through her drenched silky sweetness, I work my way back up to her clit before sucking it into my mouth and thrusting a finger inside her.

"Oh, God, Connor, I'm coming. I'm fucking coming."

Triumph roars through me at hearing her, feeling her

unravel in my arms, as I work her through a hard orgasm.

Back bowed on the bed, her tits point to the sky and tremble at the shocks rocking through her system. Instead of stopping, I make the mad swirling of my tongue even harder because I'll be damned if I don't make up for the blowjob that wrecked me.

Before the first orgasm can fully die down, I add another finger inside her and suck at her clit again, which sends another release careening through her.

She's past words now. I can barely see her, but what I do see is her mouth open on a silent scream. Satisfaction courses through me.

She falls limp as I rear up to my knees. I fist the length of my dick and jack myself to her avid gaze. My hand shuttles from base to tip, and it takes less than three strokes for my own orgasm to barrel through me.

Thick ropes of come lash her stomach and breasts, the evidence of how fucking worked up this woman has me painting her skin and making me roar with my climax.

Once the last of my orgasm fades, I topple to the sheet beside her, blindly grabbing some tissues from the night-stand to clean her up.

When that's done, I lie back down. She scooches her head to rest on my chest, and her fingers thread through the hair there. Then she asks, "You didn't want to have sex?"

I look her in the eye. "I do. But we can't. It's been a while for me, and I don't have any protection here…yet."

Bet your ass I'll be picking some up.

"Oh."

I press a kiss to her lips and ask, "I know we're going about this ass backward, but I want to take you on a real date. Let me?"

A sleepy but replete smile graces her face, causing the dimple next to her mouth to dance. "I'd love that."

ALLY

THIS MAN WANTS TO DATE ME.

Giddy elation soars through my heart at the thought.

My skin hasn't even fully cooled yet, and my desire for him sure hasn't either. I understand why he stopped; I appreciate the effort and I'll give him the highest grade for it, but I'm not done with him yet. Now that I finally have him I'm not wasting any time.

Throwing my leg over his hips, I straddle him. The hard kick of his cock butting up against the lips of my sex is enough to tell me he's not done with me either.

Delicious.

Leaning down, I pepper his chest with kisses, moving up with each one until I have his lips against mine again.

Home. This—he—feels like home, and I'm done fighting it. Done fighting against the want I have for him. The *we shoulds* or *shouldn'ts*. I'm just done.

"I'm on birth control and clean. You?"

"I'm clean." A hard swivel from my hips causes a gust of air to leave him. "Short on the birth control though."

Hands mapping his sternum, hips rocking against the

rapidly hardening dick under me, I say, "Isn't it a good thing I have us covered there then?"

I missed this. I missed the feeling of a man under me, someone just as desperate for me as I am for him.

However, I don't think I've ever experienced this level of desire, and that's enough to make me realize *this* is different. Connor and I are different together, and it's a good different.

More than ready, I reach down and grip him, moving him to where I need him. Sliding down his length, I take my time working him inside me. It's been a while for me, too, so I go slow, giving myself time to settle in to the pressure of him stretching me until I feel impossibly full.

Right. This feels so right it should be wrong, but I don't give one good goddamn right now. I'm seizing him for my own, one slow inch at a time.

"Goddamn, Als, you're so fucking tight around me."

Balls against my ass, I breathe through the last impossible inch of him disappearing inside me. Deep in my core, I can feel the muscles quivering, begging me to move, to pursue the high I didn't know was possible until his fingers were buried inside me while his tongue lapped madly at my center.

I want that again, and I'll be damned if I deny either of us.

Connor's hands find mine, and our fingers intertwine as I start to ride. Our eyes locked on each other, I work my hips against his once I find a steady rhythm. For all his dirty talk earlier, he's silent now and I am too.

This is more than just the need for an orgasm, and odds are he's feeling it also, based on the grip he has on my hands. This is *more.*

Grinding my clit on the base of him, the tightness returns to my stomach. My whole body is tense. I'm chasing my orgasm, so I don't notice his hands leaving mine until they come up to cup my breasts. He tweaks my left nipple, which sends more excitement unfurling through me.

I'm swiftly approaching the point of no return when he rears up and his mouth latches on to my right nipple. The hint of teeth in his hard suck sends me careening over the edge. I barely bite back the screech that wants to claw its way out of me.

Euphoric waves of ecstasy crash through me, the orgasm hard as I ripple along his dick, buried so damn deep inside me.

My rhythm falters as I come down, but Connor's hands find my hips, the tips of his fingers biting into my flesh, and he's physically moving me along his cock. The fact he's using me to reach his own end is enough to send me right back to the edge again.

My first orgasm quickly blends into a second, and this is either the world's longest climax or I've reached a new level because it just won't fucking stop.

"Ally." Connor's voice is a rough growl as his release rushes through him. I crash hard again right along with him.

My hips piston against his as I work us both through the tumble of bliss.

I slow as his fingers bite into my hips. I don't want his body to leave mine. Not when we've waited so long for this. I keep us connected as I sprawl over his chest.

His hands trace along my back; I don't want to move, but I know I need to. Nail-and-bail isn't my style, but I need to be there when Emma wakes up. Slowly, I rise up until he slips from me.

Leaning down, I brush my lips against his and ask, "Can I use your shower to clean up?"

"I'll do you one better." Connor holds on to me as he swings his legs over the side of the bed and, in one motion, stands and lifts me up into his arms, carrying us both to the bathroom.

If this is wrong, I don't want to be right.

LETTING MYSELF INTO THE HOUSE WITH MY HAIR STILL DAMP and my skin still singing the praises of Connor's attention feels weird. Not bad weird, but it feels like Ma's going to walk through the door and pin me with her knowledge of what I just did.

In eleventh grade I came home after a date with Johnny Wilson, and she *knew.* I don't know how she did, but she took one look at me, and after a lengthy conversation I was given the option to start birth control at my next doctor appointment.

I hope to be half the mom she is one day.

Following the sound of running water, I work my way back to the kitchen. She's standing at the sink and dropping the last dish in the dishwasher.

"Emma still out?" I ask quietly.

Ma turns, her eyes dancing over the rumpled state of my clothes and my hair tied up in a hasty bun before she gives me a small smile.

"About time you had your way with that man."

My face heats. Can't get much past Nanette Sawyer, y'all.

She winks at me. "Emma's still out. Elle's having a blast with Arik and Kate. Why don't you pour us a glass of wine, and we can get off our feet, though it seems you've already been off yours today."

"Ma!"

"What? You think I don't recognize a well-pleasured woman when I see one? I'm happy for you. You two have been dancing around each other for years now, and I for one am glad that y'all knocked that shit off."

"He wants to take me on a date." Just saying it adds to the weirdness of the day. As if merely speaking it into existence is enough to rip it away from me. I don't want to chance it.

I'm grabbing glasses from the cabinet when she says, "Well, I would hope so. We raised him better than that."

"You and Dad did kinda raise him, didn't you?"

Ma and I settle in at the table before she responds. "You might not remember, but when he first got here? James saw something in him. Jackson did too, which I suspect is why he befriended him in college and brought him home with him. Something about that boy screamed hurt when he first got here. I remember that first summer, he was even more grumpy than he is now, although Felt has softened him some over the years. The first time Jackson brought him to dinner, there was a chip on his shoulder the size of a boulder."

"How so?"

"He was painfully polite, almost as if those manners were beaten into him over the years of growing up. It hurt my heart to see. I don't know the details, but I have my suspicions—considering he rarely goes home—it wasn't pleasant for him."

Not for the first time I'm thankful for the practically idyllic adolescence Jackson and I were lucky enough to have. It wasn't always roses, but I know that not everyone in the world gets two amazing parents who have your best interests at heart. Gratitude for my family swamps me.

"I'm glad he's had you for the last couple of years then. Sounds like it did him some good."

"Oh, honey. Having me and your dad is always a good thing, but I think it was more the space, the room to grow into his own person, that helped him the most."

I can only imagine his need to get away from it all considering the disaster he lived after high school. It's logical that he took off from the hospital earlier, and while I can understand the need to get away from stress, I'm grateful that he and I were able to talk through it and move past it.

"How was the spa?"

"It was amazing. We managed to get through the bulk of the treatments that we had scheduled for this afternoon before Connor called, so there's that. I'm definitely going back soon. The massage alone is worth the mom guilt from stealing an afternoon."

Waving her hands, Ma says, "Guilt shmilt. You don't take enough time for yourself, and I'm surprised you haven't snapped yet, honestly. So to hear you plan for more of it makes me glad Connor thought it up."

"I know, Ma. It's just that I have—"

Cutting me off, she finishes my sentence, "So much going on. Yes, dear, I know. You're convinced the world will end if you don't handle everything yourself, but look around you. You have not only me and Jackson, but now Kate and Liv. You have Connor as well if the rosy hue to your cheeks speaks to anything. You need to ask for help more often. I'm not just talking about with the girls, but with everything. You don't have to do it all yourself, and while this isn't the first time you've heard me say it, maybe *now* you'll listen."

Ma's lecture makes sense. Maybe I don't have to do it all. Maybe I can rely on those around me.

I don't know when I started to be such a control freak; I've always had a solid support system in place. But more and more over the years I've settled into the idea that if I want something done, if I want to reach for a dream or to accomplish anything, I need to be the one to do it.

Maybe it was the work ethic my parents instilled in me, or it was the need to make sure I had all my bases covered before moving back home after my divorce. I don't know.

It's just gotten easier and easier to push away the offers of help, the offers to relieve some of the load I carry, over the years.

Between the fire, the Cowboy Courses, and now Emma's arm, I'm starting to realize that maybe it's not such a bad thing to take some time for myself. Some time to get myself centered before I re-adorn my shoulders with the massive list of responsibilities I carry.

"Let me ask you this. If you saw Emma and Elle trying to do it all themselves, what would you tell them?" Ma asks gently.

I hate this kind of mom logic, although I'll likely wield it in the future against my girls.

Of course, I wouldn't want them to take everything on themselves. The near-constant worry that I'm not being a good enough example for them surges.

"I'd tell them all the things you've told me over the years. That they can ask for help, that I'm here to help, and that's what family is for. It's just hard."

Ma pats my hand on the table between us as she says, "I know. You get your perfectionism from me. Took me a long time to realize that perfect isn't always best. Sometimes we have to let go of our worries and hope for the best."

"I'll try. I have been trying, but then stuff like today happens and it makes me second-guess myself."

"Emma getting hurt? How so?"

"As soon as I got to take some time for myself, Emma ended up in the hospital, almost like it's a sign."

Ma's face displays her disbelief as she waves away my concerns. "I don't believe that. Today was a coincidence. Trust me, dear. You may think it's a sign, but it was just an unfortunate incident. How's Connor doing with it, by the way?"

"We talked about it, and I think we're good now. We, uh, kinda got distracted."

Laughing outright, she says, "I bet. Now, since Emma is likely out for the night, why don't we eat some dinner and relax for a bit? You've had a hectic day, and I'm sure it's only going to get busier for you...you know, since you're getting *busy* now and all."

Palm to my face, I scoff out an embarrassed "Jesus, Ma."

She's not wrong. The addition of seeing Connor is sure to make my hectic schedule even crazier, but crazy or not, I'm going for it.

Maybe planning the Cowboy Courses will be even more fun? If anything, it means I get to see Connor more. Might as well lean into the opportunity my hometown has given me.

CONNOR

Monday morning, I'm sitting on the sandy beach of the lake, blessedly alone, when the rumble of a car engine sounds off in the distance, destroying my peace and quiet.

Purposefully driving the rougher trail to the far side of the lake, I wanted to be left with my thoughts this morning, but based on the sound swiftly approaching me, that isn't going to happen.

Should have never told Jackson about fishing this morning.

Having professionals come in and finish out the insulation and drywall meant I needed to get out of the way. The best way for me to do that? Going fishing.

Jackson's official SUV crests the last rise and drives nearly into the lake before he stops and hops out.

Goodbye, alone time. I'll miss you.

Although, he's dressed in his work clothes, so maybe he won't be staying long?

"Want company?"

I mumble, "Not really."

"I heard that. Come on, I'm bored as shit at the station,

and until the winter courses pick up, I can only drive Liv so crazy with my pestering her."

"Fine. Just be quiet about it."

Jackson sets up his camping chair and line, but before he can send his hook out into the water he's talking again. "Hal from Everette called over asking about you. You mind telling me why another ranger station is calling me about you?"

My gut tightens at the unspoken accusation, and I'm not sure how to answer him. After the call from Hal, I knew I was being considered for the position. But after this shift in my relationship with Ally, I'm less inclined to take it.

On one hand, having the position as a backup made sense. On the other—just like everything that's happened with Ally recently—I went about it the wrong way, applying for a position with another ranger station while midconstruction of an addition on the cabin and without telling anyone about it.

We're in a good place right now though.

Don't fuck it up.

The nasty little voice at the back of my mind has been sounding constantly. Telling me that whatever yesterday was, it was a mistake, a fluke. That Ally doesn't feel the same even though it felt that way at the time. That she's going to change her mind and call all this off. That I should take that job in Everette.

I haven't called Hal yet, and after last night, I don't want to.

Maybe I'll never progress further in my career by staying here in Felt, but I'm good with that.

It would mean starting over—again. Starting in a new place with a new team, learning the ropes at a new station, and honestly, I don't want that.

"Yeah, I applied for the senior ranger position there."

"Why?"

There's no animosity in Jackson's question. Nothing that gives me a hint as to what he's thinking about me moving away from Felt, but I can guess.

Jackson and I have been tight since college. Following him home wasn't even in question after rooming together for years. It was second nature. He's my best friend; I didn't tell him I applied to a neighboring station in a jackass attempt at self-preservation.

Guilt curdles in my stomach, the coffee I drank on the way out here threatening to make a reappearance.

"I've got it bad, man. I've had it bad for Ally for a long time. Me applying to that position was my escape hatch for when I needed it. Part of me thought that nothing would come of it. That I'd get a handle on my feelings for your sister, that I'd be able to go back to normal, but that didn't happen. And now..."

"Now?"

"Now that she and I are involved, I have no plans to take the position or even interview for it. Felt's home. I'm gonna keep it that way."

As soon as I say the words, the truth of them hits me.

I'm not leaving home. My growing attraction to Ally had me running scared, but I'm not that guy anymore. I ran away from Houston to college when my life exploded after losing April, and then I ran away from college to Felt to start over.

I'm done with that. It's different now. I have people depending on me. From the rangers at the station to our group of friends. I can't cut and run when things get tough. What was best for me as a hurt kid doesn't work the same for me now that I'm a grown-ass man. Nothing good ever comes from it except having to start over, from scratch, in a new environment, and I'm too old to be doing that shit anymore.

From here on, I'm sticking it out. Even if it gets messy

with Ally, even if what we have comes to an end, I owe it to myself to stick it out and see what happens.

I owe it to Ally and the girls to be *here,* to prove they can depend on me. Ally's gotten out of the habit of depending on others, and I want to change that. I want us to be a team.

After the slice of heaven I stole with Ally last night, I need to do this right.

For the first time in a long time, my mind and heart are in agreement. I'm in. Whatever this is, however long it lasts, I'm *in.*

Kissing Ally goodbye last night sucked. That, coupled with the normal appreciation I have for the silence, only highlighted how lonely it is to be on my own all the time.

I've never been one of those people who needs company, who needs noise and sound, but that's changed. I'm starting to realize I do want the noise, the chaos, the light that comes with sharing my life with someone.

Shaking his head at me, Jackson replies, "Okay, man. Just maybe give me a little warning next time so I don't get blindsided."

"I'll call Hal and let him know I'm not interested in the job. Sorry about that, man."

Waving off my apologies, he says, "No sweat."

Now I just have to convince Ally that I can be that man for her.

FIST GRIPPING A FRESH BOUQUET OF FLOWERS WHILE SWEAT beads on my hairline, I work my way down Main Street's sidewalk. Not giving myself time to second-guess myself yet again, I yank open the door to The Sweet Tooth and head inside.

I timed my visit to fall between the rushes, but even then,

I know Ally won't have that much time for me since Monday's are usually pretty busy for her.

One thing that woman never has is a lot of time. Getting her to go to the damn spa last week was a fight, and I'm not fixing to repeat that if I can help it.

Her schedule is always so packed. So what little time I can have with her? I want that. I want every minute I'm allowed and that's more than enough to slick my palms in even more sweat.

As always, stepping into the bakery is like stepping into a slice of vanilla-scented paradise. The smells of food and coffee are heavy in the air. Light streams throughout the corner building, and it's something else.

She put a lot of work into the business, slowly upgrading it over time.

It's cheerful, clean, friendly, and run like a tight ship because she would allow nothing less.

Breakfast is switching to lunch, and there's a level of efficient chaos going on behind the counter.

Normally, I'm focused on getting in and getting out. Today, I'm seeing the shop in a different light. Maybe the reason is that Ally and I are knocking down some of the walls we put between us.

Either way, I look around, and what I see is amazing.

I'm damned proud of Ally.

She took a hole-in-the-wall bakery and turned it into a thriving business in a matter of years. The fire? It could have been devastating, but she buckled down and is doing what needs to be done by organizing the repairs and maintaining the level of professionalism that's her standard.

"Hey there, Connor," Jem calls out from behind the counter, her hands busy switching the display over. "Lemme go grab Ally. Be back in a second."

Quick as a rabbit, she disappears through the double

doors that lead back into the kitchen, and before I blink, Ally's pushing through, all smiles and sunny hair twisted up in a complicated braid.

My God, she's beautiful.

Skirting the counter, Ally makes her way over to me. Before I have a chance to offer the bouquet, she's going up to her tiptoes and brushing a warm kiss across my lips.

"Hey, handsome."

Her hazel eyes sparkle up at me, and I can see Jem's eyebrows shoot up at Ally's way of saying hello.

I know the gossip mill here in town runs strong, so I'd bet that news of Ally's hello kiss is going to be making the rounds before the end of the day.

The back of my neck itches when I think about the scrutiny I'm about to undergo, but I shove it aside, focusing on the woman in front of me.

"Hey, beautiful."

She nods at the flowers I'm still holding, asking, "Those for me?"

"Yeah, I figured..." I trail off because I have no idea what I figured other than I wanted to do something for her, anything to show her I appreciate her. That I'm with her in this. That yesterday m*eant* something to me.

"Figured?"

Scratching a hand through my hair, I pull a reason for this visit out of my ass. "Figured I'd come in and see about that date we talked about."

I could have easily called her or texted her about the date —something she likely knows—but still, I'm here now, so it makes sense to get it sorted. We may have already gone to bed together, but something tells me Ally's not familiar with romance, so I'm doing my best to change that.

Reaching up, I tug at the small piece of hair that's fallen from the braided twist she's got going on. Silky smooth, the strand of hair kisses my fingertips, and I want nothing more than to get her alone again.

Alone, I'd know what to do, what to say. Standing here in her shop, in the light of day, I'm at a loss.

Socially awkward, grumpy, standoffish. I've heard them all applied to me over the years. But what I see as just being me, others see as something different, something odd. I stopped caring about the labels assigned to me years ago.

"Sure. What'd you have in mind?"

Get your head in the game, Murtry.

"How about a movie? We could go up to The Spud, grab dinner and a movie tonight?"

I watch as her expression falls a little before she responds, "Oh, uh, I'm not sure if Ma has plans tonight, but I can check with her to see if she can watch the twins."

One of the best parts of Ally is her girls, so I'm not gonna pass up the chance to spend more time with them either. "I planned on all of us going together."

"Together?"

"Yep. You, me, and Peanut Brittle. We'll grab dinner there and then I figured we'd spread out on the lawn for the movie, that is if it's okay on a school night."

"They don't have school tomorrow, long weekend for the holiday."

"Oh yeah, today's Labor Day. They have tomorrow off?"

"They do. But Connor, have you ever taken two little girls to the drive in?

"No, but I have taken them to the lake and out fishing alone, so I'd still like to take the three of you out."

Laughing lightly, she leans up to brush another kiss across my lips. "It's a date then. Now, about that house of yours. I was going to swing by this afternoon to bring over some ideas for the kitchen and the living room. I have a binder in the car. Does that work for you?"

The insulation for the addition should be wrapped by this afternoon and then the rest of the week is going to be finishing the flooring and interior fixtures before the exterior gets done.

"Sure. What time?"

She's quiet while I assume she shuffles through her mental schedule before replying, "How about three-ish? I'll grab the girls and we can leave for dinner after if that's okay?"

"That's fine."

"Okay, I'll keep them out from underfoot."

I don't care if they're underfoot, but thinking about the lack of child safety inherent in the torn-up cabin, I realize I could stand to clean up a little bit before they get there. I already have to go over the progress from today with the crew I hired to manage the remainder of the addition. Might as well kill two birds and head back to clean a bit as well as check in.

"Sounds good. I'll see you then." I brush one last kiss across her lips and head out.

Spending the evening with three of my favorite females? The day just got a whole lot brighter.

ALLY

I'M RUNNING LATE. I HATE RUNNING LATE.

A last-minute order for a late catered lunch for the community center put me behind schedule on getting out of the shop. I ended up staying past closing.

Thank God, Ma has the girls.

What I'd do without her I have no idea, but as I'm tearing down the street toward her house to change into date-ish clothes and then grab the girls and run, I can be glad she's there for me when I need her.

I thought I had enough time to get everything done before I left for the day, but you know what they say about good intentions. I texted Connor to let him know I'd be late, but I haven't heard anything back yet.

I'm going to have just enough time to run through the binder of design options I put together for Connor by the time I get over there since it's going on five now and the movie starts at seven thirty.

I wanted tonight to be perfect.

Took me a long time to realize that perfect isn't always best. Sometimes we have to let go of our worries and hope for the best.

Remembering Ma's words has some of the frazzled mess in my brain sliding away. It's gonna be okay. Even if I'm late, it won't ruin the whole date. I'll zip inside, change, and go.

Tearing into the house, I call out, "Ma, are the girls ready to go? We have to head out to Connor's."

Ma walks out of the kitchen, wiping her hands on a dishrag. I'm halfway to the stairs when I notice the quiet.

One thing you don't get without a lot of work and ingenuity with twin girls is *quiet*. Foot paused on the tread of the bottom stair, I ask, "Where are the girls?"

Ma tucks the dishrag in the back pocket of her jeans and says, "Connor came to pick them up. Said he wanted you to be able to get ready in peace since you were running late. He said for you to meet them at The Spud."

I don't have time to think about what it means that Connor picked the girls up. I barely have time to run a brush through my hair, put it up, change my clothes, and head out the door.

Driving as fast as I'll chance to avoid a ticket, I head out to the movie theater.

The sun is dipping toward the horizon when the giant truck holding an enormous fake potato comes into view. The closest movie theater is over an hour away, so this is *the place* to hang out on a Friday night in our little slice of the world.

I park in the first open spot I find and move toward the lawn seating, scanning the area for the three of them.

Once I get close enough, I can see Emma is curled up on Connor's lap, showing off all the signatures on her cast, and Elle is lying across his legs.

He's so natural with the girls. I can only hope that what we're doing, this relationship, won't jeopardize that.

I don't know that the girls could handle the letdown.

Elle catches sight of me and hops up to run into my arms.

"Mama! Connor said we can get burgers in The Spud. Can we?"

The kids live for nights out like this. Even when we've come for a movie in the past, we've eaten at home first, so dinner from the snack bar is a special treat for them.

"Sure can, baby doll."

Emma and Connor both look comfortable and not interested in getting up, so I offer, "Why don't I take orders and then go grab everything?"

He shifts Emma off his lap and sets her gently on the picnic blanket, then stands. When he's inches away, he reaches out and tucks a strand of hair behind my ear, softly kissing me on the lips.

In deference to the little eyes we have around us, it can't go further than that. I can already tell that I'm going to have to answer some questions based on my daughters' curious looks.

The rough timbre of his voice surrounds me when he murmurs, "I'll go. You sit with the girls and get comfortable. What do y'all want?"

After gathering our orders, he walks off to collect the food, drinks, and snacks that only two seven-year-olds could possibly consume in a two-hour period.

"Why'd he kiss you?" Emma asks.

Before I can even begin to answer her, Elle is jumping in. "Boys are gross. I don't ever want to kiss one of them."

Laughing, I say, "When two people like each other a whole lot, they date. Part of dating is getting to know each other, and sometimes kissing comes with that."

"Well, that was a tiny kiss. He must not like you very much. Uncle Jacks kisses Aunt Liv a whole lot"—her little face scrunches up—"like a whole lot, for hours and hours."

The exaggeration is apt. When it comes to Liv and Jackson, they're often locked at the lips. I don't even know how to begin to explain the difference between dating and being engaged.

"They do kiss a lot, don't they?"

"They do! It's so gross."

I can't say I agree with my daughter, but I also know that in a couple of very short years she's likely to change her tune on kissing, so I keep my mouth shut.

Just the memory of Connor's mouth plundering mine is enough to send heat rushing to my cheeks, but before I get lost in salacious thoughts, the previews start playing on the large screen. The girls are running off the last of their energy before sitting down to watch the movie when Connor returns.

The twins fall upon the food like they've never eaten a day in their lives.

I let them make an unholy mess while we sit back and relax. Before long, Connor tugs me to sit between his spread legs, the girls tucked in around us, while the animated film plays across the screen.

Connor's fingers trace along the backs of my arms, occasionally coming up to rest on my shoulders, where he squeezes in a massaging caress.

I don't know if I'm just starved for physical affection or if he just affects me that much, but before long, my pulse thunders in my chest, and a familiar tension takes up residence in my core.

He must notice me start to squirm. Connor breathes against my ear, his lips trailing the shell, as he whispers, "You keep moving like that, and I'm going to get arrested for public indecency."

The hot brand of his erection is evident at the base of my spine. I'd give just about anything to be alone with him right now.

Teasingly, I squirm a little more and am rewarded with a

muffled groan he bites back before his hands drop to my legs to still my movement.

"Enough of that now."

"Or what?" I don't know where the brazen challenge comes from, but I toss it out before I think better of it.

"Or I'm going to have to fuck my fist tonight, when I'd rather be fucking you."

The low tone of his voice, coupled with the grip on my thighs, is enough to send a quiver through me.

Why is that so hot? The thought of him getting himself off drives me to distraction. I forget all about our audience, the children's movie playing, my girls rolling around on the grass, and turn my head to kiss him.

His mouth clashes with mine. Cedar invades my senses, making me lightheaded.

Like always, Connor takes control of the kiss, his hand abandoning my thigh to cup my face. But instead of the kiss spinning out of control, he slows it down until it's sumptuous. Like molasses rolling through me and I'm caught up in him.

He's the first to pull back after one last peck, his chocolate gaze searching mine. Both of us are breathing a little heavier now, and the knowledge I can affect him like this is heady.

"Ally…" His speech falters, and I couldn't agree more.

The speed of our *relationship* has been fast. Just last week he was trying to push me away, but now here we are, out on a date with my two girls in tow.

"I know. One day at a time, okay?"

He only nods, but I'll take it. This is new territory for both of us. We're still finding our feet and figuring each other out. Considering how long we've been in each other's lives, we still don't know very much about each other, but we're getting there.

I can say there isn't another place I want to be tonight than here with him and my girls.

Now, if I could convince my heart to slow down when it comes to Connor Murtry, this would be perfect.

~

THE NEXT MORNING, I'M SITTING IN MY OFFICE AT THE BAKERY, swearing like a sailor while temper tears trail down my cheeks.

Colby called first thing this morning, letting me know there's a holdup with the permits I need in order to repair and renovate the shop.

Because of the delay, my kitchen won't be done for four more weeks.

Four weeks of carting my baking supplies and ingredients over to another kitchen and dragging the finished products back here.

Should I even stay open that long?

The damned preservation society in this town moves so freaking slowly sometimes. That plus the need to not disturb the businesses on either side of me have hamstrung me. My workload has doubled by cooking off-site, and I just need a freaking break.

I'll be running right up to the Cowboy Courses by the time Colby's team can get in here, but I was hoping to have this taken care of so it'd be off my plate of things to do.

The door at the back of the shop opens, and I wipe at my cheeks before turning to find Liv and Kate shoving their way in.

"Hey, guys. What's up?"

Kate looks at Liv before saying, "Nope, we're not going to pretend you're not crying. What happened?"

"The permits to repair my kitchen are delayed. They treated the mold, so we're good there, but I can't have the wall fixed or the work on the studios above done until middle of next month."

Sympathy covers their faces. Kate had to deal with her own renovation hell just over a year ago, so she knows how frustrating it can be to have a solid plan in motion only for it to be stopped midprogress.

Liv asks, "Did they say what's holding them up?"

I shake my head. I wish I knew.

"Four weeks—shit, that's right in the middle of the Cowboy Courses. What can we do?"

Having friends is the best.

I want to handle this all on my own—it's my business, after all. I want to be able to get my life squared away without having to rely on others, but like I promised Connor, maybe it's time to ask for help. Lord knows I need it now.

"I don't know yet, but as we get closer, I might need help with the store or the courses depending on what's going on."

Nodding, Kate says, "You got it. We'll do our best to jump in when we can. Just let us know what you need, and we'll figure it out."

"Thank you. I really appreciate it."

The ease with which they offer their help isn't surprising, nor is the small feeling of failure that comes along with needing help.

"What brings you guys by?" I'm pretty sure I know why they're here, but I'm not in the mood to beat around the bush after the morning I've had.

Liv rolls her eyes. "Like you have to ask. Tell us how the movie went last night!"

"It was good. The girls had a fun time, and it was just a really...*good* evening."

Kate's eyebrows climb her forehead. "That's all you're going to say? That it was *good*? Lady, I need you to dish. We need details."

Liv jumps in. "She's right. I'm an incurable romantic, and the sexy tension that's been floating around you two was almost too much to handle. Are you going to see him again? If so, when? Have you guys made any plans for a kid-free date yet?"

The questions come rapid-fire, and Liv is nearly out of breath before she finishes peppering me with them.

Holding up a hand, I say, "Slow down there, Cupid. We're taking it a day at a time right now. Feeling each other and this out. I think..." I don't want to talk out of turn, but I need to share my concerns with someone else. "I think this might be overwhelming for Connor. He was so dead set on not looking at me romantically that this is throwing him for a loop. I'd rather not rush ahead and mess him up."

"That's understandable. It's hard when you expect one thing and then something completely different comes out of left field to throw you off course," Liv says. "Plus, when you think about him applying for that position over in Everette, I can see how you'd want to take it slow."

Hard stop.

"Wait, what? He applied for a position over in Everette?"

Liv's brows furrow and she looks at Kate, both silently communicating with small shrugs and blinks.

Liv turns back to me. "You didn't know about him applying for the senior ranger position?"

My voice won't work, so I shake my head. I sure didn't know.

Maybe he applied before we got together. Maybe he isn't considering the position anymore. Maybe...

The mental montage of hopeful positivity sings through

my thoughts, battling the insecure parts of me that want to jump to all the bad conclusions.

I'll bring it up with him, see what's what.

And hope for the best.

CONNOR

STANDING OUTSIDE MY NEARLY FINISHED HOUSE BRINGS AN insane amount of pride. What started out as a small one-room cabin is now a three-thousand-square-foot home. The relief of being *this close* to done is astounding.

The timing couldn't be more perfect. With less than three weeks until we're set to start the weeklong celebration, I'm fucking relieved I won't have to juggle both projects.

Ally and I are meeting later to get a finalized list of the participants for each of our events before we go over some of the design ideas she has for the house. I haven't seen her much this week. Between the ranger station and the house, it was a busy week.

I sent her a text this morning, confirming the plans for us to get together today. Maybe it was because she's busy at work, but she seemed off. The short one- and two-word replies were completely different from the woman I had in my arms at the drive-in the other night.

I could be reading too much into this. They were text messages for God's sake; there wasn't a tone to infer anything from.

Why am I so nervous when it comes to us? Maybe we should define our relationship more and that'll put my mind at ease? On the other hand, I'm leery of rocking the boat when we're in a good spot—or at least I think we are.

The crunch of gravel behind me has me turning my head, and before the SUV is turned off, the girls are out and running for me.

For the second time in as many weeks, I wonder if I should put a swing set or something in the back of the house for them.

If I have my way, they're going to be spending more time over here, which is why I have some ideas for the other rooms in the house.

I might be moving too fast, planning to design the girls a bedroom so they can stay over, but I got a little carried away once the thought popped into my head. I managed to stop myself before buying the paint and furniture.

Swinging Elle up, I hitch her onto my hip and get hit with how much the girls have grown. A couple of years ago, I could fit both in one arm, but now Elle's foot damn near hits my knees when I'm holding her.

Emma's arm pops around my waist in a half hug. She's still getting used to the awkwardness of the cast, and a moment of guilt hits me before I shove it off.

Accidents happen, and if you beat yourself up over that, you'll end up perpetually black and blue.

"Peanut Brittle, what's happening, captains?"

They both tell me about their week at school. I soak in the attention they give me. Once Mom died and I went to live with my dad, the only people who cared about my day was the staff.

And maybe it's silly, but the excitement I get from hearing about a pop quiz in math and the schoolyard politics during recess brings the same absurd amount of joy that having my house finished does.

Ally's slower about getting out of the car, and when I see why, I set Elle on her feet and head over to give her a hand.

"Here, let me take that." Pulling one of the large totes off her shoulder, I can't help but wonder what the hell she has in there, because it's heavy.

I'm leaning down to brush a kiss across her mouth when she turns her head to give me her cheek.

That's odd, because it's not like the girls haven't seen me kiss her. "Everything okay?" I ask.

She won't meet my gaze, and the pinch between her eyebrows is enough to answer my question even before she says, "Can we talk?"

Fuck.

What happened?

"Sure. Later?"

Nodding, she says, "Yeah, let's get this inside so we can get started." Looking to Emma and Elle, she says, "Girls, grab your backpacks so you can work on your homework."

Abandoning me, she and the girls grab the rest of their gear before making their way inside. The icy slither of apprehension creeps up my spine.

Something's up. I don't know what it is yet, but something's up.

I follow them, and once Ally's inside, she stops dead in her tracks. "Holy wow, Con. It looks so good."

"Yeah, Jackson and Arik came out this weekend to help out. There are a few things left, but we're getting close."

Hazel eyes finally meet mine, but the openness I normally see in them is absent as she says, "That was nice of them."

Everything about our interaction right now is odd, like shoes that don't fit quite right. Have I done something wrong or upset her?

I'm not one to beat around the bush, so I tell the girls, "You guys go ahead and get set up in the kitchen with your homework. I'm gonna show your mom something."

Not giving her a chance to back away—I can see the desire to do just that on her face—I grab her hand and tug her down the hallway after me.

Pulling her in through the pocket doors of the office, I ask, "Okay, now, you wanna tell me what's wrong?"

"Let's talk about it later. I just have a lot to get done today, so if you don't mind?" She waves her hands at the door, but I'm not gullible enough to fall for that.

"I do mind. I know you, beautiful. Talk to me."

I run my hands down her arms before catching her hands in mine, hoping the contact will make her comfortable enough to open up to me.

With a huff of breath, she asks, "Why didn't you tell me about the job in Everette?"

Ah, now it makes sense. She heard from Jackson about me applying for the job. I don't know why he didn't tell her I wasn't planning on taking it, but that's okay.

"I applied for it after I kissed you at the fairgrounds. My control around you was dwindling, and I thought your brother wouldn't approve, so I made plans to leave if I needed to. Things have changed since then, so I called Hal and withdrew my application."

"You turned it down? When?"

"Last week. Jackson knows I turned it down, so I don't know why he didn't tell you that, but I'm not going for the position anymore."

"Jackson wasn't the one who told me about it. Liv was."

Coasting my fingers along the back of her hands, I say, "See, she probably didn't know I withdrew. Did you think I'd just up and leave and not talk to you about it first?"

Biting the corner of her mouth, she sucks her lower lip in. I drop her hand to pull the abused flesh from her teeth.

"I don't know. I mean, I don't think you would, but you didn't say anything about the interview in the first place, so I have no idea."

I drop my lips to hers in a brief peck, definitely not the kiss I want or need, but it's enough of a reassurance that I explain, "There wasn't anything to tell. I got the call for it, but decided I didn't want to move, that I'm where I want to be."

"Really?" A smile starts to kick up her cheeks, her dimples coming out to play.

"Yeah, and if that changes, then you'll be the first to know. But, Als"—I hesitate because I don't know quite how to say this—"if you have concerns like this, or questions, you can come to me. We can talk them out and then figure out how to move forward together. I want that. I want us to be a team."

Her smile grows until she's practically beaming. "Okay."

"If I'm with you, then I'm *with you.* You can talk to me about anything, and I hope I can with you."

Nodding, she says, "Of course."

"Good. So we're okay?"

"Yeah, we're okay."

Kissing her lips again, I know we aren't going to get much more uninterrupted time, so I make the most of it, tasting the sweetness of her mouth before pulling back.

"Let's go get the plans out of the way, and you can show me your ideas for the house, okay?"

"Let's."

~

By accident or subconscious design, Ally and the twins eat dinner with me that night. It's nothing fancy, just takeout, but it's enough to cement the rightness of my decision to turn down the ranger job.

I know we just started seeing each other, that this is still new for both of us, but sitting across from Ally at my new dining room set while the girls pig out on burgers and soda is enough to convince me to go all in.

"And then Cindi made a milk bubble out of her nose when she hiccupped. It was so funny."

Emma's animated as she recounts her day for us. Elle is less so, but still involved in the conversation.

"That sounds like it would be funny. What about you, Elle. How was your day?"

Turning to me, Elle's little shoulders shrug in a move that looks so much like something her mama would do I can't help but smile.

"It was okay. We got to play dodgeball in PE and that was fun."

"Oh, yeah? Is dodgeball your favorite?"

"Not really, but I got to throw a ball at Alex and not get into trouble for it..."

Ally interjects, "Elle, I know you and Alex don't get along, but that doesn't mean you should be mean back to him. Remember that we tell adults when we have a problem with someone?"

Grumbling, Elle replies, "I know."

I don't know this Alex kid, but in my opinion, if he's giving Elle a hard time, then a foam ball to the face is the least of his worries. I look at Ally, and the question must be evident on my face because she waits until Elle looks back to her pizza before mouthing "school bully" at me.

I fucking hate bullies.

I wasn't bullied in school, but that was more because you

have to give a damn to be bullied. That doesn't mean I don't know the damage they can wreak, and I'll be damned if my girl is picked on.

Ally is shaking her head for me to drop it, but that's not gonna fly with me. As soon as I can, I'm going to get her alone and have her break down the situation for me.

I see my chance after dinner, while the girls are in the living room packing up their stuff, and Ally and I are in the kitchen.

"So what's the deal with this Alex kid?" I shove leftovers into my fridge and carefully keep the irritation out of my tone.

"He picks on Elle because she's shy and doesn't talk much. I don't know why, but I do know that it has to stop because Elle is starting to dread school. I have a meeting with the principal later this week to discuss it." Under her breath, she mumbles, "Took him long enough to get back to me."

"Hmm. Who are his parents, and what do they have to say about it?"

"Jason and Lisa Bennet. I don't know what they have to say because I haven't been able to get them on the phone or into a meeting with the school administration."

I know Jason. I know he travels a lot for work and when he is home, he's usually at the river on the weekend.

Plans are forming in my head. I know it's not the mature thing to do, but changing my weekend plans to include a trip up to the river sounds just about right. I'll talk to Jason and get to the bottom of it. I can get Jackson and Arik to go with me to stop anything from escalating.

"I don't like that look in your eye, Connor Murtry. Just what are you planning?"

Adopting the most innocent expression I can, I answer, "Nothing."

Hands fisted at her hips, she looks adorable, replying, "Nothing, my foot. I know when you're scheming."

"Don't you worry about it. You get home and put those girls to bed."

Lips pinched, Ally wants to argue with me but wisely doesn't. Out of the two of us, I don't know who is more stubborn, but I'd rather not beat my head against her temper tonight.

"Girls! Let's go."

The chorus of pleas to stay longer is drowned out by Ally saying, "It's a school night. You both still need baths, and I have work to get done."

Ushering the girls through the house, I follow Ally and watch as they climb into her SUV.

"Text or call me when you get home."

"Connor—"

I pinch her chin between my finger and thumb and drop my lips to hers.

As a method for shutting her up, it works wonders. The taste of her invades my senses, and it's not long before I get swept up in the feel of her in my arms.

Ally's the first to pull back, saying, "Fine, fine. I'll text you when I get home. Happy now?"

"Very." I drop another brief kiss on her lips before I step back, taking a deep breath to get myself under control. I know the girls have school and she has work in the morning, but the desire for them to stay here with me is intense and immediate.

One day. Hopefully one day soon I'll have them with me for more than a couple of hours.

ALLY

THE WALLS OF FELT ELEMENTARY SCHOOL HAVEN'T CHANGED since I was a kid. The cinderblock walls are covered in art and projects from the students, and the hallways still sport ugly maroon and beige linoleum.

"Ally? Principal Woods will see you now."

The same ancient front office receptionist sits at the same desk as twenty years ago, and I stifle the urge to flinch.

I didn't go to the principal's office much as a kid, but the few times I did left an impression.

It's strange that I'm walking to the office alone when I asked for Alex's parents to be present so we're all on the same page when it comes to handling this situation.

"Ally, thanks for coming in." Principal Woods pumps my hand in an enthusiastic shake before I can cross the threshold into his office.

"Thanks for accommodating the meeting." Looking around I ask, "Where're Jason and Lisa?"

Eyebrows pinched, he says, "They declined to attend the meeting."

Declined to attend.

How can parents decline a meeting request from the school administration? That sets the last ounce of patience I have on fire.

"What is the school prepared to do when the bullying doesn't stop?"

I'm done playing nice. If my daughter comes home crying because of that little turd nugget one more time, someone is going to answer to me.

"Now hold on a minute, Ally…"

I hold up a hand. "No. I will not hold on. I have sent numerous emails to Elle's teacher and this administration. I have asked for a meeting for weeks, to be put off over and over again, until finally we got today's meeting on the calendar, only for Alex's parents to *decline to attend.* I would like to know what you intend to do to ensure my daughter has a safe environment to learn in. This is not a new circumstance; this did not *just* happen. It is a known issue, and I am done sending email after email to not be given an answer."

Higher and higher his eyebrows climb until they all but disappear into his hairline, and I realize during my tirade my voice climbed just like those caterpillar-looking bushy brows did.

"We've tried to get Jason and Lisa in here to discuss this, but without them being present, we have no way to gauge the best course of action—"

"I'm going to stop you right there," I spit out. "If his parents can't be bothered to attend a school meeting, what makes you think they're going to have input on the changes needed to ensure he stops tormenting my daughter? If Jason and Lisa won't come to the school to meet with us, then I'll take this fight to their goddamn door. I will *not* have my daughter come home crying one more day because of the negligence of the school. Figure out a course of action or you'll be hearing from my lawyer."

Temper has me striding out of the room and building before I can rein it in enough to take a full breath.

How fucking dare they? They are his *parents*, and they couldn't care less that he's responsible for hurting a little girl every single day.

If I have to, I'll yank both of the girls from the school and homeschool them while running my business.

Tearing out of the parking lot, I head out of town. I can't go back to the bakery with my temper so close to the surface, or I'm likely to go off on some unsuspecting customer who complains their coffee isn't right.

When I come to the turnoff for Connor's place, I don't even think about it, I just turn down his road. We never got to talk about the design ideas I have for the second floor of the house. Now's as good a time as any, and it'll give me a chance to calm down.

Jackson's department SUV is parked in front of the house, and I have a moment of hesitation before quashing it.

Jackson knows about Connor and me dating. This shouldn't be weird.

But standing on Connor's porch, knocking on his door? That's another thing all together. I'm just here to talk about paint and calm down. Nothing more, nothing less. When the door opens to my brother's smug, asshat face, I know I'm in for it.

"Well, well, well. If it isn't my little sister."

Shoving his shoulder, I push past him. "Shut up, you. Is Connor here?"

"Yeah, we're out back. I was just grabbing beers for us."

"Great. I'll take one too." With my drink order taken care of, I head out to the back deck where the eye candy of all eye candy awaits me.

Shirtless, a defined chest with just the right amount of hair dusting it greets me. The ripple of washboard abs shift and move with each hefting swing of the splitting awl in Connor's hand.

If I had known this would be my view when I headed out this way, I would have sped—potential ticket be damned.

Jesus fuck.

He's splitting wood for winter, and I'm drooling over the man.

Connor looks up, and my lusty thoughts must be apparent on my face because the most egotistical snarky smirk shifts his mouth as he asks, "Like the view, beautiful?"

Nodding silently is all I can manage. Every single drop of spit has dried in my mouth until I'm certain the sheer sexual masculinity of the man in front of me has dehydrated everything but my panties.

He sets the awl down and makes his way to me, and with every step he gets closer, I lose more brain cells to his appeal.

How is it even fair that he looks like he does shirtless? I'm over here in yoga pants and a nicer blouse—my one concession to the meeting at the school—and he looks like a centerfold model for a naughty lumberjack ladies' catalog.

Less than an inch away he stops, his hand coming up to tuck my hair back, and I'm two seconds away from jumping his bones.

"Hey, you two! None of that until I leave. Connor, put a damn shirt on. Ally, his eyes are up there."

I swear to heaven above, Jackson is always in the wrong spot at the wrong time. Is it too much to ask to let me ogle in peace, for the love of Pete?

Jackson hands out the beers, sure to get in the middle of us, and Connor just shoots me a conspirator's wink while we both sip.

It's one in the afternoon, and I'm having a beer with my brother and my boyfriend.

Is this my life right now?

"How'd it go at the school?" Connor's the first to speak. The reminder of why I'm out here brings the irritation and temper right back to the forefront of my mind.

"Alex's parents didn't show up, so there wasn't a meeting."

"What?"

I ignore Jackson's question when I see the spark of temper ignite in Connor's chocolate gaze. He's just as pissed as I am.

"They didn't show up, so I asked Principal Woods what he was planning on doing about it the next time Alex starts in on Elle. He didn't have an answer for me, but that's okay. I'll go up to the resort and try to talk to Lisa next week and see what's what."

"Well, shit. Let me know if you need any help," Jackson says to me, but his eyes cut to Connor. Those two are up to something.

Setting my beer down, I pick up the splitting awl and load a chunk of wood onto the stump. If I can't resolve something for my daughter, how good of a mother am I? If I can't protect her when she's young, then how can I teach her to stand up for herself?

"Als, that's heavy. Here, let me..." Connor's offer to take over trails off as I swing the axe up and over my shoulder, letting gravity pull it down until it crashes into the log, splitting it cleanly in two. My eyes find Connor's.

"Bro, she's been splitting logs our whole life. She's got this." Jackson's vote of confidence doesn't drop Connor's eyebrows an inch, so I do it again. Another log goes up on the stump, and keeping my eye trained on it, I heft the awl, let it swing, and slice it in half. Lips curling in a smirk, I say,

"Just because Jackson usually cuts the wood for Ma and me doesn't mean I don't know how to do it or I'm not capable."

Connor sucks in his bottom lip and says, "I can see that."

I don't ever want him to think I'm incapable even though that's exactly how I feel right now knowing there isn't much I can do to deal with the issue Elle has to deal with every day.

If I weren't trying to raise happy, healthy, productive members of society, I'd tell Elle to go cowgirl on the kid the next time he tries to pull some shit. But that would only exacerbate the issue.

He's not physically touching her, and my hands are tied when it comes to what I'll let her do in retaliation.

Handing the axe off to Connor, I grab my beer and chug a couple of swallows.

"I'm so fucking mad. That little shitstain thinks he can get away with coming after *my girl*? His mother better do something about this because I won't be held responsible when I give Elle permission to rock his shit the next time he starts something."

Jackson looks at me in astonished shock. While he's seen part of the pissed-off mom come out once or twice, he's never seen it to this degree.

I do my best to keep my feelings about the girls to myself. There's no one who needs to know I worry about being a good enough mother every day. But I've just about had it with the whole situation.

"As she should."

Connor's quiet declaration derails my train of thought.

Laughing weakly, I say, "Yeah, but she shouldn't have to, and that's the whole point of this. Why are kids so frickin' mean?"

With a deep sigh, I hand Jackson my barely touched beer. "Well, this was fun, but I've got to get back to the bakery."

"How're the repairs going there?" Jackson asks after taking a drink of my abandoned beer.

"They're not. There's some holdup at the permit office, so Colby won't be able to work on the bakery for another few weeks."

"Where are you doing the baking then?"

"Up at the inn. They're letting me use their kitchen early in the morning. I just have to be done before they start breakfast. It sucks, but it's working for now."

"Well, shit. Lemme know if I can do anything."

Looking at my brother, I know his offer is automatic, off the cuff, and genuine. I can count on him for just about anything, and I know for a fact that the hero complex in him is trying to figure out how to fix this for me.

"Can't do anything without the permits, and we have to wait for those. It'll be okay, but thank you."

"Here, let me walk you out," Connor says.

Giddy elation takes flight in the pit of my stomach as his hand reaches for mine and we skirt the exterior of the house.

"Is there anything I can do for Elle? Or Emma? Or you?"

Thinking about it for less than a second, I shake my head. "No, you're already doing it. Thanks for letting me work off some steam and split some of your wood."

Heat creeps into his gaze, as he drags his eyes from my head to my toes before saying, "You're more than welcome to work my wood anytime you want."

The sheer seriousness of his tone sets me off. Before I can stop myself, I'm laughing at him, bent over double.

"You did not just say that. Oh, my God! That was the worst line I've ever heard in my life." I can barely get the words out around my laughter. I know he meant to be suave or sexy, but that was definitely not the way to go about it.

He scrubs his hand through his beard and looks away, a

wince playing across his face. "Yeah, that was kinda rough, wasn't it?"

I pinch my fingers close together, holding them up, and say, "Li'l bit. Next time, throw in a lewd wink, and that might sell it a little more."

He chuckles, and I add his smile to the tally I've been keeping over the years. Each one gives me a little more insight into the man and tunnels him a little deeper into my heart.

Reaching into the pocket of my yoga pants, I pull out my key fob and unlock my doors.

Connor advances on me until my back meets the side of my SUV, and when he leans down, the scents of clean male sweat and cedar surround me.

"I want to see you again. When can we make that happen?"

Shuffling through the mental files of my obligations, commitments, appointments, and the girls' lives takes me a few seconds before I say, "How about Saturday? We're meeting to go over your study and order materials. I can see if Ma will watch the girls for me so I can maybe stay the night?"

"Sounds like a plan to me. Are you sure Nan will be okay with…"

"Me coming over for a booty call, or me spending the night with you?"

"Either. Both."

"She knows we're seeing each other. She guessed it after the first time when I came home. And unless she has plans, she won't have a problem with wrangling the girls for me. I'll talk to her about it when I get home."

After a quick kiss, I hop into my car and head back to Felt. I'm ready to get home and finagle a sitter so I can have a proper sleepover.

~

HOW DOES ONE ASK ONE'S MOTHER TO WATCH HER GRANDKIDS so her daughter can get laid? As much as I want to just ask, the embarrassed daughter in me knows she's going to see right through my request for what it is.

I mean, how hard can this be? She asked me to make a damned dick cake for her book club not even a month ago, so surely I can ask her to mind the girls while I spend time with the man I'm seeing.

"What are you muttering about over there?"

I'm midplacement of a plate in the dishwasher when Ma's question takes me off guard.

"Uh..."

"Well, spit it out. What's got your knickers in a knot?"

Well, shit. I guess I have to ask now. Ma's always been able to see through my lies from a mile away.

"Can you watch the girls for me this weekend?"

"That's what you were muttering about? Of course, I can. Do you need to get more work done on the Cowboy Courses?"

Hedging, I say, "Uh...not really?"

"Ally Ann Sawyer, I am not a mind reader; just tell me already."

"I'm going to Connor's. I want to have a sleepover so I can get laid and not have self-administered orgasms for a change."

Ma's mouth drops open for a split second before a peal of laughter shoots out of her. I didn't mean to say all that, but the full name got me. There's nothing more terrifying than your mother saying your full name. I don't care who you ask, that shit is still effective as an adult.

"Well, in that case, of course I can watch the girls."

Heat flies into my cheeks, and I need a second before I

mumble "thank you," all while staring at the floor. I don't have a lot of triggers for embarrassment, but apparently asking my mom to watch my kids while I go have sex is one of them.

Remembering Connor in his shirtless glory today makes the little bit of embarrassment I'm feeling right now *worth it.*

CONNOR

FISHING AT THE RIVER IS DIFFERENT FROM AT THE LAKE. AFTER cajoling Jackson and Arik to come out with me, I got Jackson to grab the girls from Ally.

This should be interesting.

When she came over and started splitting wood in frustration over what's going on with Elle, I decided to take matters into my own hands.

Jackson and Arik are backup in case things get heated, which is the opposite of what I want.

Luckily, I know Alex's dad, Jason, from occasional poker nights. He's a steady guy.

It doesn't take us long to set up on the bank, nor does it take us long to get our lines in the water before Jason makes his way over to us.

"Hey, Connor." With a nod to us, he continues, "Jackson, Arik, how's it going?"

"Not bad, just decided to get some fishing in this morning. You remember Ally's daughters, Emma and Elle, right?"

Elle spots Alex and tucks herself closer to my side. Emma just glares in his direction. I love that they stick together.

Jason nods to the girls after saying hello and then starts talking with Jackson about the next poker night. Looking down, I nudge Elle and say, "Why don't you go play in the shallow water, but don't go out too far."

After the incident at the lake, I have both girls in life vests because the river water can move fast if you're not paying attention. I'd rather be safe than sorry.

Elle steps away from me with a wary eye on Alex, who is poking at the mud with a stick.

Soon the girls are splashing, and we're all sitting on the bank when I turn to Jason and ask, "So Ally told me y'all had a meeting at the school, but you and Lisa couldn't make it. I hope everything's okay?"

A puzzled frown covers Jason's face, and as his mouth opens up to respond, Alex chooses that moment to fling a handful of mud at the girls.

Without missing a beat, Emma scoops up her own handful and tosses it at Alex, but her aim is better and she manages to catch him right in the face with it.

"Dad! Did you see what she did?"

Emma hollers back, "You threw the mud at us first, Alex!"

The kids dissolve into arguments, and I take the chance to say, "Apparently Alex has been bullying Elle, and Ally requested a meeting with y'all and the school administration."

Jason holds his hand up to me before turning to Alex and saying, "Alex, I saw you throw that mud at Elle. You apologize right now, you hear me?"

"But Dad."

"Don't you *but Dad* me. You say you're sorry right now."

After Alex offers a grumbled apology, Jason turns back to me, saying, "I didn't know about a school meeting, and Lisa never said anything."

I don't know if he's lying or just ignorant about what's

going on in his own house, but I give him the benefit of the doubt and explain, "He's been giving Elle a hard time at school, sent her home crying a couple of times, and Ally reached out to the school to have a meeting to handle it."

"Alex! Come here."

The irritation and anger in Jason's tone lead me to believe he had no idea this has been going on.

Alex walks over to us, and Jason drops a hand to his shoulder, asking, "Have you been picking on Elle Sawyer?"

Green eyes turn contrite before he responds, "Yes."

Jason's mouth pinches in disappointment before he says, "Connor, man, I'm sorry. I didn't know. Lisa gets all the emails and calls from the school, and as you know, I'm not in town that much. I'll talk to Lisa about this tonight, and we'll call Ally to get this resolved. I can promise you that Alex won't be a problem for Elle." Jason turns to Alex and continues, "Isn't that right, son?"

Alex nods, and Jason ushers him away to pack up their fishing gear.

Jackson says, "That went a lot better than I thought it would. Do you think he's going to handle it?"

"I hope for his sake he does, because I'm not letting that shit slide anymore."

Arik chimes in, "Well, look at you, going all papa bear for the girls."

I kick sand in his direction. "Shut up, man."

But the truth of it is I do feel like a papa bear when it comes to anyone hurting or causing problems for those girls.

Glancing over to make sure the girls are preoccupied, I ask, "What's the deal with their dad?"

Jackson frowns. "You know how he and Ally got together, right?"

I shake my head. Maybe I should be asking her about this,

but I'm not going to turn down information I can get from Jackson.

"They started seeing each other when she worked up at the resort. But he kept it super hush-hush and didn't tell anyone he was seeing her. I don't know her side of it beyond what she and Ma have told me, but they were involved for a good bit of time before Ally found out she was pregnant with the twins. When his parents found out, they demanded he propose. She said yes and they moved to San Francisco where the bulk of his family's business is located."

Jackson pauses to reel in his line. Once he recasts it, he continues, "She was there for about a year when she walked in on him and his receptionist. Packed the girls right up and came home."

"What a fucking idiot." What kind of man throws away a woman like Ally?

"That's not even the worst part. He didn't even fight her for any type of custody for the girls. He sends a check each month and considers his duty done."

What a fucking bastard.

My poor girls. I don't know whether I want to play ignorant and pretend I don't know what's going on or scoop them up and promise I'll protect them from all the hurts in the world.

The bright pink cast on Emma's arm is calling me a liar, and I know for a fact that regardless of my intentions to protect her, I can't save her from *all* the hurts in the world.

What kind of dad would I even be to these girls? I sure as hell didn't have a good example growing up, never mind I've never considered having kids of my own.

What if I can't be what these girls need? What if I'm only hurting them more by getting involved with their mother?

What if they come to hate me when I can't be a good role model for them?

The more I think about it the more I like the idea of being a family with them. I love them…

Holy shit! I love Ally.

“Hey, man. You okay?” Arik’s question pulls me away from the bomb that just went off inside my head.

The girls are still splashing in the river, their sunny hair dancing in the breeze while their laughter peppers the air around us.

I want this. I want these girls, Ally, and everything that comes with them, and I’m prepared to work my ass off for them, for her, and for us.

I’m an okay cook. I don’t starve. I’m more suited to opening a can of soup than gourmet meal planning, but I decided to cook for Ally and myself tonight since the kitchen is finished. I’m only slightly regretting the decision.

I have steaks marinating and ready to go on the grill with potatoes in the oven when the first fire alarm sounds.

Well, at least I know they work.

Running from my bedroom to the kitchen, I see smoke pouring out of the oven. I dash to the window and am opening it up for the smoke to escape when the doorbell rings.

“It’s open,” I yell over the smoke alarm while I use a dish-towel to fan some of the smoke out of the kitchen.

Sitting on the rack of the oven are two charred spuds. I have no idea what I did wrong.

“Holy shit, Con. What the hell happened?”

Ally’s in cut-off shorts that show a mile of leg, her hair down and loose around her shoulders. I lose my train of thought when I catch sight of the lace of her bra peeking above her tank top.

Ally grabs the cutting board from the dish drainer and starts to fan it through the air to get the smoke to disperse faster. Why didn’t I think of that?

"I don't know. I was just trying to bake some potatoes for dinner."

"Did you calibrate the oven temperature?"

The shriek of the alarm cuts out just as I yell, "No. Was I supposed to?"

She gives a muffled snort, and I feel my own cheeks crease in a grin before we both lose it.

"Oh my God," Ally tries to talk through her laughter. "Were you *trying* to burn down your new kitchen? You have a brand-new oven and didn't calibrate it? No wonder the potatoes are hockey pucks."

Her laughter is a balm on my soul, and the earlier apprehension and nerves I had surrounding tonight melt away.

I drop the dishtowel, and in two steps I have my arm wrapped around her waist, dragging her into me, and am pressing my mouth to hers in a hello kiss I didn't know I needed.

"Hi, beautiful."

Hazel eyes sparkle with laughter. "Hi, handsome."

"Since the potatoes are a loss, how do you feel about steak? I promise my skills on the grill are much better."

"If you have more potatoes, I can whip up some to throw on the grill with the steaks."

"Sold. They're in the pantry. You want some wine? I got a merlot Liv recommended."

Ally's head cocks to the side. "You asked Liv for a wine recommendation?"

"I did. I don't drink the stuff, and I didn't want to ask you."

"Why not?"

Mulling over my answer, I go for total honesty. "Well, I can't imagine you get many nights where you're not the planner, conductor, and implementer, so I wanted to give you a night where you don't have to think or do anything. That's kinda ruined now that you're in charge of the potatoes, though."

Expression softening, Ally rises up on her tiptoes and locks her mouth to mine in a brief kiss before pulling back. "Thank you. Even though I'm making the potatoes, I appreciate it and you."

I don't know what to say to that, so I just stay silent.

Ally doesn't get enough breaks. She piles everything on herself and then runs herself into the ground. If I can take a little of the weight off her shoulders by planning a meal and a quiet evening in for us, then I'm going to do that.

"So, I got a call from Jason today. He said something about running into you at the river. You wouldn't know anything about that, would you?"

"What? Me? No. I have no idea what you're talking about."

Eyes narrowed at me, she says, "Mm-hmm. Well, thank you for saying something. Lisa didn't want to bother Jason with the school visit. They both assured me they'd be talking to Alex about how he treats his classmates moving forward."

"Do you think it'll fix the issue?"

"I hope so, but if not, I'll handle it. I appreciate you saying something, but I don't want you to feel like you have to step in on my behalf. I could have handled this, and while I appreciate it, the girls are my responsibility—"

"Ally?"

"Yeah?"

"Shut up. Just accept the help. I have no illusions that you can't handle anything the world throws at you, but just accept the help."

"Connor—"

"Ally, are we or are we not involved?"

"We are, but —"

"No buts. If you're with me then you're with me, remember? To me, that means you have every right to handle things the way you see fit, but if I can make your life easier, then I'm going to. Okay?"

"Okay." The agreement is hesitant, like she doesn't quite believe me. I'm not surprised, but I'm going to do my damnedest to make her see that we're a team, that I'm here for her and those girls no matter how uncomfortable the change makes me feel.

ALLY

All day long I debated about bringing up the conversation he must have had with Alex's dad at the river today.

I almost left it alone, just went with the flow and didn't stir up trouble, but I don't want him to think I'm incapable, that I don't know how to take care of me and my girls, because I do.

It's ridiculous. A holdover from the time when Daniel had me convinced I couldn't do anything right. That I was classless, ignorant, and not worth a damn. I should be over it by now—it's old news, and I know my value—but as this is my first serious relationship since him, some of the old insecurities are coming out to play. I really wish they wouldn't.

Connor's reminder to just accept the little bit of help he gave is weird for me.

Don't get me wrong. I had a solid support system growing up, and it wasn't until Daniel that I started down the path of control freak extraordinaire.

Moving to a new, large city and feeling so completely alone was hard for me. It was nearly a relief when I caught

Daniel cheating on me because it gave me the excuse I needed to go back to my comfort zone. To return to Felt and put the whole sordid short marriage behind me.

But the ordeal changed me. I went from being footloose and fancy-free to having two infants depending on me. I learned really fast that I couldn't count on Daniel for anything.

Now with Connor? Him stepping in to protect my little girl? He just stole a part of my heart that I didn't know he could.

After my agreement to just *accept the help,* Connor shifted the topic to the Cowboy Courses that are swiftly approaching and the to-do list we are still working on accomplishing prior to the event.

"I confirmed with the participants their time slots and the dates they'll be at the fairgrounds. There shouldn't be any issues there as long as we stick to the schedule I drafted."

Connor takes a swig from his beer before asking, "That's in my email, right?"

"It is. I also forwarded it to Ben and Hedy to see if they had any input."

I've given up on my idea to get Hedy's confirmation that she put Connor up to this in a blatant matchmaking attempt. We're together now whether she did or not. If this was her goal, then I've got to give her credit because she not only managed to get him involved with the courses, but she convinced the universe to conspire along with her in sticking us together.

"You're still on vacation the week of the courses, right? You should be able to be there for the full event?"

"Yeah, I don't go back to work until the Monday after, so I'm at your disposal."

"Hmm. I like the sound of you being at my disposal."

His only response is a saucy, cocked eyebrow.

Once my plate is empty, I move to take it to the sink, but Connor snags it away from me and says, “Let me.”

“I can do dishes, you know.”

Dropping a kiss on my lips, he says, “I know, but no arguing. Pour yourself another glass of wine and relax. I’ve got this.”

I don’t know what it is about a man doing household chores, but the competence is sexy, and my pulse kicks up in appreciation.

I pour myself the wine and wander toward the sound dock he has set up. It’s currently playing a ballad of some kind, but flipping through his playlist, there’s an eclectic mix of just about everything.

Clicking over to a pop song I haven’t heard in years, the familiar intro of Jason Mraz’s “I Won’t Give Up” fills the room.

Connor looks back at me over his shoulder and, seeing me at the sound dock, dries his hands and walks toward me, setting my wineglass down and wrapping me in his arms.

He starts to shuffle us across his kitchen floor while my hands come up to rest lightly at his shoulders.

Under his breath he starts to sing, and I can’t tear my eyes away from him. I know they’re just lyrics, but the promise in them is evident as we dance.

“You’re making this so hard for me.”

Pausing midlyric, he asks, “What?”

“Not falling head over heels in love with you.”

His eyes flare in surprise or fear, and I wish I could rewind time and take back the words because I don’t know what’s going to happen now.

His expression softens, and I hold my breath waiting for him to respond. He leans down, and the tip of his nose brushes along mine before his lips come to rest against my own. His whispered question ghosts along the sensitive flesh. "What if you did?"

I pull back slightly, just enough to look into his eyes, and ask, "Fall for you?"

He only nods, and all the air gets sucked out of the room because what started as me blurting out something I've held deep inside for years is turning into a *what if* that I'm not sure I'm prepared for.

"I don't know. What if I did?" I honestly don't. We just started this, and with every inch of his heart I uncover, I fall deeper and harder for him.

His forehead resting against mine, he says, "You're not asking the right questions, beautiful."

"I'm not?"

"No, a better question is what if I told you I've already fallen for you?"

I back away from him, my eyes finding his. The earnest adoration shining at me floors me.

"Ally Sawyer, I've loved you for as long as I can remember, and I'll love you until I leave this earth. No amount of time is going to change that."

Tears gather in my eyes, and despite my best efforts, they fall down my cheeks. I can't hold them back, just like I can't hold back the rising tide of feelings that swamp me.

This man.

This beautiful man, whom I get to claim as my own for whatever time we're given.

How I ever came to deserve him I'll never know.

I reach for the hem of his shirt and drag the material up his torso. He quickly gets with the program and helps me remove it.

My shirt and bra quickly follow, and we sway side to side with the music as we undress each other. I don't care that we're in his kitchen, that there are still dishes to be done or leftovers to be put away. I'm focused on the feel of his skin under my greedy fingers, the way his breath hitches when I drag my nails along his abs. All my focus is on the man in front of me.

Wanting to adore, wanting to worship him, I fall to my knees in front of him, pulling his shorts and boxers down until the heavy length of his cock brushes against my cheek. The heated slide of his skin sears my own flesh.

Gripping the base of his cock, I swirl my tongue around him. His masculine scent goes straight to my core, and I'm not sure if it's the act or him that's drenching my panties.

"Fuck, Ally. That's so good. Suck me."

The guttural request lights me on fire. My nipples pucker against the air as his fingers tunnel into my hair, providing a provocative bite of pain before he scratches my scalp, massaging away the sting.

The sounds that erupt from his throat give away how close to the wire he is. But instead of letting me yank him over that line, he tugs harder at my scalp and pulls his hips back, leaving my lips with a pop.

"I'm not finishing in your damn mouth tonight, baby. I'm going to be buried deep inside you when we both go over that edge."

I stand, bringing my breasts flush to his chest, the oversensitive peaks brushing along the slight dusting of hair covering his pecs.

One strong forearm bands under the cheeks of my ass and he lifts me, urging my legs around his hips, before he starts out of the room. Unable to wait another second without the feel of his mouth on mine, I drop my lips to his in a heated kiss.

We barely cross the threshold of his room before he's dropping me to my feet and walking me backward toward the bed.

The cool sheets feel like heaven against my heated skin. I scoot back, and Connor follows me down, his lips never leaving mine.

There's an urgency to the kiss. A need to consume and be consumed, neither of us getting enough of the other.

His hands coast up along my sides, and his fingers tweak my nipples and pull. What should hurt doesn't—I'm too caught up in him.

Continuing their path up my body, his hands fist in my hair. His lips leave mine to trail down my neck, and he sinks his teeth into the tendon between my neck and shoulder.

"You taste like cookies and sunshine." The gruff confession against my skin causes goosebumps to race down my arms.

My hands come to rest at his shoulders, my short nails biting into the skin under them as he sucks at a particularly sensitive spot behind my ear. Without urging, my legs come up to wrap around his waist. With the motion, his cock brushes along my folds. There's just the slightest pressure against my center, and my hips shoot forward in search of more friction.

Connor pulls back, his eyes locked on mine as he dips a hand down to my pussy. Fingers teasing at my slit, his thumb plays with the bundle of nerves at the apex of my sex.

Dead set on slow, he takes his time with me. No matter how I shift or fidget, he doesn't budge from his agonizing exploration of my center.

"Connor, please." There isn't enough pride in my body to stop the plea from escaping. I'm on the razor's edge of exquisite agony, and any shame I had has flown out the window.

"Slow, baby. Slow."

I can't take much more of this slow business, not without

going up in flames. The little bit of patience I had left snaps; I sit up, forcing his hands away from my body.

Twisting, I tug, turn, and push him into a prone position under me.

"Ally, I'm on the edge here…"

I know exactly what he means, like the years of denying our feelings for each other, the denial we forced our bodies into, are over. The overstimulation from waiting is a revolt of our senses, making it nearly impossible for *slow.*

"Fuck the edge." Reaching down, I line him up and sink onto him in a single hard thrust.

Head tipping back, the veins in his neck stand out. Mouth open, his face twists into a euphoric grimace even as he says, "Goddamn, you feel fucking perfect."

I give myself three seconds to adjust to his size before I can't take it anymore and I have to move, to ride.

Connor's hands are still locked on my hips as I take the first shuddering slide along his dick. His girth lights every one of my nerve endings on fire.

With slow, sweeping grinds of his hips against mine, his legs lift and his feet plant behind me, providing better leverage for us to work together in a duet of mind-bending pleasure.

Hand sliding along my ass cheek, his fingers dip into my crease before gliding past my rear to circle where I'm speared on him. Gathering my slick arousal, his fingers retreat to press against the puckered ring of my back passage.

"Jesus, fuck," I groan. The slight pressure there has my hips jerking forward hard. The dual sensation of his finger-play coupled with my clit grinding at the base of his cock sends the flash fire of my release through me.

My toes curl with the intensity of my climax. Each wave of pleasure is sharper than the last. Connor moves his hands to bracket my ass, and he starts to thrust, carrying me along his cock in search of his own release.

The clench in his jaw and the tension running through him are the only signs he reached that peak, and the symphony of pleasure in my core starts to die down.

I'm sprawled on him, my head resting on his chest and my breath panting out of overtaxed lungs, when the first giggle overtakes me.

Maybe it's a delayed response to the endorphins running rampant through my system, or perhaps my brain has had time to catch up with his earlier declaration. But before I reconsider, I lever myself up until I can look into his sleepy chocolate eyes.

"I love you too, Connor."

My declaration of feelings isn't as poetic or lyrical as his, but it's real. The only thing I have to offer him is my truth, and for better or worse, that's what he'll get from me.

The timeline of our relationship isn't standard, and for some reason that makes me appreciate it all the more. It's ours. It's unique, and while we still have things to learn about each other and figure out, I have faith we can do it, together. As a team.

CONNOR

The Friday before the Cowboy Courses are set to kick off, I'm at the fairgrounds moving tables, carts, and benches around. There are about twenty of us out here—but the work is going fast.

After the last few weeks, I've been on cloud nine.

Ally is nearby with coffee and muffins laid out on a folding table for us while we work on getting the bones of the event set up for vendors to come in tomorrow.

Between this and the repairs at her shop over the weekend, we haven't had as much time together as I would have preferred, but we're managing.

The girls are "helping" me by following me around, so it takes twice as long as it should to get the tables into formation, but it's amusing work with my two shadows.

I didn't know there wasn't school the day before the courses, but I can see the appeal, as families are gearing up to compete, and a week of fun is about to be underway.

We've managed a couple of family dates since the drive-in, most recently bowling in Idaho Falls, and if my surprise plan works out next week, the girls and Ally will be able to come home with me at night and hopefully stay whenever they want to.

Things are settling for us, despite our busyness, and it feels good.

I never thought I'd be the guy to settle down or the guy who gets the girl, but I guess I was wrong. My day starts with thoughts of Ally—how to see her, how to lighten her load, how I can be there for her and the girls—and usually ends the same way.

Emma and Elle are running circles around the chairs that still need to be moved, their giggles and laughter filling the air around us, and I wonder again what kind of man would willingly give up the rays of sunshine these girls are.

One who doesn't recognize what he has.

I stomp toward the twins, skirting tables and making low growling noises in my throat. Their giggles and laughter turn into shrieking howls of delight as I chase them around the grass.

They run to where Ally's working with Maeve, one of the volunteers. The kids claim sanctuary against her, but I'm not about to let them get away with it.

In two quick steps, I've got my arms around all three of them, smooshing them together in my arms as I lift their combined weight off the ground. Elle's poor face is smashed against her mom's ribcage, but based on the snickering laughter that's coming from that side of Ally, she doesn't have a problem with it.

I drop them all back to their feet with a triumphant declaration. "I win!"

Ally's hazel eyes sparkle up at me before she stands on tiptoes to press a chaste kiss against my lips.

"Well, aren't y'all the cutest little family." Maeve's tone is sugary sweet, like a new grandma cooing over a baby.

The girls scamper off, squealing and chasing each other.

We may not be going about this in a traditional sense, but countless times over the last few weeks, I've thought about what it would mean for me and Ally to be more than just seeing each other. What I want out of the relationship, what I can give her, what I want from her.

One thing I want, one thing that's nonnegotiable to me? I want all of her, and that means her girls too. I may not be their biological father, but I want the chance to be their daddy. To pick them up when they fall, to cheer them on when they succeed. I want it all.

I thought Ally wanted that too, but the strained smile on her face says otherwise.

I brush my hand down her arm before coasting my thumb along the back of her hand in reassurance.

"Thank you, Maeve. I'm gonna steal Ally for a second to get her opinion on the tables." It's a bullshit excuse, but I don't want Ally to be uncomfortable, so I make it all the same.

After we're a few feet away, Ally turns to me. "Connor—"

"Shh. It's okay. It's no one's business but ours what we've got going on."

Pinched eyebrows frame serious hazel eyes that map my face before she responds, "Okay. I just…" She trails off and I leave it alone.

I'm not one to talk endlessly about my feelings and thoughts, so I can wait until she's got it put together in her mind. If she needs a little time, then I can give it to her, no matter how full steam ahead my heart wants to be.

I want to make them mine. It doesn't matter what hurdles we have to jump to get there.

Still, I can understand her hesitation. This has all been so fast. Striving for patience when I've always been an action-oriented guy is a struggle, but this is worth it.

Her phone chimes in her pocket, reality intruding on the quiet moment between us.

"Colby got the permits. I need to head to the store."

Her head swivels, likely looking for the girls, and I say, "You go ahead. I'll take them fishing with me after we're done here."

Indecision crosses her face, but before she can argue, I say, "This way they aren't in your way or bored while you try to get things going there."

"Are you sure?"

"I am."

"Okay, let me switch over their booster seats—"

"I bought some for my truck, same brand you use, and Jackson helped me install them."

Her lips pinch and her brows furrow again. "You bought booster seats?"

"I did. I figured it'd be easier to have a set. This way we don't have to swap cars or move them around all the time."

It was one of the things I thought would maybe make her life easier, but based on her frown, I might have made a misstep.

Frown lessening, she says, "Okay. How about I pick up pizza for dinner?"

"That works." And it'll give me a little time to bring the girls around to my surprise.

After saying a quick goodbye to the twins, she heads out, and I quickly finish the setup for the tables.

With not much more to do before the festivities kick off tomorrow, I'm free for the rest of the day. There's a new rooster tail lure I'm eager to try out.

~

"Peanut, Brittle, I wanted to talk to you girls about something."

The boat rocks gently on the lake in the cool afternoon. Their fishing poles are propped against the side of the canoe, forgotten, as their little faces focus on me.

My throat feels drier than a desert right now. I'm so fucking nervous. What if they say no? What if they don't love me as much as I love them? How can anyone say no to these two mini Allys?

"It's about Mom, isn't it?" Elle's quiet voice cuts through my thoughts.

Ignoring her question, I plow ahead. "I love you girls. You know that, right?"

I'm so out of my depth here. I've never imagined having a conversation like this with two seven-year-olds. There's so much of Ally in these girls, both in looks and mannerisms, evidenced by the sassy way Emma's hazel eyes shoot for her hairline in a roll that's gonna get them stuck there someday.

"Everyone loves us." Emma is all cocky confidence.

"You got me there, Brittle. See, what I wanted to talk to you about is..." I don't even know how to explain what I want.

But Elle, the little mind reader, jumps in. "You love us, but you love Mom too, right?"

"I sure do. Your mama..." I want to make sure they understand my feelings. "Your mama is special to me. The three of you are the most special people in my life, and I wanted to ask if you guys would be okay with all of us being a family."

Their silence is deafening, and the water slapping at the canoe's hull suddenly sounds harsh. I'm also pretty sure the sun just jumped a million miles closer because I'm starting to sweat the longer they just stare at me.

Emma's the first to break the silence. With her eyes locked on her fishing pole, she says, "Our dad didn't want us."

Right there. This minute. My heart shatters with one whispered declaration from a girl who's too young to have to understand or deal with the letdown of a shitty father.

Kneeling in a canoe isn't the easiest thing to accomplish, but I do it anyway, reaching for Emma's hands. "Look at me, Brittle. That's not your fault, baby girl. What your dad does or doesn't do isn't your fault, and it's his loss if he doesn't see how amazing and lovable you two are. You understand that, right?"

Her eyes fill, and she nods before looking out over the lake. From the far seat, Elle has her serious gaze trained on me.

"What about you, Peanut? You know your dad's choices aren't your fault, right?"

"I know. I don't really like Dad. We barely talk to him, and he's not a good guy. Not like you."

I've never been more in love with these girls than I am right now. No matter what happens between Ally and me, they'll always own a part of my heart.

A sniffling hiccup comes from Emma, and I reach for her, my own eyes burning. Bundling her into my arms, I let her cry it out. I wish my arms were enough. I wish they could shield her from the world's hurts, but they can't. Ally's words after Emma broke her arm take on a new light. I may not be able to protect them from everything out there, but I can be there for them when something comes along to hurt their hearts. I can be a balm, a solace for them when they need to be steadied.

"I know it hurts, baby. But it'll be all right."

Elle asks, "How do you know?"

"My dad used to be really mean to me and my mom. It hurt a lot when I was little, but now that I'm older I understand that him being mean and hurtful was his fault, not mine. The only thing I can do is try to be a good person and learn from his mistakes."

Maybe this is too heavy for little kids. Maybe they should be talking to their mom about this. I don't know. I'm in the deep end here.

I want to find their father and pound him into the dirt while also thanking him for getting out of my way so I can have the family he didn't treasure.

Emma wipes her face, her casted arm coming to rest around my middle while I hold her in my lap. "You want to be our family? Like Meemaw?"

"Kinda like Meemaw, but something more."

Elle eyes me while asking, "Like a stepdad?"

Nodding, I can't quite get the words out to say that yes, I want to be their stepdad. I want to be there for them, love them, hold them, teach them, and guide them.

Emma's hands come up to rest on my cheeks, turning my head so my gaze meets hers. "You want to marry Mama and live happily ever after in your castle?"

"I do." My voice nearly cracks on the promise.

"That means you'll take us to the father-daughter dance at school?"

I brush a kiss against her tiny forehead. "I'd be honored, Brittle."

Elle scoots closer to me, asking, "You'll take me too. All of us?"

Looping my arm around her shoulder, I drag her into me. "You got it, Peanut. We'll all go dancing."

"Okay, and we love you too, Con."

Heart cracking against the battering emotions slamming against it, I let the tears pool in my eyes. One slips past my defenses to trail down my cheek before disappearing into my beard.

"Happy tears?" Emma's little thumb brushes the moisture away.

"The happiest."

My future has never looked so bright, and I'm raring to get Ally on board.

I hope the path forward remains as easy as it has been. I'll talk to Ally tonight about taking the next step, about us moving forward together, as a family.

ALLY

BLUEPRINTS AND SCHEMATICS COVER MY DESK AT THE BAKERY.

Colby swung by with the permits he needed to replace the wall and implement all the changes I'd drafted for him, and it's finally time for the next step of my dream to start. I'll have a larger workspace with room for an additional walk-in. It'll cut into the available seating at the front, but we'll be able to offer more lunch and to-go options with the expansion in the back.

My favorite part is the joining of the two apartments above the shop. That remodel is going to take a bit longer, but according to Colby, it won't affect business downstairs.

It's weird to know that in a few short months the girls and I are going to have our own home. Other than the year I worked at the resort right after high school and had a small efficiency apartment, I've always lived with someone. First it was my parents, then Daniel, and then back home again when he and I divorced.

I'm a grown adult, though. I should have my own space for me and my girls. And no matter how much Ma claims to love having the girls at home, it'll probably be nice for her not to have three people underfoot all the time.

Our bakery apartment won't be as large as Ma's house, but it'll be mine.

I won't have to get Ma's opinion or approval on changes and decor. The timeline even meshes well with decorating Connor's house because we can save time shopping for both places at once.

Eager to share the news with him, I pack up the plans and shove the canister in my purse before closing down the shop.

Baking off-site and transporting everything in has been going better than I anticipated, but we sell out faster each day with limited cold- and dry-storage areas around the construction team, so I've been closing earlier.

Not that I mind the early afternoons. For the first time in years, I'm home with my girls every day after school. I get to help them with homework or cook dinner with them like I did with Ma and Dad growing up.

Connor has been involved in more dinners over the last week or two also. Spending time with him and the twins has made me realize how much time I was devoting to work even after I left the bakery each day, and I don't want to continue that trend. I like knowing my evenings are for family rather than spreadsheets.

I need to talk to Jem about a promotion to manager. Giving myself steady hours, a schedule that has me home at the same time every day with weekends off, would be wonderful.

Additional labor costs right now might not be ideal, but the siren call of spending more time with my girls and Connor is strong. I want more time. Even with the Cowboy Courses and the off-site baking, my plate is lighter than it has been in years, and a large part of that is thanks to Connor.

He's been so helpful, taking the girls off my hands on the weekends, when they usually come to work with me if they don't have plans, and I appreciate him.

The sleepover when we shared our feelings changed things. No more hesitation or feeling each other out. We both jumped in feetfirst, and his effortless way with my daughters isn't different from the past, but it means so much more now.

Learning that he bought booster seats for his truck nearly left my heart in a messy puddle while we were at the fairgrounds.

The consideration, courtesy, and caring in his actions make me wonder why the hell I ever settled for less in the past.

After a stop at Louie's to pick up Italian for dinner, I leave Felt and drive up the mountain road to his house. That's another change that's quickly becoming routine for me. The girls and I have spent more dinners at his house than at home this week.

I let my windows down, and the crisp fall air fills the cab of my SUV. I realize it's been only six weeks since Connor kissed me at the fairgrounds.

For such a short passage of time, a lot of big changes have happened.

Tomorrow, all our hard work is going to coalesce into the start of the courses, and while our events aren't until later in the week, we're both expected to be out there each day to lend a hand.

It was easier for me to close the actual bakery and have Jem work the cart at the fairgrounds knowing Colby and his crew will be in and out all week. After that, he'll be moving to the second story.

Jackson will have to clear out the stuff still in his old apartment up there before Colby can get to work.

I add it to the mental list of things I need to get done this weekend while working the festival crowds.

Hopefully I'll get a chance to participate in some of the events. That's really the only downfall to being on the planning committee. I'm used to being a spectator—to playing games and scarfing down snacks with Emma and Elle—but I'm not sure I'll have the opportunity to do that this year.

I know my daughters are excited for the magic carpet rides and the mutton scramble. Ma and Jackson have already offered to stuff them full of locally brewed root beer and buckets of cotton candy while I'm on my volunteer shifts. For once, I feel like I can take a deep breath without the weight of my responsibilities shifting the wrong way.

Connor's house comes into view with light glowing warmly from the front windows. I park and gather the plans and my bag before making my way up to the porch.

The sound of shrieks and laughter is muffled through the closed front door, and I smile, knowing I'm stepping into a party.

Stress, exhaustion, expectations—they all fall away as I crack open the front door. Elle is jumping on the couch while Connor is making his way across the living room floor on all fours with Emma perched on his back.

"Baby Shark" is screeching through the house's surround sound, and the sight of Connor's large frame playing horsey with my daughter has me snorting with laughter.

He whips around while trying to stand, Emma slings the other way on his back, and just before she crashes to the floor behind him, his arm reaches back to snag her and gently lower her to her feet.

"Mama!"

I grin at them but keep my eyes on Connor. His cheeks are adorably pink, and I can't help but tease, "You don't have to get up on my account."

Stalking toward me, he leans down and brushes a kiss along my lips.

Just as he pulls back, I say, "I mean, I'd like to ride you right about now too."

Instantaneous heat shifts his gaze, and with a quick look to see that the girls are occupied, his tone drops. "Ditto."

SHORTLY AFTER DINNER, THE GIRLS SCAMPER OFF TO WATCH A movie, and I pin Connor down at the dining room table to get his opinion on some of the paint swatches I brought from the hardware store for his spare rooms.

"What do you think of these?" I hold out the soft beige colors, one slightly whiter than the other, and he shakes his head.

"I have colors picked out for the two rooms. Here, let me grab my tablet, and I'll show you what I have bookmarked."

As he gets up, I call to his back, "I thought I was supposed to help with the design, but you'd have the final say. You been planning without me?"

He sits back in his seat and shifts his tablet toward me. The first color is a soft pink and the second a pale lavender. My heart starts to race, and I can't quite catch my breath as my eyes shoot up to his.

Chocolate eyes lock on mine. There's a slight curl to his lips when he says, "I want these colors for the rooms."

"Those are the girls'..."

"Their favorite colors. Yeah, I know."

"Con—"

He holds his hand up to stop me, and I fall silent. I'm too scared to hope, too cautious by far to make assumptions about his meaning. Panic steals my air while nerves swirl in the pit of my stomach.

First the *family* comment. Then the seats. Now this.

It's all—all so fast and I can't keep up.

"Let me tell you what I'm thinking. I want you and the girls to be comfortable here. You don't have to move in, not until y'all are ready."

Move in? My brain hadn't gone that far down the road yet.

"But I want you to have a space here—I want those girls to have a space here—so you can stay when you want to."

He shifts the tablet and taps the screen a few times before showing me the next bookmarked page. "This is what I was thinking for furniture. The white one for Emma since she has the princess fascination."

I can't keep up. My mind races, and I guiltily glance toward the front door where the canister with my plans is sitting. The tablet displays the perfect furniture for my daughters. One is a tufted white gem-studded headboard and matching dresser, vanity, and night table. The other is an earthy sage green that would go well with the pale lavender Elle favors.

We're moving fast all of a sudden, and I'm scared I'm getting caught up in the moment. That none of this is real. That I'm going to be left in the dust when Connor decides it's time to move on with his life.

Sure, I'm in love with him and he says he loves me too, but how much of that was in the heat of the moment, the carefully crafted bubble of intimacy we cultivated that night?

How do I know if what he says is real? That this is the forever kind of love I'm looking for?

I don't know. And I'm not sure I can take that risk this quickly again. My last relationship ended in disaster when I didn't take the time to think it through.

Because if this were to go wrong? If this isn't the forever kind of love, it'll wreck me. And I don't just have myself to worry about anymore—I have the girls to consider now too.

What kind of mother would I be if I just slid us into this life because a man swept me off my feet?

Maybe I should have thought of this before falling for him. Before we made our relationship public. But the girls have seen us together. They've gone on outings with Connor, and he's become *their person* over the last month, not just another surrogate uncle like Arik.

Emma and Elle are already in this just as much as I am, and if it goes wrong, what'll it do to them? What'll it show them? That it's okay to rush in feetfirst, that it's okay to get swept up, to think with their hearts instead of their heads?

I don't know if that's what I want to teach my daughters.

"You hate it."

The stark declaration from Connor brings my eyes up to his face. His expression is shut down, and that stings for some reason. I've gotten so used to seeing into him that being on the other side of whatever wall he just put up hurts.

"I don't hate it."

A mirthless chuckle leaves his lips. "Yeah, your face is broadcasting nothing but excitement right now."

"Look, this has all been really fast—"

"Als, don't. Don't turn this into a cliché. If this doesn't or isn't working for you, I need you to shoot straight with me and tell me. If I'm not what you want, if this isn't what you want, tell me. Please."

The plea in his tone unmistakable, I rush to reassure him. "No, Con, that's not it. I do want this, want you. I just want to slow down a little. We went from barely talking to full-fledged relationship in the blink of an eye, and now you're talking about me and the girls moving in, buying booster seats for them. We've been together less than a month, and it's…it's a lot to take in."

Standing, he grabs his forgotten plate from dinner and walks it to the sink. He rinses it and puts it in the dishwasher before turning back to me, asking, "How much of this response is in reaction to the family comment Maeve made?"

My breath hisses out before I can stop it. "Does it matter?"

Connor scrubs a hand through his hair before saying, "It does. How much of that is playing into this?"

"It's not." Shaking my head, I feel tears gathering in my eyes. "Okay, so some of it is. Can you blame me for being hesitant to jump headfirst into a relationship, one that has the potential to wreck my girls—"

"Don't fucking do that. You know I wouldn't hurt them under any circumstances. And you make it sound like you and I are so sudden when everyone but us has seen this coming like a runaway freight train. Don't make those flimsy excuses, Ally. Be honest with me; I deserve that much."

He wants honesty? Fine, I'll give him honest. "I'm scared. What I feel for you is so much bigger than what I've ever felt for anyone other than my daughters, and that's terrifying to me. I want to greedily grab everything you're offering, to snatch it all up, because happiness can disappear in a second. But I can't do that, Connor. I have to be smarter, work harder, and think with my head and not my…" I trail off before I can finish my tirade.

"Your head and not your heart. That's what you were going to say, wasn't it?"

Rolling my lips in, I don't say anything. Connor comes to me, squatting between my spread knees, knees that shake in fear that he's going to end this, end us, because we disagree.

"Beautiful," he whispers as his hand lightly touches my forehead, "all *I'm* saying is that you're letting what's going on in here"—his hand comes to rest at my breastbone, right above my thundering heart—"stop what can happen in here. And that's a damn shame because I'm all in."

CONNOR

THE SMELLS OF SWEETS AND FRIED FOOD PERMEATE THE AIR AT the fairgrounds. People are out in droves, and the world is a steady static of voices, excited yells, and event announcements. Kids are lined up for the carnival games, participating in turtle races, and eating goodies from the various food carts.

In about twenty minutes, we've got the mutton busting, and I'm queasy at the thought of Emma and Elle getting up on the back of the sheep and hanging on for dear life.

Is there protective gear for the kids? Yep. Is it enough for *my* girls? Not a chance.

Emma just got out of her cast, and part of me wants to forbid her from participating at all, but I know I can't.

After my talk with Ally last Friday, I'm uneasy about overstepping or doing too much. The eggshells I've been walking on since then are enough to make my shoulders tense in uncertainty just thinking about it. We're in an awkward sort of stalemate—still spending time as a couple and finishing work on the Cowboy Courses, but it's stilted.

Our previous intimacy was easy, and I don't know how to rekindle that.

The effortless affection, the excitement at being together —that's all strained now. It's got my hackles up, and I'm preparing for the worst.

I'm standing out at the makeshift corral where the races are taking place. Ally's girls are in the first heat. The number of kids participating is large this year, so we're having to do multiple rounds to determine the winners for the various categories. I'm hoping the girls don't do well in their first heat and won't have to go multiple times.

Maybe that makes me an asshole, but I don't care. The thought of them getting hurt in any way is enough to send my blood pressure through the roof.

"Hey, man, you okay?" Jackson's palm comes down hard to slap my shoulder.

With a slight shake of my head, I respond, "No. Why the hell is this an event?"

Easy smile in place, he says, "It's tradition, bro. The girls will be fine. This is, like, their third year doing it. They even wear helmets and padded safety vests."

I shrug and don't say anything because a helmet isn't doing shit to alleviate my concern where Elle and Emma are concerned.

"They'll be okay. You'll see. Ally over at her cart?"

I nod. She's been working almost all morning, helping Jem with the crowds. There will be a lull in the early afternoon when they can replenish some of the stock, but they've been slammed this morning. I offered to bring the girls over here, even though I'm regretting it now.

No, it's better I'm here if anything goes wrong. I can get to them in a minute or less.

Elle is practically bouncing with excitement, her normal reserved manner falling to the wayside when she spied the trophy they have displayed. Who knew the kid was so competitive?

Her sister is more subdued, fidgeting a little here and there. It's like their personalities have swapped, with Emma now quiet and withdrawn.

I squat next to them, asking, "You ladies ready?"

Elle's smile stretches her cheeks wide, while Emma's is more like a grimace, but both nod.

"Okay, well, I want you to be extra careful."

Something's up with Emma, so I nod to Jackson to distract Elle while I pull Emma off to the side. "Hey, you good, Brittle?"

Her breath is panting out of her chest, and she nods hard. "I'm fine."

Locking my eyes to hers, I say, "You know you don't have to compete if you don't want to, right?"

Her sunny eyebrows scrunch up. "Yeah, I do. Elle is doing it, so I have to."

Cocking my head to the side, I ask, "Who says?"

A little of the spitfire I'm used to shines through when she rolls her eyes at me. "She's my twin. We do everything together."

Ah. I guess that makes sense. She's so used to doing everything Elle does that she might be scared to back out.

"Okay, so you can do all the same things Elle does, but only if you *want* to. If you don't want to do all the same things, you don't have to." A glimmer of hope sparks in her gaze, and I capitalize on it. "No one will be mad at you if you wanted to just hang out with me and Uncle Jackson."

"You promise?" Her hands are already coming up to unbuckle the strap of her helmet. "They won't think I'm a wuss, will they?"

"No, baby. I'll make sure of it." Taking the helmet from her, I help her out of the padded vest before taking it over to the gear that's arranged on the tables and hand it to the volunteer. "Emma's going to withdraw."

No questions asked, likely because I'm glowering at the attendant, she says, "Sounds good. I'll adjust the heat."

Emma's hand comes up and tucks into my larger one. Her face is all real smiles when she says, "Thank you."

"You're welcome, baby, but you don't have to thank me for that. If there is ever anything you don't want to do, you just come to me. Deal?"

"Deal."

I scan for Elle and find Jackson's gaze trained on me and Emma. He smiles and nods in my direction.

Elle's heat is one of the first up, and watching her climb into the chute, her blonde braid trailing down her back, is enough to send me into an early heart attack no matter Jackson's reassurance otherwise.

Before I can snatch her off the back of the sheep, the buzzer sounds. She flies into the corral, clinging to the back of the animal that's trying to dislodge the little girl from its back.

Elle puts up a good fight though, her grip strong on the rope, her face twisted with determination to stay on the sheep.

Bucking and weaving, the sheep tries its best to kick her off, but she's just as dead set on keeping her seat. When she starts to slip to the side, her knees grip the sheep until one of the volunteers plucks her from the animal and announces her score.

As the event wears on, Elle's time is enough to advance her to the next heat until she's one of the last of four kids competing for first place. My palms are sweaty, and there's a lump of concrete in my throat from watching her get tossed around over and over again.

The only thing keeping me from storming over there and

demanding she stop is the smile that lights up her face each time she hits the ground and rolls out of the way before popping back up. Both arms shooting in the air, crowing her victory over the sport to the onlookers.

She's first to compete in the last heat and does a fantastic job of staying on the sheep. The next kid doesn't even get out of the makeshift gate because the sheep stumbles and rolls the second the door is open. The third manages to stay on the sheep but falls short of Elle's time by three seconds.

The final kid up to ride is Alex, Elle's personal enemy. He's in the chute getting ready for the buzzer to sound when Elle finally starts to show some nerves.

Standing next to the dusty girl, I ruffle her hair in encouragement as we watch Alex's sheep scramble out of the chute with the boy's legs clamped tightly around it.

In less than a second, the sheep sidesteps sharply while throwing up its hindquarters, and Alex falls off the back.

The announcer calls out his score, and everyone starts yelling Elle's name. I turn to her, pride lighting my heart on fire, and say, "You won, Peanut! You won!"

Swinging her up in my arms, I hug her to me and then throw her up on my shoulders, trotting around the corral while they prepare my girl's trophy. We're both laughing with elation as she gets high-fives from the spectators.

I drop her to her feet, and she turns to me, saying, "I beat him. I can't believe I beat Alex."

"You sure did, Peanut. I'm so proud of you."

Screeching, she yells, "I can do anything!" before she makes her way over to the small winner's platform while I stand back against the fence. The announcer calls out her final score and her win before handing over the gold and blue trophy.

Looking back to Emma and Jackson, I see Ally standing

there, her eyes locked on mine and the biggest smile I've ever seen on her covering her face.

~

HOT DOGS, HAMBURGERS, COTTON CANDY, AND SODA MAKE UP our dinner that night. The floodlights illuminating the park have just kicked on in the dusk while the moonshine races are being set up.

Just as we toss the last of the garbage away, I snag Ally's hand and look over her shoulder to give Nan a nod and ask, "You got the girls?"

"I do. You guys go. Have fun!"

I tug on Ally's hand and pull her toward the starting line where there are horses and carts lined up. People mill around the area, getting ready for the last event of the day.

"What are we doing over here?"

"We're gonna race."

Ally yanks on my hand, bringing us to a stop, and says, "What? No, we aren't. We're not on the participant list."

I twist her until I can wrap my hands around her waist and say, "We're not on the list you got, but I signed us up for it last week."

"Why?"

"Your mama told me how much you liked racing as a kid, so I thought it would be fun. Although, I've never done or seen this one, so you'll have to explain what exactly we're doing."

Smiling at me, she asks, "You've never watched the moonshine races?"

"Nope. I have no idea what I'm getting myself into here."

Slyness slides into her smile and she says, "Okay, partner. Let's go race." Placing her hand back in mine, we work our way over to the stands beside the starting line.

Based on the name alone, I have to assume moonshine is going to come into play, but I wasn't lying when I told Ally I've never watched this before. I'm usually at home, tucked in with a book or watching ESPN by the time this runs.

Ally signs the liability waiver confirming that she's driven horse-drawn buggies in the past and won't sue the owner if there's trouble before I grab the reins from a volunteer and usher her onto the seat next to me. "You want to tell me what to expect here?"

"So, we'll race the buggies around the track." Pointing to tables set up along the road, she says, "But there are checkpoints where you do a shot of moonshine and complete an activity before you can continue. They range from spinning around in a circle with your head on a bat before tossing a ring to beer pong but without the additional drinking."

"Is that safe?" I can't help but worry about the effects of drinking and then trying to drive a buggy.

"Yeah, the driver doesn't do any shots. That's all on the passenger. The horses know to stay on the track."

Well, that's kinda reassuring. I'm no slouch in the drinking department—I can hold my own—but I have to ask, "How strong is the moonshine?"

She mulls over the question before answering. "Probably about as strong as a hard whiskey, but it's brewed by one of the locals, so it depends on how the batch turns out each year."

Jesus Christ.

Ally shifts in her seat, saying, "I've had the moonshine. My limit is a solid three shots before things go tits-up for me. You think you can handle them?"

I nod, saying, "I think so," just as someone from the neighboring buggy calls my name.

I look over my shoulder; Arik is waving at me before he flips us the bird and yells, "Get ready to lose!"

Kate's messy curls are just discernible next to Arik's bulk. Then from directly behind us, I hear Jackson call out, "I've got twenty bucks that says Arik tosses his cookies like last year."

Ally and I turn in our seat to find Jackson and Liv in the carriage behind us. Kate yells out, "Have you still not learned your lesson with bets, Jackson James Sawyer? I'm the one drinking for our team this year anyhow. You're all going down."

Liv's face blanches and she mutters, "Oh shit," just loud enough for us to hear while Jackson yells, "We'll just see about that, Kate Belle Palicki!"

Arik shifts in his seat and shouts, "That's Kate Belle Beaumont to you, asshat!"

Ally's face gets stony in her determination. Turning to me, she ignores the ribbing that flies back and forth between our friends. "I assume you've never driven one of these buggies before?"

Sarcasm coats my reply. "Oh, yeah, it's the only thing we drive down at the ranger station." In a serious tone, I continue, "This is the first time I've even seen a buggy, Ally."

"Shit. That woman has a sky-high alcohol tolerance. I'm gonna open these bitches up, though, so you have to be fast with the activities."

Some of the determination and competitiveness I saw on Elle's face earlier today is written all over Ally's, and I can see where her daughter gets her grit now.

Five shots of moonshine, on a bumpy circular track, while doing God knows what before we can keep going.

Lord help me.

Other buggies around us start to fill up. Some are two-person teams, though I see others in groups of three.

Ally grips the reins, and her eyes lock onto the track in front of us.

What started out as a way to have fun has quickly turned into something super serious for her.

I'm never challenging Ally to a competition, ever.

The sounding shot startles me, and I jump in my seat even as the force of the horses lurching forward throws me back. The wind whips at Ally's hair, but she's a machine, watching the track in front of her.

We're neck and neck with Arik and Kate when we come up to the first table. Jumping out of the buggy I run to the table and grab one of the mini mason jars of hooch and slam it back.

It burns like hell going down, but I manage it before looking at the table and seeing Kate trying to flip up a Solo cup. I hop over to it.

College with Jackson prepared me for this very thing.

I manage to nail my cup with my third flip, and Kate gets hers at the same time.

As we're running back to our carts, Jackson's barreling his way toward us. Right before I'm about to reach him, he sticks his foot out to trip me.

Vaulting over the extended limb, I rush back to the cart and am hoisting myself inside when Ally gives the reins a flick of her wrist, and we're flying down the track again.

If that's the way he wants to play, fine. We'll play.

Kate and Arik are right in front of us, dust flying from their wheels until Ally slaps the reins down and our horses pull up alongside theirs.

In a clear calm tone, Ally says, "Connor, reach beneath the seat; there's a box. Inside it will be Silly String or other prank stuff."

Sure enough, I reach a hand down and encounter a wooden box. I pop the lid and see confetti cannons, Silly String, and filled water balloons nestled in newspaper along with a glitter bomb. With a can of Silly String in my hand, I ask, "What am I supposed to do with this?"

With a quick glance at me and a devilish smile playing across her face, she says, "What do you think? Hit 'em with it!"

"Okay, but I need you to get closer!" I have to shout to be heard over the thundering hooves. We're about to head into our next turn when Ally lines me up with Arik, who's watching his pair of horses.

I aim the can, but Kate catches sight of me. Just as I depress the trigger, she yells as she jumps in Arik's lap, shoving his head to the far side of her shoulder, acting as a human shield.

"That's playing dirty, Connor Murtry!" she shouts while batting away the aerosolized plastic string smooshed in her hair and face.

Ally shouts back, "You know you'd have done the same thing, Kate Belle," before giving a testy flick to the reins, and our buggy shoots ahead of theirs on the inside corner of the track.

At the next table, Ally yanks back on the horses' leads, and our buggy comes to a shuddering halt. I jump out of the cart, my laughter trailing behind me. This shot goes down a little easier, now that I know what to expect, but the challenge gives me pause.

A series of cowboy boots is lined up on the ground behind the table, which holds a bunch of beanbags. The goal? To throw one of the beanbags into a boot. I couldn't be worse at this if I tried.

I grab one of the bags and toss it underhand. It bounces off the rim of a boot before falling to the ground.

Kate's buggy pulls up behind us, and she comes tearing up next to me, grabbing a beanbag while tossing back her shot.

She nails her beanbag on the first attempt and hurries

back to her cart. By some act of fate, Jackson and Liv's cart pulls up, and Jackson swoops Kate up and over his shoulder, holding her hostage, while Liv runs for the table.

I take the chance Jackson's unwittingly given me and take a deep breath. I line up my beanbag with the boot closest to me. Miraculously, it goes into the boot, and I sprint for the cart even as Ally whoops and hollers from her seat.

Just as I reach for the cart handle to jump in, Ally tosses a container at me. I spin while my ass meets the seat and fire off the glitter bomb into Jackson's face.

He's coughing and hacking when I shove him back and yell for Ally to go.

The others aren't far behind, but we maintain a small lead through the next two challenges. The first one is the beer pong table, where I nail the cup with my Ping-Pong ball in one shot, and the next requires spinning in a circle ten times before we're allowed to continue.

The six of us are neck and neck as we approach the last table. Ally halts the horses and is out of the cart before I can even grab the reins from her. I down the shot while she grabs one of the premade lassos on the table.

She takes a running leap onto a spring-loaded horse contraption, rocking back and forth a second to steady herself, then tosses the loop around the head of the rocking horse that sits about ten feet in front of her.

Jumping off the fake horse just as fast as she jumped on it, she sprints back to me, scrambles into the buggy, and has us careening down the last straightaway.

Jackson and Liv are hot on our tail, so I reach into the prank box for the water balloons and confetti cannon.

I have to time this just right if it's going to work.

Cocking my arm, I take aim at Jackson's ugly mug. He glares at me, and just as he opens his mouth to no doubt warn me against my course of action, I let the balloon fly. I manage to smack Liv in the shoulder, water exploding everywhere.

Her outraged scream is enough to pierce my eardrums. Before she even finishes the last note, I'm firing the next water balloon, which splatters and splashes against Jackson's forehead. As soon as I hit my target, I grab the confetti cannon and fire it in their direction. With confetti sticking to his face, he's forced to slow down as he swipes at the mess on his head.

Just as I'm turning back around, Ally's steering us past the finish line, and the buzzer sounds.

Kate and Arik are the next to cross the finish line, followed closely by Liv and Jackson, who are still wiping confetti from their faces.

As the other racers cross the finish line, I look over at Ally, who is a little windblown, and we both succumb to gut-busting laughter. Out of the corner of my eye, I see Jackson and Liv walking up to us.

Pride filling her tone, Ally says, "What? I told you we'd win."

The laughter dies in my throat at her declaration.

Maybe it's the fair food for dinner with the bumpy ride of the race or the adrenaline dump coupled with the laughter, but my stomach gurgles hard before lurching painfully. I manage to bend over the side of the cart before losing my dinner all over Jackson's shoes.

Deadpan, Jackson says, "I see I put my money on the wrong stomach."

ALLY

By Thursday, I'm Cowboy Coursed out. This week has been amazing and fun, but I'm exhausted.

With no ill effects from the moonshine races, I have one more day of events and then the barn dance tomorrow night before I can pack it in.

Juggling the shop and the festival has me passed out as soon as my head hits the pillow each night. I haven't had time to do anything other than run from one place to the other, never mind think about the conversation Connor and I had prior to the courses starting.

Today we're running the cowboy dash, a short, mud-filled obstacle course, with flags tied around our waists. The goal is to finish the race without a rodeo clown yanking your flag and disqualifying you.

My preferred method of cardio is hiking since I have neither the stamina nor the tatas to make jogging comfortable.

Hell, the last time I sprinted was to the oven to avoid burning cookies.

We're lined up at the starting line with what feels like every other person in town. I sincerely hope the girls don't want me to pull some win out of thin air for us.

Emma and Elle stand next to me wearing their bright pink numbers on their shirts. They're looking around as if they expect someone to show up. I rack my brain trying to remember whether I planned for anyone else to run this with us.

Just as I'm about to ask who they're looking for, I catch my bearded lumberjack ambling over to us in a pair of gray jogging shorts, and the spit in my mouth dries to dust at the sight of his powerful quads flexing while he walks.

"Connor! You came!" Emma cries when she spots him.

"Sure did, Brittle. Wouldn't miss it for the world."

I, however, am confused. He's supposed to be helping with the calf scramble for the kiddos under the age of ten.

Some of my confusion must be on my face because he says, "Jackson's helping out so I can be here."

The announcer calls us all to the starting line; I'm not optimistic enough to work my way to the front. We crowd somewhere in the middle, people jostling around us, while we wait for the siren to sound.

My daughters get their competitiveness from me. The looks on their faces are enough to convince me this is serious for them. With that, I prepare myself for some serious cardio.

Here's to hoping my sports bra holds up.

A loud bang sounds, and the crowd starts to move, narrowing down the path as we come to the first obstacle, which is a series of tall wooden walls to scale.

"Ally, come here."

Connor's cupping his hands, and before I think about it too much, I place my foot in the cradle of his palm, and he launches me to the top of the structure. Swinging a leg over, I straddle the wall while he passes Emma my way. I hoist her up with me.

"Hang on to my waist, baby." Like me, she's straddling the wall.

Reaching down, we repeat the movement with Elle and then Connor scoots back before running and jumping.

His palm slaps against my hand before locking onto my wrist. Using every inch of strength in my thighs to hold us on the wall, my arm yanked tight, I pull while he scales the wall.

Once he's on the wall, he lowers me to my feet before passing me the girls. Just as he jumps down, we turn to continue down the course and find we're surrounded by rodeo clowns.

Their faces painted in white-and-red streaks with oversized lips give me the creeps.

If we pull their flags before they pull ours, they have to let us pass. Charging at one, I feint right just as the clown goes left, and I manage to snag his flag before he gets mine. Connor is pulling a similar move with his clown when Emma lets out a cry. Tears brimming in her eyes, she starts to limp toward the last clown. He hunkers down, asking, "Are you okay, honey? Did you twist your ankle?"

As he's about to reach for her, her face clears and she lunges for his flag, grabbing it triumphantly and holding it in the air.

Connor laughs next to me and says, "That's my girl! Let's go!"

Emma and Elle run past us, and we jog after them. Luckily, there are no more clowns as we come up to the next obstacle, which is a mud pit. Lifting Elle onto my back, Connor throws Emma on his, and we work our way through the mud. I'm climbing out of the other side when Elle jumps off my back a second too soon and topples into the muck.

Golden hair now a dark brown, she's laughing uproariously when she surfaces.

The sound of her tinkling laugh sets me off, and I wait until Connor and Emma get closer. Under the guise of helping her off his back, I get a good grip on her and push them both over.

Emma manages to land on her feet, abandoning his back at the last second when he dips under the water.

He resurfaces and wipes his face. His teeth gleam in a feral grin as he says, "Oh, now you're going to pay for it."

Lurching toward me, he gets his hands around my waist, and we both go back down into the muck.

When our heads pop above the surface, both of us spitting out mud, we're all laughing and breathless. We help the girls up the bank and then follow them.

At the last obstacle, a rope bridge over another mud pit, two clowns have us pinned down. I look at Connor, and he gives me a nod while scooping the girls up.

They head for the bridge, and just as the clowns start toward him, I lunge for their belts and snag a handful of flags before they get farther than a foot or two in the direction of my girls.

A third clown chooses that moment to come up behind me and yank on my belt. The flag comes free, disqualifying me from the race.

Jumping up, I shout, "Run, Connor! Run!"

The clowns whip around and number three gives chase, but Connor's fast. He and the girls run onto the rope bridge as he calls, "Peanut! Brittle! Attach!"

Elle latches onto Connor's front leg while Emma jumps up into his arms. Connor bounces on the rope, causing it to shift and shake enough to send the clown down into the mud pit below.

Righting the girls, Connor rushes across the distance. I'm

running on the sidelines as all three cross the finish line. There's an old fire truck hosing participants off at the end.

Connor's bent at the waist, his breath gusting out, as the girls yell and run in circles around him.

We definitely didn't win, since our whole team needed to cross the finish line, but we had fun together, and that's all that counts in my mind.

Once we're all hosed down, we head to where I parked at the end of the trail in anticipation of having to dry the girls off.

They change their clothes behind the privacy of a towel. When it's my turn, I ask Connor to hold the beach towel up while I keep my back to the door panel of my SUV to get into dry clothes.

I'm standing there in wet panties and a bra when Connor curses, "Jesus Christ."

I lift my head. Connor's eyes are positively devouring me, running over my damp skin. The heat in his gaze is unmistakable, and his tongue darts out to swipe across his bottom lip.

My nipples pucker against the fabric of my bra as my breath hitches in my throat.

"Beautiful, if you don't get dressed right now, we're going to jail."

The threat does its job. I glance around and see no one, but I pull on my cut-offs and T-shirt in double time. Connor hangs on to the towel, though, wrapping it loosely around his own waist to hide the ridge of his erection in his now wet and clinging shorts.

Backing me to the side of the SUV, he keeps one hand locked on the towel at his waist and brings the other up to my face, holding my chin in place as he drops a carnal kiss on my lips.

The evidence of his arousal presses against my belly, and

a needy whine sounds between us as my core ignites in want for him.

"Mama, can I have water? I'm thirsty."

At Elle's question, Connor sharply pulls back. With a whispered "To be continued," he disappears into the back of the SUV, presumably in search of the cooler of drinks and snacks I have stashed back there.

I may still be apprehensive about a lot of the aspects of our relationship, but I'm more than ready for the day to be done so I can have him to myself.

~

WE'RE AT CONNOR'S KITCHEN TABLE AND WATCHING THE GIRLS devour their roast chicken. Today was a light day event-wise —most of the activities are more game-related—so Connor and I were able to break away early enough to put a full dinner together.

Emma and Elle are wrecked. I'm surprised Elle isn't sleeping in her mashed potatoes, considering how heavy and glassy her eyes are.

Emma tries to get a bite of spinach into her mouth and misses completely. The fork tines stab her cheek, and she jerks back before managing the bite on the second attempt.

I stand, intent on clearing some of dinner before getting the girls and heading out, when I feel Connor come up behind me.

"Stay?"

My shoulders stiffen at the whispered plea. I shouldn't. I know I should pack the girls up, take them home, and let them sleep in their own beds.

We're supposed to be slowing down.

"They need a bath and bed. They don't have any pajamas here."

Connor counters, "I have multiple bathrooms. They can wear some of my old T-shirts, and we'll throw their clothes in the wash. Come on, Ally. They're wiped out."

Over his shoulder, I see Elle's head resting on the table, and I wouldn't be surprised if she started snoring then and there.

Relenting, I say, "Okay."

Skirting him, I scoop Elle up and usher her to the bathroom for a quick bath. While I rinse her hair, Connor knocks on the door, then cracks it open to pass me a T-shirt for her to wear.

I repeat the process with Emma, who's slightly more awake.

Once she's out of the bath, I leave her to get dressed and go in search of Connor. I assume the girls are going to crash on the couch, but I hear quiet voices in one of the spare rooms.

I push open the door. Connor's in bed with Elle, the same bed he had bookmarked. Walls the palest lavender are illuminated only by the dim lamp on the nightstand. The room is fully furnished, down to rainbow drapes over the window.

Propped open on his chest is a kids' book about a cat and his groovy buttons.

He's reading to Elle. The last shaky barrier I had around my heart shatters and disappears entirely as I listen to his steady voice rumble through the children's story.

He's reading my baby girl a bedtime story, and she's curled up on his chest, breathing evenly in sleep.

Tears brim and trickle down my cheeks. Each drop of saltwater is full of love, hopes, dreams, and the sliver of bittersweet heartache that comes from knowing these girls aren't just mine anymore.

He might not be their father, but he's more of a daddy to them than anyone else.

Slowly, his head lifts, eyes locking on mine, and he smiles. Looking down before his gaze meets mine again, that grin is full of love and a little bit of wonder.

I'm done.

The last holdout of my anxiety-riddled brain falls away.

I back out of the room and find Emma in her own bed, fast asleep. Tucking the covers up and over her shoulders, I brush a kiss across her forehead and sneak out of the room.

The house is dark when I make my way down the stairs. The only light is coming from the stove light in the kitchen and the door to Connor's room. When I push through the door, he turns from the dresser where he's emptying his pockets. He's also removed his shirt; if I had to guess, he's on his way to the shower.

I cross to him, the heated feel of his skin under my hands shocking in a way that only happens with him.

His hands come to my waist, and he shifts us away from the dresser before swaying us to a beat only he can hear.

"Dancing in your house is becoming a thing for us."

"Hopefully not just my house."

"What does that mean?"

His lips kick to the side in a purse before he says, "I was hoping I could convince you and the girls to go to the barn dance with me tomorrow night, you know—kinda like practice for the daddy-daughter dance next week."

I didn't even know he was aware of the dance at the school. But I can't deny him. He's more than earned the right to take them.

Not just in the last few weeks either.

His love and devotion to my girls has been apparent for years now, but in the misguided notion of putting space between us, of me trying to shove my feelings for him away when I mistakenly thought he didn't look at me "that way," I didn't acknowledge just how big his presence is in our lives.

False blinders fading away, love for him saturates me. I reach my arms up around his neck, dragging his lips down to mine to breathe my answer against his lips. "We'd love to."

CONNOR

THE RINGING OF MY CELL PHONE WAKES ME FRIDAY MORNING. Bleary-eyed, I watch the sun dance and shift through the windows. I can't remember the last time I slept past sunrise, but feeling as rested as I do, I can't really complain. It's one of the last days of my vacation, and going nonstop for the Cowboy Courses has been exhausting.

Rolling over, I glance at the readout of the buzzing device to see Jackson's name floating across the top of the screen.

"Yeah," I answer.

"I just got off the phone with Hal over at the Everette station. He's short three rangers today due to a stomach bug and wanted to see if we had anyone to spare. You feel like driving up there for a few hours?"

I pull the phone away from my face and glance at the time. It's just after eight, and the neighboring station is about an hour and a half away.

"How long do they need someone? I told Ally I'd take her and the girls to the barn dance tonight."

"Hal said he's got some night shifters coming in early, so just a few hours. You'll be able to make it, no problem."

"Okay. Yeah, I can be there. Lemme just text her and let her know."

"I'll text her. You go ahead and get ready."

We disconnect the line, and I'm not surprised to find Ally and the girls gone. She gets up at the ass crack of dawn to bake. I'm not sure she would have left the girls with me even if she could have.

We're still figuring our way after the discussion last week and finding the girls' rooms done last night probably threw her for a loop.

I'm all in. I want her and those girls with me all the time. Maybe I'll bring up her being able to leave them with me in the mornings. That way she can stay at the bakery after her morning duties are completed instead of taking them to school and then going back to the bakery.

I start earlier than I need to at the ranger station, but I can push that back to drop them off for her.

Plans and ideas to lessen her load for the future circle my head as I get dressed and grab my gear. The drive is a long one, so I shoot off a text to Ally before leaving.

Hey, did Jackson call you?

He did.

OK, so I'll see you later then?

Yep. Don't forget you're supposed to get Hedy and Ben from the airport tonight after the dance.

I won't. Thanks for the reminder.

I love you

My heart beats a little harder at that message. She hasn't said she loves me other than the one time, and after the hiccup with the girls' rooms, I worried she rethought it and changed her mind.

I love you too

Climbing into my truck, I throw it in reverse and head out. While the drive is tedious, it's not boring. The fields are changing in anticipation for the winter and the day is all clear blue skies.

The station is a flurry of activity when I arrive, but Hal still takes a moment to greet me with a handshake.

"Where do you need me today?" I ask.

"We just got reports of a fire starting up on Big Elk we need to check out. Based on the initial report, it's pretty small—likely a campfire that's starting to spread. So suit up, and you're going with me."

He hands me fire protectant gear I slide on over my uniform. It's late in the season for fire, so my fingers are crossed that it's small, otherwise I won't make it back to Felt in time for the dance like I promised.

The only thing I can do right now is get through the next couple of hours and hope we put this thing out quickly.

I'M SATURATED IN SWEAT, AND EVERY INCH OF MY BODY IS sore, achy, and tired.

Small fire, my ass.

A campfire got out of hand and spread to the surrounding area. Luckily, there wasn't a lot of forest debris to feed it, and the site was right at the edge of a lake, but containment and extinguishing it took longer than they should have.

The sun is starting to go down by the time I'm hauling ass

back to the station with Hal. Since he's driving, I whip out my phone and gape at the time. The barn dance already started.

I have missed call after missed call. I don't bother listening to the messages before trying to call Ally back, but it goes straight to her voice mail, so I hang up and dial mine to listen.

"Hey, Con, not sure where you are, but we're ready whenever you are. I thought you'd be here by now, so just give me a call when you get this."

I click over to the next message.

"Connor, I called Jackson, and he said you're at another station but should have been back by now. Please call me when you get this."

One of the girls is in the background asking for me, and that's like a cannon blast to the heart.

"Well, we're headed to the dance." Her voice drops like she's trying to avoid the girls overhearing when she says, *"They are really upset. They've been looking forward to this all day—seeing you and you taking them was a big deal for them. Listen, Con...I think we need to talk."*

The irritation and sadness in Ally's tone rips at me. As soon as the voice mail disconnects, I try to call again, but like the first time, there's no answer.

Disappointment and self-castigation eat at me as we pull into the station.

I drop off the gear, and with a few quick goodbyes I'm almost out the door when Hal calls my name.

"Yeah?" I'm in a hurry to get out of here, can't he see that?

"We need to file the report for the fire. Think you can stick around long enough to get that done before you take off?"

Fuck. Fucking paperwork. I can't leave without dealing with that no matter how much of a hurry I'm in.

I check the time again when I remember I still have to get Hedy and Ben from the airport. The Idaho Falls airport is on the way back to Felt, but it'll be too late to make it in time if I stay and deal with the paperwork.

Hal says, "I don't have any other rangers here to deal with it. I'd appreciate it if you could stay. Unless you have something more pressing?"

My sense of responsibility tells me to stay, but my need to get home is urging me to leave. Jackson would probably be able to get Hedy and Ben from the airport if I asked.

"Let me make a call."

I'll make this up to them. I swear it.

I try calling Jackson, but when he doesn't answer, I try Ally again.

This time she answers. "Connor"—her voice is a pissed-off whisper—"where the hell are you?"

"Als, I'm so sorry. There was a fire, and I got held over."

"I see. So why are you calling?"

Holding my phone out, I scowl at the thing. I'd rather be having this discussion in person with her, but I can't so I have to settle with an impersonal phone call.

"I tried calling Jackson, but he didn't answer. Is he there?"

"No, he and Liv already went home. They're doing the last dance now and then we're cleaning up and packing it in."

"Shit. I have to finish the paperwork here, so I won't make it in time to pick up Hedy and Ben. I was going to ask if he could grab them. If he leaves now, he should make it in time."

A heavy sigh comes through the receiver, and Ally says, "If I leave now, I can pick them up."

"Can you? I know you're mad at me for missing the dance, and I'm sorry that I have to ask. I'll make it up to you."

"Sure, okay." Her voice is hesitant, like she doesn't quite believe me, and I hate that I put that uncertainty in her.

Before I can respond, she disconnects from the line, and just like that, she's gone.

And for some reason, I don't think it's just from the phone call.

Paperwork takes forever—the Everette station's computer equipment is more outdated than ours. When I finally make it out of there, the trip back home crawls and crawls no matter how I speed. I can't shake the feeling that Ally's request to *talk* really meant she's ending things. The foreboding that settles into my bones is unwelcome, uncomfortable, and chilling.

I'm just leaving Idaho Falls hoping Ally was able to pick up Hedy and Ben without a problem, when I see flashing lights in the distance and traffic slows to a crawl.

Of fucking course it would be just my luck that the one time I want to get home, there's an accident that's stopping all traffic.

My phone buzzes, and Hedy's name flashes. Fishing the phone out of the cup holder, I answer as I creep closer to the flashing lights.

"Hello?"

"Connor? Are you still coming to pick us up?"

Confusion has me cocking my head. "I got called to another ranger station today. Ally said she would pick you up." Glancing at the dashboard clock, I continue, "She should have been there by—"

The words die in my throat as I reach the accident. On the other side of the road, a paramedic van is parked in front of a horrifically familiar SUV, and the blood in my veins freezes to ice.

The entire front end of the car is crumpled like an accordion, the vehicle sitting crooked in the road. Spiderweb cracks cover the front windshield, and the nylon of the airbags hangs limp over the steering wheel and driver's side window.

Glass, steel, and plastic litter the ground around the fire of the emergency flares.

Dark fluids—please, God, let it be fluids from the car—stain the ground. I'm just barely close enough to make out the rear license plate: TWNBK3R

Yanking the wheel of my truck, I pull on to the shoulder, heedless of the traffic behind me. I don't even bother to shut the truck off before I vault out of the vehicle.

I'm running across the highway when one of the highway patrol guys stops me. I fight uselessly against his arms.

Please, God, let her be all right.

The words of the police officer don't register at first. I can't hear anything over the pounding in my ears; it takes me a second to focus on his words.

"Sir, you can't go over there. Do you know her?"

"Ally Sawyer. She's my…uh, my girlfriend. Is she okay?"

Sympathetic gaze trained on my face, he doesn't answer me as the paramedics wheel a gurney to the back of the ambulance. She's too far away for me to see, so I fight off the arm holding me back and run over to her.

I reach the gurney just as they lift her to the back. Her eyes are closed, and she's so fucking pale she could pass for a ghost.

"Ally! Ally, beautiful, can you hear me?" She doesn't so much as twitch in my direction. I realize it's because she's either sedated or passed out.

What the fuck happened?

One of the paramedics stops me with a hand on my arm. "Are you family?"

Shaking my head, helplessness stealing over me, I croak out, "No, she's my girlfriend."

Again with the sympathetic gaze, the paramedic says, "You can't ride with us, only family."

"Where are you taking her?"

"Eastern Idaho Regional Medical Center," he says as he shuts the door in my face.

I pivot and run for my truck.

Fear is a greasy ice pick in my stomach. I don't realize I'm holding my breath until my head starts to pound and my heart thumps harder.

Ignoring the highway patrol, I follow the ambulance as it makes a U-turn in the road and stay behind the flashing lights all the way to the hospital.

I illegally park in the first reserved spot I come across—they can tow my truck for all I fucking care. I dial Jackson as I jog across the parking lot.

He answers on the third ring, and I say, "Ally was in an accident. We're at EIRMC. Call your ma and get down here."

"Wait! What? What happened?"

I disconnect the call and shoot off a text to Hedy, letting her know what happened. I feel like shit, but they're going to have to find a different way home from the airport because I'm not leaving the hospital until I find out what the fuck is going on with Ally.

Storming the receptionist desk in the emergency room, I say, "Ally Sawyer was just admitted by ambulance."

"Your name?"

"Connor Murtry."

"Are you family, Mr. Murtry?"

Fuck this.

"She's my fiancée."

The nurse clicks a few keys and says, "We don't have information on her yet. Have a seat, and I'll call you up when we know more."

Suffocating impotence swamps me.

I'm never where I'm needed when I'm needed.

This is all my fault. If I had just told Jackson no this morning, that I couldn't work at Hal's station, this never would have happened. I would have been *there*.

Wishing with my entire being that she's okay, my head falls into my hands. I dig the heels of my palms into my eyes until fireworks shoot behind my closed lids.

How could this happen to me twice? My best friend's sister. A car accident. The only reason they were behind the wheel is *me*.

Just like before, if I would have been the one driving, someone I love wouldn't have gotten hurt. Just like before, it's my fault someone I love is hurting. Instead of learning from my first mistake with April, I went ahead and compounded it by doing the exact same thing with Ally.

I let down people who matter to me by not being there tonight, and then I hurt those girls by putting their mama in the hospital. It might not have been my direct actions that put her here, but it was me all the same.

I don't deserve the sunshine Ally has illuminated my life with. I don't deserve good things when all I do is cause pain.

I crush, I destroy, and no matter how much I wish that wasn't true, it's time to face the facts.

I'm better off alone. Everyone else is better off if I'm alone.

Hatred and self-loathing circle in my head. I can't fight back the recriminations anymore. By the time Jackson, Liv, and Nan come through the door, I've shut down my emotions, locked them tight behind a wall so thick it's impenetrable.

Standing, I say, "They haven't given me any information on her condition. But if you want to try, you might have some luck, Nan."

The fear in her face destroys me. I'm responsible for that

too. Every ounce of heartache and panic she and Jackson are feeling right now can be laid at my feet.

Breath backing up in my lungs, the need to run, to get away, to leave twitches through me until I'm bouncing my leg, fidgeting with the need to *move.*

I can't be here right now. I can't be what they need. I'll never be what anyone needs.

With that last thought cemented in every fiber of my being, I leave the hospital.

ALLY

Hushed voices wake me. Everything aches, and there's a relentless pounding behind my still-closed eyes.

When I swallow, the pinch in my dry throat is just one more ouch to add to all the rest.

Even my fingernails hurt. What the fuck happened to me?

I clearly got into a fight with a semitruck and the truck won.

Wait.

Did I?

The lights of an oncoming car crossed the center line.

Before I could swerve, we collided. Metal screeched and then everything went black.

I try to open my eyes, but they're weighted down, and no matter how I try, I can't pry them open.

"Kate says the girls are fine. They're watching a movie." I can barely make out Ma's voice. It's like she's talking while driving through a tunnel.

"Okay. Can they keep them for the night?" Jackson's question is just as fuzzy. I try to move my hand from where it's pinned against my chest. When I can't, I use my other hand to drag my fingers across the bedding while croaking out a noise.

A cool hand finds mine, fingers wrapping around my palm. "Ally, baby, are you waking up?" Ma sounds like she's trying to whisper.

"Mm-hmph." That sounded nothing like what I was going for, but it'll have to do.

"Here, sip some water." A straw is pressed against my lips, and I greedily suck the cool liquid into my mouth, letting it chase away the dry.

"Thanks." My voice sounds as rough and patchy as my throat feels.

"Do you know where you are?"

The beep of a monitor somewhere behind me is enough to clue me in. "The hospital."

"Yeah, baby. You were in a car accident. You're in Idaho Falls."

"Hedy and Ben?" My brain is so muddled I can't remember if I picked them up before or after the world imploded in a fiery explosion of pain.

"They're out in the waiting room. They came here straight from the airport."

I guess I hadn't picked them up.

"What's wrong with me?"

"Well. You have a concussion and a fractured collarbone to start."

No wonder it feels like my head is splitting like an overripe tomato.

"Girls?" It's the only thing I can focus on.

"They're at Kate and Arik's for the night. Last I heard they were making popcorn and building a blanket fort."

I finally manage to peel open my left eyelid. The lights are turned off in the room, probably in response to my concussion, and I'm grateful I'm not being blinded.

"Connor?"

Mom's eyes cut away, and her lips purse.

"What?" I ask.

Jackson's voice cuts in. "He was here…but he, uh, he left."

"He left?"

Ma nods, and my heart splinters in my chest.

He's not here. The man I love isn't here with me, when I'm hurt and broken, and that makes me cry. Not the pain that's amping up and reverberating through my skull, not the dull ache of my shoulder, or the fact that I feel like a bruised banana all over. No. My stupid eyeballs are leaking because once again I let a man into my life and he hurt me.

"Oh, no, baby. Don't cry. Are you hurting? It's okay. I'll page the doctor and let them know you're awake. They should be able to give you something for the pain." Ma's hands lightly swipe at the tears that spill from the corner of my eyes down into the hair at my temples. I don't have the energy to tell her that it's not the physical pain that has me crying. It's the shattered remnants of my heart.

The door opens and closes softly, then it's silent for a minute before I feel the warm callus of my brother's hand come into mine.

"Connor drove past the accident scene. He followed you here and waited until we showed up before taking off."

Somehow, that hurts more. That he would know but still not be here when I need him most. I thought him standing us up for our date tonight was bad, but inexplicably, this is so much worse.

How can he claim to love me, claim he wants me and the girls in his life, but can't even be bothered to stick around when I'm in the hospital? No matter how much I don't want to believe it of him, the glaring facts tell a different story.

He was here. He left.

It's not the first time he left me in the dust. I don't know why I'm surprised or shocked it happened again.

"I don't know why he left. He's not answering his phone, but he looked pretty shaken—"

"Please don't," I interrupt. "Don't defend him right now. I can't..."

"Okay."

We sit in silence until the door opens, admitting a slice of blinding light, and a forty-something man in a white coat follows my mom in.

"Ms. Sawyer? My name is Dr. Richards."

I answer the questions he asks by rote. Yes, I know what my name is, what date it is, where I am. No, my hearing and vision aren't wonky.

He tells me, "X-rays of your collarbone show a clean break, hence the sling. We set the break, but you'll be uncomfortable for a while. The sling will stay on for five to six weeks. Your CT scan shows a mild concussion. We're going to keep you here tonight, but if all is well, we can discharge you in the morning."

Once the doctor covers my injuries and treatment, he leaves me, Ma, and Jackson alone.

"My car?"

"I got the information from the highway patrol on the way here for where it's being towed. Don't you worry about that right now."

I can't help but worry; it's what I do.

I'll need to contact Jem and see if she can handle the baking until I'm out of this sling. I have to arrange for a rental car immediately and a replacement before too long. My insurance company will need the information for the accident claim.

It's easier to focus on the next steps of my life than the

heartache that Connor left the hospital as soon as my family showed up.

This is probably similar to his old girlfriend and Texas, but I have no sympathy for him. He could have stayed to make sure I was all right, but no, he bailed at the first sign of trouble, much like he did after Emma broke her arm.

Chasing him down back then started us on this path. I knew I should have listened to my misgivings when it came to letting him all the way into my life. That was the first red flag I ignored.

Our friend group is close, but if I never saw him again it would be too soon. I let the anger at his asshole-ishness chase away the pain of his abandonment.

He's going to make me break my girls' hearts again, and I could punch him for it.

"Hey. I can see the wheels turning. Shut that shit down. You're supposed to be resting."

Jackson's admonishment yanks my mind away from the bubbling devastation waiting to creep in.

"Where's my phone? I need to call Jem."

Ma crosses to a cabinet and pulls out a bag of my belongings. The front screen of the device is severely cracked and doesn't turn on when I press the power button.

Great. Just one more thing in my life that's broken.

It goes great with the sucking wreckage of my heart.

FOR A WEEK AFTER I'M DISCHARGED FROM THE HOSPITAL, MA and my brother do nothing but chase me around, telling me to rest, while I ignore them and work when I can. Hedy and Ben closed out the Cowboy Courses committee and jumped right into helping pack up the fairgrounds at the beginning of the week.

I've seen neither hide nor hair of Connor, and, frankly, it's a relief. I don't have my head or heart screwed on correctly, and I don't trust myself not to rage at him if I were to see him.

Distance is best right now.

I'm fighting with the zipper bag for the bank deposit on Sunday night. The newly repaired kitchen was done a whole week ahead of schedule. Whether it was Colby's super-efficient team or speed born of pity due to my accident and breakup, the bakery is back in tip-top shape either way.

Now if only I could get there.

Arm throbbing as I wrestle with the bent teeth on an ancient bag, I let my frustration at nearly everything in my life take over. Just as I'm about to throw it down, the back door opens.

Liv and Kate I expected, but...

"Taylor? What on earth are you doing here?" No one mentioned Kate and Liv's friend from Arizona coming to visit.

She wraps her arms gently around my shoulders, and the spicy floral scent of her perfume envelops me.

"Hey, lady. How're you feeling?"

Well, that's a loaded question.

"I'm fine," I reply.

Dark brown eyes dance behind her glasses, and a shit-stirring smile tweaks her lips. "Mm-hmm, I'm sure. As for what I'm doing here—I'm at your disposal."

"What do you mean?"

"Kate and Liv told me about the accident and you being laid up because of your shoulder, so I'm here to help. I can't bake worth a shit, but I can keep your business running until you're back on your feet, so to speak."

"What about Rob? Doesn't he need you?" Liv's brother

runs his own gym empire in Phoenix, and Taylor's his right-hand woman.

Waving that away, she says, "I can run his business from anywhere. Don't you worry about that. Just consider me your business manager for the next few weeks."

Tears that I'm sick of crying start to burn, and I can't grab the tissues fast enough.

My knee-jerk reaction is to decline her offer of help, to reassure my friends I can handle it, but I'm done with that. I toss in the towel.

I am not okay. I can't handle it, and I'm done trying to do everything myself.

I need help. A lot of it.

Swallowing hard, I point to the current bane of my existence. "You think you can get that closed for me?"

"I'd love to," she says with a kind smile.

The question I've been dreading comes up later, when we're all crowded around a pan of brownies, the girls have cracked open a bottle of wine, and I'm sipping tea since I can't drink with pain meds.

"So what happened between you and Asshat McGee?" Kate scoops up another bite of brownie and chases it with a sip of wine like her question didn't turn the sweets in my stomach into a ball of greasy refuse.

I shrug because really? What is there to say?

"I don't know. I haven't heard from him since the day of the accident. Jackson hasn't said anything about him either, so I have no idea what happened."

Liv's eyes narrow. "But the accident was a week ago."

I nod. "I know."

"And he hasn't tried to call you? You haven't tried to call him?"

Taylor punctuates the question by tossing her fork into the mostly empty pan of chocolate.

I take a sip of my tea to stall a moment. "No, he hasn't called me, and no, I'm not going to call him. I chased him last time he left. I'm not doing it again. If he has something to say to me, then it's his turn to figure it out and come find me. Until then, I'll be doing what I always do—working and taking care of the girls."

"How are they?" Kate asks quietly.

Cocking my head, I consider how to answer. I told them Connor and I had a fight, and we might not see much of him. It wasn't their fault, and he loves them just as much as always. They didn't take it well.

Emma still isn't talking to me, and Elle asks to go to Connor's at least once daily.

I knew they would get more attached to him, but instead of heeding the warning signs when shit started to go sideways, I let this happen. If I had just listened to my instincts when he started talking about bedroom furniture for them, maybe we wouldn't be where we are now.

I put off my plans to move us to the apartment over the shop.

I'm still having the space renovated because I'm not doing anything else with it right now, but it's going to sit empty since I don't want to submit the girls to yet another change in life while they're still reeling.

From here on out, my children and this bakery are my only priorities. Relationships, love, and everything else be damned.

CONNOR

TUESDAY MORNING I'M AWAKENED BY THE SMELL OF COFFEE and bacon. For one blissful second, I think Ally is making breakfast before I remember the accident, my cowardly reaction, and the fact I haven't talked to her in eleven days.

Yes, I'm counting.

I fucking miss her.

Extending my vacation with sick time, I took last week off, scared to see Jackson at the station. Scared of the censure for leaving while Ally was in the hospital I'd see when he looked at me.

Today's supposed to be my first day back, but I'm still a coward, so I swapped shifts with Boone and won't go in until night shift.

I emailed Hal at the end of last week and asked him if the senior ranger position is still open. I figure it's for the best I get the hell out of Dodge before the Sawyers come after me with pitchforks.

I hate myself enough for all of us, so it's probably better that I leave while I can.

Shoving my legs into a pair of boxers, I grab the baseball

bat by my dresser and creep down the hall. If someone broke in here intent on doing harm, they likely wouldn't be making themselves breakfast first, but I'd rather be prepared.

Of all the people who could be in my house on a Tuesday morning making breakfast, Nanette Sawyer is the last person I expect.

The floorboard under my foot creaks just as I cross the threshold into the kitchen, and she turns. She says nothing, just cocks one of those silvery blonde eyebrows and nods at the table.

Her expression is stern. She's not here to play around. I don't feel like getting skinned by my best friend's mama, so I heed the silent warning and slink over to the table, ignoring my state of undress in front of the mother of the woman I love.

"You really fucked up."

Disappointment saturates her tone, and my shoulders instinctively hunch. I don't refute the words, though, because I did fuck up.

Nan is likely here to warn me away from her son and daughter, and I can't fault her for it.

"Nothing to say?"

I look up from the wood grain of the table to find her standing next to me with a plate of food in her hands. Setting the plate down, she turns back to my cabinets before grabbing a mug and filling it with coffee.

When she drops it on the table, I finally find my voice. "No, ma'am."

Nan pulls a chair out and sits, motioning to my plate. "You better eat while it's hot. I'm fixing to be here a minute."

The bite of scrambled eggs tastes like sawdust and regret on my tongue. Still, I swallow, then sip the coffee she left at my elbow.

"Connor, I'm going to level with you. You broke my baby girl's heart. Why?"

The small bite of food I managed threatens to reappear as my gut curdles in shame and disappointment.

"She's better off without me."

Quick as a flash, her hand comes up to cuff me in the back of the head. "Boy, don't you pull that mopey shit with me. Why'd you break her damn heart?"

"Nan, shit. What do you want me to say? That I didn't mean to hurt her? I didn't, but it still happened. That I wish I could take it back? If I could, I would."

"For starters, you'll watch your mouth around me. I've got one question for you. Do you honestly think that accident was your fault? That you're the reason she got hurt?"

The reprimand and force in her tone tell me she believes there's only one right answer.

"It was my fault she got hurt. It was my fault she was even on the road that night. If I had just turned down the request from the other—"

She smacks me in the head again. "I can all but hear the useless thoughts bouncing around in that pea brain of yours, Connor. You didn't cause the accident. You didn't make the other driver cross the center line. You didn't make her go to the airport to pick up Hedy and Ben. None of that was your fault. Do you understand me?"

Her saying it and me believing it are two very different things, so I don't answer. I don't agree with her or even nod.

I know the truth.

"If you got into an accident and Ally was blaming herself, what would you tell her?"

Fucking mom logic. Even as a grown-ass man, it trips me up. My mom's been gone for years now, and I don't appreciate the pseudo mom I have wielding the strongest weapon in her arsenal against me.

Gritting my teeth, I say, "This is different."

I'm waiting for that fast hand to pop up again when Nan leans back in her chair, smirk in place, eyebrow climbing as if to ask, "Oh, really?"

"It is different. She was only on that fucking road that late at night because I—"

"Was helping a neighboring ranger station with what almost turned out to be a forest fire." Nodding at me, she continues, "Yeah, I got the story from Jackson. So, no, you're not allowed to take responsibility for the circumstances that led up to the accident. You can't even blame yourself for the accident. Now, isn't that a bitch?"

Man, I don't think I've ever seen Nan this mean, and I don't relish being the recipient of it right now.

"What you can blame yourself for? You leaving the damn hospital when you knew she was hurt. You letting the misplaced blame come between you and my daughter. You letting that old hurt, guilt, and fear come between you both when it's clear to anyone around you that you love each other."

She stands up and grabs her purse. "Now, I'll only say this once. If you want my daughter, you better be prepared to fight tooth and nail for her. You better lay it all out on the line and fight for her love, her devotion, and her loyalty every single day. You fight for my grandbabies because they deserve a daddy who's worth a damn. They deserve to have someone who doesn't run at the first sign of trouble. If you can't do that, then I ask that you let her and those girls go, because they deserve happiness, love, affection, and family."

With those parting words, she leaves the kitchen and me to stare over the cold remnants of eggs and coffee.

~

GALVANIZED INTO ACTION, I HAUL ASS TO THE RANGER station. I'm terrified I'm going to get a fist to the face at best and the end of a decade-long friendship at worst, but it's time for me to stop running from my problems.

Jackson deserves an explanation for my behavior, and I need his help.

Nan's rebuke lit me on fire once I thought of someone else getting all three of my girls because I didn't step up.

No one is ever going to love them like I do, so it's time to let go of the past, cherish every minute of the present, and plan for the future.

Our future. Together.

I want to track down Ally and talk to her, but I need a better plan than that.

The station is pretty empty for a Tuesday morning.

"I need to talk to you," I say as I walk through the main entrance.

Jackson doesn't respond to me, just stands and makes his way to the conference room.

I pass him, and he shuts the door behind us. Just as I turn to speak, he grips me in a bear hug. Hand slapping against my shoulder, he doesn't let me go immediately, and I feel the forgiveness for my foolishness in the hug.

When we break apart, my eyes are stinging.

"I'm sorry," I say as we sit down at the conference table. "I left, and I shouldn't have. I didn't think about anything other than myself. I'm a selfish asshole."

"Con, man, it's okay. If Liv ended up in the hospital, I wouldn't be in my right mind either."

"Yeah, but I thought you'd be mad. I thought…"

"You thought I'd break up our bromance because my sister ended up in the hospital and you couldn't hang?"

Well, that sums it up.

"Yeah."

Punching my shoulder, he says, "I'm not Del, man. I know Ally getting into that accident wasn't your fault; it was just something shitty that happened. What I'm mad about is you thinking I'd be mad at you for it, though."

Oddly enough, I understand what he's saying.

"It shook me. The same thing happening twice—it was like the universe was telling me something, and I let it get to my head."

"But you're done with that bullshit now, right?"

"I am. How is she?"

Head cocked, he thinks for a second before responding, "Like she was before, working herself into the ground."

The words are a sharp stick poked right into the oozing wound of my heart. I might not be responsible for the accident, but I am for everything that came after it.

So I do the only thing I can do.

"What do I do?"

"How good are your groveling skills?"

NERVES JUMP AND BOUNCE IN A JIGGLED MESS AT THE BASE OF my stomach as I raise my hand to knock at the door.

Swallowing back the thick saliva that usually predicts vomit, I try hard to steady myself.

Inside, young voices are quiet and then louder as they get closer to the door.

For just a second, I want to cut and run.

To get away from this, because I'm not sure I can put myself out there, make myself as vulnerable as I need to for what's going to come next.

No.

I have a plan.

I'm doing this.

She deserves it.

Elle and Emma deserve it.

I can do this.

The girls open the door, and like a radio being shut off, the instant silence I'm left with is so loud I clam up.

"Jackson, they're almost ready—"

Ally's voice is like a ray of sunlight after being in perpetual darkness for the last two weeks. Her eyes widen when she sees me.

This is just phase one of the hastily arranged grovel plan I came up with.

Lips tightening and eyebrows pinching over pissed-off hazel eyes, she doesn't say anything. I devour her with my own gaze, taking in the disheveled hair, the sling that holds her arm immobile, all the way down to the painted toes of her bare feet.

For the first time in forever, I feel like I can breathe again. My heart stutters and pumps back to life, and colors are suddenly vibrant. The sweet country air tastes like heaven on my tongue while I stand on her front porch.

"I'm here to pick up the girls."

Emma's in a rainbow-colored dress, her hair hanging in blonde ringlets. Elle wears a buttery yellow dress with her hair piled on top of her head. They've both been in their mama's makeup based off the cherry pink cheeks and the slightly crooked lipstick.

Pure love for them drowns me.

I drop to my knee and set aside the two plastic containers of flowers so I can I pull them into my arms.

The hug seems to break them out of whatever paralysis they were under before, and they both start to animatedly talk at the same time.

"Connor, you came!"

"Are these flowers for us?"

"Why are you wearing a suit and tie?"

"Can we go now?"

The questions bombard me, and I let their bird-like voices float around us as I look up at Ally.

Her eyes are shiny and wet, and I'd bet every dollar in my bank account she's fighting back tears. I hate myself for hurting her like this.

Just like the girls in my arms, I want to protect her, hold her, and safeguard her from the hurts of the world, but I can't. I'm the one who hurt her. The only thing I can do is try to make it right and hope she gives me—gives us—another chance.

"Peanut, Brittle, why don't you go get your sweaters? I'm going to talk to your mama for a minute."

They run off, and I know I don't have long. "Als, I'm sorry. I know you don't want me here, but I promised I'd take them to the father-daughter dance. Please let me?"

Her throat bobs in a hard swallow but she doesn't say anything. She just nods and turns away from me, disappearing into the house.

God, please let this work.

ALLY

WHEN JACKSON TEXTED, TELLING ME TO GET THE GIRLS READY for the dance, I thought it was him, that he was taking them, doing what he does best and being a good uncle.

Never in a million years did I expect to find Connor at my door in a tuxedo.

Where the hell did he even get a tux?

The strange stalemate we've been in these last two weeks came crashing down, and now that he and the girls are gone, my brain won't shut up.

What does this mean?

What's going to happen next?

Is he just keeping his promise to the girls?

Are we even going to talk about what happened?

Minutes after he drives away with the twins, Kate, Liv, and Taylor swoop in and hustle me through a makeover.

I have no fucking idea what's going on, but based on the evening dress Taylor unzips, it's something fancy, and I just don't have the energy to question it.

Did I forget about a party or something?

Ever since the accident, it's been impossible to focus. I get tired ridiculously early, and my memory is like Swiss cheese. If I don't write it down, it gets lost in the mess of my jumbled thoughts.

My doctor said that's common after a concussion and that it'll go back to normal as time goes by, but it's been endlessly frustrating.

I shower, then Taylor works on my makeup while Liv does my hair. Kate is picking through my minuscule jewelry offerings.

"So, what am I getting primped for again?"

They share nonverbal communication, then Kate says, "It's a surprise."

I don't want to be surprised today. I've had more than enough of them to last me into the next four lifetimes, but I don't say that. They've been so intent on cheering me up that I don't have it in me to snap at them.

I just want a good book, some food, and my bed.

But here I am, being plucked, brushed, and dressed like a Barbie doll.

It takes an hour before I'm declared *ready* and bundled out of the house. And in that time, the three of them have done their own hair, makeup, and dresses also.

We drive out of town toward the fairgrounds, which makes no sense, since there's definitely nothing out here that a freaking evening dress is appropriate for. But sure enough, we pull into the packed parking lot, and there are women in dresses and men in jackets and Stetsons walking to the tent-covered concrete area where the barn dance was held.

Twinkling lights cover the outside of the old structure, and music and people spill out of the space.

"What are we doing here? Why are all these people here? What's going on?"

"No questions. Come on." Grabbing my good arm, Kate gently drags me through the crowds, Liv and Taylor at our backs. The twang of country music can be heard all the way out here in the parking lot, and a dull throb starts up at the back of my head.

Inside the barn, tables line the outer walls, a dance floor is open in the middle of the building, and a local bluegrass band is playing at the back.

People circulate with food and drink, the buffet set up along the left side of the space. If I didn't know better, I'd think we hadn't had the barn dance because just about everything is identical.

Liv ushers us through crowds of couples who are dancing and laughing to a table holding a "reserved" sign.

"Ally, you want something to drink? Eat?"

I yell, "What I want is someone to tell me what the hell is going on here," just as the song ends.

My cheeks heat, and I feel bad for snapping, but my patience is at an all-time low right now.

Instead of doing what I want, which is lying around my house like a lazy heifer, a pack of well-meaning friends descended upon me and dragged me out on a Friday night.

Before any of them can speak up, the screech of a microphone being turned on cuts through the room.

"I can answer that."

Chills shoot down my spine at the rough rumble of a familiar voice. I whip around, and Connor's standing on the makeshift stage at the back of the barn in front of the band. His face is two shades lighter than fluorescent, and even from here I can see the sweat beading at his hair line.

"Ally, I never got to take you and the girls to the barn dance, and for that I'm sorry. Then I wasn't there when you needed me after your accident. I was an asshole. I'm sorry for my cowardice after your accident. I'm sorry I didn't talk to you, that I ran and hid instead of coming to you. I'm sorry you got hurt and couldn't depend on me to be there for you, but most of all, I'm sorry that those actions might have cost me you and the girls, my family. When I told you I want all of you, I wasn't lying. But instead of being there when you needed me, I cut and ran, afraid of causing you more hurt, when in the end that's just what I did. I'm so sorry, beautiful."

My pulse is through the stratosphere, and I can't catch my breath the longer his speech goes on.

Like a short circuit, my brain isn't computing what he's saying. All I know is that a man who hates public speaking just bared his heart in front of loads of people.

Audibly swallowing, he continues, "I know I don't deserve you or those girls, but I want to. I'll fight for you, cherish you, love you, and hold you close for every day you'll give me. I'll be there for you, Emma, and Elle because no one is ever going to love you or them like I do."

I don't even realize I'm crying until the tears distort my vision. Falling silent, he hands off the microphone to the band and walks toward me. With each step, his form becomes clearer and more defined until he's standing right in front of me.

I can barely make out the scent of cedar through my runny nose, and I swipe at the tears on my cheeks before asking, "Do you mean it? Because I can't do this again, Connor. I can't put my faith in you to have you let me, let Elle and Emma, down again. I can't do that."

A flash of sorrow comes into his gaze. "I can't promise not to let you down because that's what love is. It's opening yourself to the possibility of letting down the people you love no matter how much you try not to. I promise to love you, to protect you, and to pick up the pieces of any hurt I cause and to make it right. I promise to not run when things get tough and to weather the storms life throws our way beside you."

Lifting my arm, I wrap it around his neck and drag his lips to mine. His heady masculine scent invades my senses, and ignoring the cheers and claps behind us, I kiss him with every ounce of love for him in my heart.

"I love you, Connor Murtry, and I accept."

A brilliant smile breaks out on his face as he wraps his arms around my waist in the gentle hug I've needed for the last two weeks.

Once he sets me on my feet, I ask, "I thought you were going to a dance at the school."

Chuckling, he runs a hand through his hair as the girls attach themselves to our legs.

"Yeah, I had a little help with that. Jackson called Arik, who called the school and got the planning committee to move the dance out here instead of at the school. One call from Hedy and the word about a repeat of the barn dance started to spread, so we kinda hijacked the school dance for this."

"Mama! Mama! Does this mean Connor's going to be our daddy?"

Elle's quiet question sobers both of us. Looking into the chocolate gaze of my forever, I match his vulnerability and ask, "What do you think? Wanna marry us and be a family?"

Unexpectedly, a tear tracks down his face at the same time his lips curl higher. He drops down so he's eye level with the girls. Wrapping an arm around my waist and the other around the girls, he drags us into him. "I'd be honored to be your daddy, Peanut. What about you, Brittle? What do you think?"

My feisty little firebrand bursts into tears, and unable to speak, just nods against Connor's shoulder. He wipes her face, and like he promised, he holds her as she cries.

We might have gone about it backward, but there isn't a single part of me that would fall in love with Connor Murtry a different way.

EPILOGUE - CONNOR

THE GLINT OF THE SUN OFF MY WEDDING BAND NEVER FAILS TO surprise me. Somedays I wake up and Ally being in bed next to me is a lightning strike of revelation. She's *mine.* I'm *hers.* A small December ceremony last year tied her to me, and now I have my own person to come home to each night.

Life is good.

The four of us are in the car on the way home from the airport. A trip to Arizona was in order for Rob and Taylor's wedding.

While we were busy here in Felt, they were falling in love in Phoenix.

The early March breeze dances through the windows, and my left hand tightens on the steering wheel catching more of the sunlight. Ah, it's good to be home.

Emma and Elle are chattering away in the back about the wedding. Both of them being included in the party is something they'll remember for the rest of their lives.

We have a lot to catch up on after two weeks away. We extended our time in Arizona to take a small family vacation so the girls could see the Grand Canyon and what Arizona has to offer. Now that we're home, I know Ally's itching to get into The Sweet Tooth. Though she'll deny it, she was nervous since this was Jem's first time flying solo as manager.

Jackson and I already planned on spending the week catching up on the paperwork at the station, but Jackson and Liv's honeymoon prepared me for what to expect there.

The girls are due back at school on Monday which gives us this weekend to get everything in order before we're back to our regularly scheduled program. They're also starting on the valley's softball league, and I plan to be at every game and practice.

Ally asks, "Can you swing by the post office? It's probably full from us being gone for so long."

"Sure."

We're both eagerly awaiting a specific document from the lawyers, so I understand her wanting to stop before we even get home.

After the wedding, I broached the topic of the girls taking my last name and me legally adopting them. Ally was on board with the change since their father didn't do anything above sending financial assistance each month. We didn't need the money, but I wanted them to be completely mine.

The process has been ongoing, and we're waiting on the last step before I can adopt the girls. I hope that we hear from the lawyers soon.

The Welcome to Felt sign comes into view minutes later, and I pull down Main Street toward the post office.

"Want us to come in with you?"

Ally smiles and says, "Nah. I should be able to get it all."

She hops out of the car and disappears inside.

The sounds of YouTube come from the back, both girls now engrossed in the toy reviews playing on their tablet.

Ally exits the post office, and with the way her purse is bulging, she was probably right in the amount of mail we got.

Please let it be here.

Once she's buckled in, I ask, "Did it come?"

Lips downturned in a frown she says, "No. Nothing yet."

I feel like a kid waiting for Christmas to come every day and when it doesn't it hurts just a little more.

I pull out of the parking spot and turn down Main. Once we're on the road that heads up to our house I say, "It's okay. We'll get it taken care of eventually." Maybe I can call the lawyer and see what the holdup is. I didn't think it would take Ally's ex this long to agree to terminate his parental rights, or to get that pushed through the court system. But here we are months later with no word, and I'm impatient to move forward.

Ally's hand lands on my thigh, and I know she's trying to give me comfort, but my dick didn't get that memo.

It twitches behind the confines of my jeans, and I will it to chill the fuck out. The best part about family vacations is the uninterrupted time we get together. The worst part is the shared hotel room.

It's been a long two weeks and another reason I'm happy to be home. Tonight, Ally's all mine, in the privacy of our room, and I'm not planning on getting much sleep.

A quick glance over at Ally and the little minx knows I'm struggling based on the smirk she shoots my way.

We pull into the driveway and unload the car. There's a sticky note on the door from Meg, Arik's mom, who graciously offered to take care of all of our houses while we were gone since the whole pack flew down to Arizona for the nuptial event.

"Well, looks like dinner is taken care of. There's a casserole in the freezer for us to reheat. That was nice of her." Ally reads the note and pockets the piece of paper.

"It was. We'll have to return the favor."

There used to be a time when I'd hide away up here, but since falling for Ally, I've been slowly coming out of my shell, stretching myself and trying to be a bigger part of the community.

One of the biggest changes was signing on to the Cowboy Courses committee early this year.

Since we're not coming in at the tail end of the event there'll be more work, but I'm okay with that.

Unloading the car doesn't take long, and I work on separating laundry to get that started while Ally unpacks the rest of the suitcases. It's been a long day of travel, and we're all pretty wiped out.

She's slowed down a lot over the last few months. Once the renovation to the bakery apartment was done, she went to work on beefing up her staff. The increase in event desserts she's commissioned from word of mouth after Jackson and Liv's and then our wedding justified the expense of more part-time staff and promoting Jem to manager.

I shut the lid on the washer and start it up before heading into the kitchen to pull out the casserole left for us.

Ally calls from the living room, "Connor, come here."

I step through the door from the kitchen, and the girls have their new softball jerseys on. They look so damn grown up.

Just yesterday they fit into the crook of my elbow, and now their heads almost brush my chest and I'm not ready for them to get any bigger.

"Wow, they look great, you guys."

Ally's grinning at me when she says, "That's not even the best part."

With that, the girls turn around, and the large numbers dominate the back, but that's not what makes my eyes sting and my nose tingle.

It's the name across their shoulder blades. *Murtry* is there in bold lettering, and my heart soars.

My girls.

And then I remember that it's not official yet.

My smile falters, and before I can recover it, Ally's reaching into the bottom of the cavernous bag she carries and pulls out a manila envelope.

Elle takes it from her, and she and Emma bring it to me.

The seam is torn, and I ask, "What's this?"

Emma rolls her eyes—sassy little thing—and says, "Read it."

The sheaf of papers inside is thick when I pull it out but the words at the top threaten to take me out at the knees.

Petition of adoption.

I drag my eyes to Ally; her outline is blurry and I blink rapidly to bring her into focus.

"Als. Is this..." I don't want to assume. Or get my hopes up.

Ally comes to stand next to the girls and grabs one of the sticky tabs on the side of the document, flipping the pages over to show me where my name is printed *right there.*

"It was so hard keeping it a secret from you. I found out that they were mailed while we were down in Arizona, and I wanted to surprise you."

I drag her into me, overwhelmed, and kiss her to the sounds of enthusiastic gagging from *our daughters.*

Ally has tears in her eyes when she pulls back, and I'm crying with her. The liquid drops of joy spill over and disappear into my beard. I don't bother wiping them away because they're falling faster than I'd be able to keep up.

Emma pulls a pen out of her back pocket and asks, "Ready to make it official, *Dad?*"

Snagging the pen from her, I can't scrawl my name fast enough.

Finally.

Ally pulls out her phone and fires off a text message, and two seconds later, the door opens and everyone is pouring into the living room cheering.

I get a few backslaps but even more hugs. The four of us get passed around our friends and family, and I should be surprised that she pulled this off without me knowing, but I'm not.

After all, our romance has always been a family affair.

THANK YOU SO MUCH FOR READING! FOR MORE OF CONNOR and Ally you can grab their extended epilogue here!

Or turn the page for a sneak peak of Meadow Ridley and Griffin Gallagher in All's Fair in Love and Leaderboards, an enemies to lovers, forced to work together to catch the bad guy, spicy and steamy first book in my Phoenician Heat series.

EXTENDED EPILOGUE

CONNOR

Peppermint and pine scent the air at Hedy's place. She's taken to hosting the holidays for our ramshackle group over the last few years.

Garland, twinkling lights, and mistletoe decorate the living room, but no matter how festive the environment is, the jovial mood is brought low by the amount of tension floating in the air.

Eight adults are standing around the Christmas tree, and there's not a smile in sight.

There is a crocheted baby blanket under the tree and no tag on it.

Why would a baby blanket be unsettling, you ask?

The last three times someone has come up pregnant in our group, Gram has announced it by making them a baby blanket.

Before they got pregnant.

She somehow knows who's next, and at this point, yarn within a fifty-mile radius of her is enough to make our collective group sweat.

Rob and Taylor are the last couple standing, and I'm

personally hoping that super soft, plush, cuddly omen of dirty diapers and sleepless nights goes to them, but then I think back to the Russian roulette that Als and I played with birth control this week and my stomach gurgles an *oh hell no.*

Ally's IUD fell out, and she didn't realize it until *after* we had unprotected sex.

Is another baby a bad thing? Not necessarily. But considering the fact that we have two almost teenagers and two toddlers about to come out of diapers, I thought that we were done.

We're two for two on multiple birth pregnancies, and I don't have the cojones to consider going three for three.

After the boys were born, I scaled back at the station and Ally hired in more help, but colic and acid reflux wrecked any semblance of rest that we could possibly get.

We're both still recovering from the sleep deprivation, and I for one am not ready to go right back into it.

The peppy yellow blanket has to go.

I nod to Jackson, my partner in crime of nearly a decade. His face is tinted green, and his eyes keep straying back to the sweet sleep destroyer.

The irony isn't lost on me. That simple item that helps babies sleep is a symbol of the deprivation the parents will feel until they're mainlining caffeine and their memory has more holes than Swiss cheese that's sat in the deli drawer too long.

Please God, let Rob and Taylor get knocked up.

Now, it may seem like I'm picking on them, but they live in Arizona. That means that if they get pregnant we'll go visit them when the cherub is born but then we get to make an escape. When Kate and Arik's son was born, we passed him around households for three months, and there wasn't a wink of sleep to be found between the six of us who live in the valley.

Jackson sidles up to me and hisses, "Watch the kitchen. If Hedy starts to come out, I need you to distract her."

He squats next to the tree, and untucking his button-down, he shoves the whole thing under his shirt.

The man has bigger balls than I do, because I'm too scared to actually touch it.

"What is going on in here?"

In unison we whip around, and Hedy is standing at the entryway to the kitchen. Glares from the friend group are all aimed my way, and I stammer out the best response I can come up with. "Um... he was just looking..."

A red eyebrow cocks over disbelieving eyes, and my shoulders get tighter in response.

"Jackson James, you put that blanket back before I hide you."

"Yes, ma'am." Jackson is the picture of contrition as he slips the square back under the tree.

Hedy turns around and disappears back into the kitchen, and the whisper yells start.

"Way to keep an eye out, fucker." That's from Jackson.

"I swear to God, if that comes to us I'm going to cry. I will actually cry," Arik says.

"You need to get a vasectomy, honey," Kate says while rubbing Arik's back.

"We have that climbing trip next month; we can't be pregnant. It'll mess up the whole belay structure," Taylor says absentmindedly.

Ally crosses the living room to me, and I wrap my arms around her. I need the comfort of a hug from her.

Whispering between us, I say, "We can handle it, don't ya think? I think we'll be okay. We should be okay. We're handling the girls and the boys pretty okay."

Ally goes to her tiptoes and hisses, "Are you kidding me?! Every day I wonder if orange would be a better color for me because I'm three seconds away from sending Emma and her sarcastic ass to live with Meemaw. The boys are like tiny tornadoes of chaos, energy, and maniacal laughter. We cannot be pregnant again." Ally points at my dick, which has pretty much pulled a disappearing act at this point. "You keep him far, far away from me. We are officially celibate until the threat passes."

My soul wants to cry at the thought of celibacy no matter how critical it is currently.

There's a booming crash from the playroom, and Ally goes to investigate, the blanket forgotten for a few minutes at least.

EXTENDED EPILOGUE

ALLY

I AM ABSOLUTELY ONE HUNDRED AND TEN PERCENT KNOCKED up. I tried to keep my cool earlier, but the wet dog, dead ferret, deviled-egg-fart smell coming out of the playroom at Hedy's house has the precursor-to-vomit saliva pooling in my mouth.

Under normal circumstances I have an iron stomach. The only time I've ever been known to not be able to hold my cookies is during the dreaded first trimester of my pregnancies.

With the girls I couldn't eat anything sweet. I could, however, eat anything pickled in vinegar by the jar. With the boys it was the opposite. I couldn't look at something sour, but I almost ate myself out of stock at the bakery more days than I didn't.

Oh God. What are we going to do?

The boys are just old enough to start preschool, the girls are in their own world of ignoring us as much as they can, and I am not prepared to start all over again.

We were in the home stretch and then a tiny piece of hormone-filled plastic flew the coop that is my vagina, and here we are. Me trying not to vomit while I see which of our kids got into something that rolled around in something that died.

I push the door open, and there's three seconds where my eyes do not compute what I see and time stands still.

Like a rubber band snapping back into place, time resumes, and I vault into the room dragging one boy up by his arm and catching Liv and Jackson's little girl by the back of her shirt while she tries to make a break for it with the rotting varmint in hand.

"What in the world.... Where did you get that?"

Abigail's pixie voice says, "Cletus brought him in. We didn't do nothing."

The evidence of all the *nothing* they did is covering both of them and the room.

I yell, "Jackson!" while keeping a tight leash on our troublemakers.

About ten seconds pass before Jackson enters the room with his shirt over his nose. "What the heck is that smell?"

My hands full with the kids, I gesture vaguely with my pointer finger toward the mangled, black, *wet,* piece of fur sitting on the ground near the Playskool toy yard.

"You take them and hose 'em down; I'm going to get that and get rid of it."

I pass off the kids, and he disappears with them down the hall. Knowing that the hall closet will have the cleaning supplies I need, I head that direction.

The door is within sight when the first burping gag escapes the stranglehold I have on my stomach.

Ripping the door open, it nearly takes off my toes before I can wrest the roll of trash bags and rubber gloves from the shelf.

I swallow thickly, forcing the small lunch of a muffin and coffee back down. I will *not* be sick at Gram's place. That just gives them more ammunition to work with in addition to that blanket.

My composure is hanging by a thread by the time I have the creature bagged. Carrying it through the kitchen and then into the backyard, I make it to less than ten feet away from the trash can when I lose the fight and start to gag again. With my only other choice to throw up in the rose bushes, I rip open the trash bag and stick my face as close as I dare.

My stomach turns hard, and I vomit everything including what I ate for lunch in seventh grade into the bag. Focused on hitting my target, I don't realize I'm not alone until it's too late.

"It's you!" Taylor's voice can barely be made out over the sound of my retching and the plastic bag shaking.

I spit a couple of times until most of the grossness is out of my throat and mouth and close the bag again. Taylor's standing off to the side, and the whites of her eyes are visible with desperation at the prospect of being pregnant.

Normally she'd be babying me into the kitchen, plying me with saltines and ginger ale, but right now? We're all on high alert.

"It's not me. The kids dragged in a dead creature, and I was getting rid of it when the smell got to me. Here, smell this." Like a twelve-year-old boy, I hold out the bag.

"Ew, no. I'm not smelling that. It's totally you. It *has* to be you."

No matter that I agree with her, I'm not going down without a fight.

"It's not me. You'll see."

Taylor gapes after me, and I leave her there.

Shortly after the kids are clean. and the dead-animal smell floating around the house is gone, we gather in the living room.

The kids rip into their presents like a Category five hurricane, all the parents snapping pictures.

The adults are a little more laid-back in our opening extravaganza, but we quickly get down to the single present under the tree. The present no one wants to acknowledge.

Hedy gets up, and after gently grabbing the bomb of fabric stands in front of us. The kids are quiet, not because they understand what's about to happen, but because their parents have terror written all over their faces. Seeing eight adults collectively horrified has them stumped.

Connor grabs my hand, and I look over into those chocolate eyes that I love so much.

I don't know exactly when I lost my IUD, but considering the level of friskiness that we ascribe to, it's a safe bet that we're going to have a new blanket in the linen closet tonight.

A smile tries to break through, but Connor's eyes widen in further horror as Gram approaches us.

The soft afghan drops to his lap, and he looks down at it before his eyes find mine again.

Voice scratchy, he says, "Okay. It's gonna be okay. We've got this. We can absolutely handle this."

Yeah. I don't believe him either.

But there isn't another person on this earth that I'd rather go through these adventures with even as I lean over and lose Christmas breakfast on his lap.

THANK YOU SO MUCH FOR READING!

Turn the page for a sneak peak of Meadow Ridley and Griffin Gallagher in All's Fair in Love and Leaderboards, an enemies to lovers, forced to work together to catch the bad guy, spicy and steamy first book in my Phoenician Heat series.

SNEAK PEAK OF ALL'S FAIR IN LOVE AND LEADERBOADS

THERE ARE THREE THINGS IN THE WORLD I CAN'T STAND. THE obscene cost of nut butter, EagleEyeBeastPI, and Griffin Gallagher.

Now those might seem like weird things to hate. But I promise they all make sense.

Let's talk about nut butter. The deliciously smooth and never ever crunchy—because that's a travesty—peanut butter is pennies on the dollar in comparison to the cost of the specialty nut butters my palate prefers. Almond, cashew, hazelnut…the list of deliciousness goes on and on.

I can pick up a tub o' peanut butter for under ten bucks at my local chain grocery store, but try that with Nutella or pistachio butter? Not possible. Even walnut butter is massively more expensive than plain-Jane, stick it between two pieces of bread and go about your day peanut butter.

One might call me a snobby nut butter consumer, but I've been known to get down with a solid peanut spread when I have to. It all depends on the day of the week and how I'm feeling. Let's face it. Some butters are just made better than others. My pantry holds more than enough options on the worst of days to keep my addiction to high protein, high fat, high calorie options alive and thriving.

Finding the jar of my go-to almond butter depleted is enough to blip my heart rate—but this morning the scrape of my butter knife along the plastic container of deliciousness causes irritation to slice along my shoulders. Which means a trip to the warehouse style bulk grocery store is in my future —because it's the only place I can get the best almond butter in existence. I'm an amazing neighbor, so I'll check with the other people on my floor of the apartment complex to see what they need.

I already have the membership card, so they might as well benefit from it, right?

I snag a pad of paper and head down the hallway, starting at the farthest apartment from my own. Owen Garcia answers his door. Shouts of laughter echo behind him from his kids and husband, Miguel. They've lived in the building for about three years, the longest out of everyone, and their daughters are the cutest kids I've ever seen in my life.

"Hey, Meadow, how's it going?"

I hold up my notepad. "You guys need anything?" Owen's an editor for the valley newspaper, and Miguel is a public defense attorney, so they usually have a list for me since they're both busy and I'm happy to help.

"Oh my God, yes. Thank you. One second. Let me get you our list."

When I first started offering to grab them anything they needed while I was out, they didn't want to take advantage of me. But after Maddy, their six-year-old, came down with a stomach bug when Miguel was in court, a panicked Owen asked me to run to the store for them. Now? They have a standing invite to the block parties my parents throw.

"How was the ride this morning?" Owen asks as he hands me the list.

I scoff. "Second place—again."

"You'll catch him eventually." There's a crashing sound in the background, and Owen spins to find the damage, his door shutting behind him.

Tanking my ride this morning brings us to the number two thing I can't stand. It used to be I could strap on my riding shoes and clip in to my favorite heavy metal, EDM, or groove rides and sweat myself into my happy place for the day.

Now, I wake up and sign in to my favorite classes and trail behind EagleEyeBeastPI. Every. Single. Day. When I first got the follow request I approved it because I'm always down to make a new friend, and one that's in the same line of business as I am was welcome.

What I wasn't ready for was him skunking me every morning and leaving me in the dust on the leaderboards. I'm used to being the top dog on those leaderboards. But no longer. Now I have him to contend with.

I tuck their list in my pocket and knock on Mr. Hadid's door, though he almost never answers. He's lived here for about a year, but I haven't been able to make a lot of progress with him.

Mrs. Nelson is my last stop, and I inch my way to her door like a ninja on a stealth mission.

Which brings us to hate number three. I hate that I can't ask my eighty-year-old neighbor, Mrs. Nelson, diagonally across the hall if she needs a jumbo pack of toilet paper or incontinence underwear without *him* hearing.

Griffin Samson Gallagher. The bane of my existence.

He moved in six months ago, and it's been hell ever since.

As a private investigator, I see some of the worst people humanity has to offer, and yet Gallagher still managed to hit my "irks me beyond imagination" list. And he ends up on the "can't kill him because I look terrible in orange" list at least weekly.

Last month I was prepping for the store run, and there he was, leaning against the wall, hipshot, arrogant, and the ultimate pain in my ass. I passed him with the intention of ignoring him when he requested I pick up a jumbo pack of magnum-size condoms.

Did I buy them? You bet. I didn't even charge him. If his mission in life is to annoy me with his very existence, then mine is to ensure he doesn't reproduce himself. Really—it's my duty to humanity. Some people volunteer at charities; some build houses in countries that lack running water or food. I make sure my neighbor has more than enough birth control to survive a nuclear war.

As of right now, I'm out of almond butter, tanked my ride, and am actively avoiding the bane of my existence.

My hand is poised to knock when the door at my back opens, and I kiss any hope of this day being okayish goodbye.

"Well, lookee what we have here. If it isn't Flower Power herself."

Goddammit.

Twisting, I take in the most evil being in creation. Trademark smirk in place, there he is, leaning in his damn doorway, and I clinically absorb his appearance. Gallagher's not handsome in a traditional sense. It's almost as if his features formed in a "this is what you get" way and his genetics said "challenge accepted" on making them work. The hawkish nose, the most stubborn jaw line, and a mouth so lush it's in direct contradiction to his arresting features shouldn't work, but they do.

Another thing, he's not tall. I'm five six, but if I wore heels, I'd likely match him in height. Whipcord lean, he looks skinny, but he's not. That's a red herring for fools who underestimate him—like I did.

The first time I came across my neighbor wasn't in the apartment building. Oh no. It was at the end of a twenty-minute skip chase where Gallagher jumped out from around a corner and clotheslined the perp. Then he had the audacity to challenge me for the contract completion. I ended up claiming the bounty, but ultimately he got the last laugh when I came home from work to find him moving in next door to me. In the six short months since he's moved in, we've gone head-to-head on a number of jobs, so I see more than my fair share of his face. The case leaderboard my sisters and I use to track our case completion and compete in a fun family manner in the office is a visual list of my losses right along with my losing streak on the bike every morning. It's starting to sting. I used to run both boards and now I can barely keep up on either.

"What do you want, Gallagher?"

"You shopping again?"

Is it possible to roll my eyes so hard I give myself a concussion? Asking for myself.

"Yes," I say. I'm so going to regret this. I know that I'm going to. "Did you need anything?"

A sinister twinkle brightens his cognac-colored eyes, and today is going to be the worst Thursday in existence.

"Now that you mention it, I could use some more condoms, but also some lube."

"Lube?" I sputter. Also, how in the hell was he able to go through a mega pack of prophylactics in less than a month?

You know what? Never mind. I don't want to know.

"Yeah. The one with the industrial-sized bottle and pump lever. I'd go myself, but I have an appointment with a beautiful woman this morning."

Oh. My. God. He cannot be for real. Ew.

Wait a second. I smirk. "I didn't know that you had that much trouble arousing your partners, Gallagher."

"Oh, it's not for me, Flower Power."

I ignore the juvenile nickname he thinks is hilarious or cute. As if I haven't heard it all before. "Then who's it for?"

"You, of course."

"What do you mean, it's for me?" I haven't dated in who knows how long, and that's not something that I have the time or the willingness to change in the near future. And I buy my own lubrication, thank you very much.

He opens the door at his back and fires his parting shot. "I figure it'd be easier to remove the perpetual stick shoved up your ass if you had a little gliding help. See ya later, Flower Power." He shoots me a smug grin and jaunty salute. Before I can flay the skin from his bones with a scathing retort, he turns back into his apartment and closes the door.

Motherfucker.

I hate Griffin Gallagher.

PHOENICIAN INVESTIGATIONS HAS BEEN HOUSED IN THE SAME small house-turned-office in downtown Phoenix since my mom announced she was pregnant with triplets and my dad realized more than just their one-bedroom apartment was about to change.

My sisters and I basically grew up here. As kids, we cleaned, filed, and probably made more work for our dad than we cleared, but we eventually moved to our own cases and have leaned into our individual strengths.

The slate-blue front door slams behind me as I snarl and stomp my way back to the converted kitchen we use as a breakroom.

I yell, "I'm going to go to jail for murder. Don't post my bail because I will be guilty."

"I'll grab my shovel," Willow calls.

"I've got the hydrofluoric acid," Fawn says.

I slide the coffees I picked up on the way onto the counter with more force than is necessary and drop into the chair next to Willow.

Fawn and Willow share a speaking glance. Fawn asks, "Gallagher or EagleEye morning?"

I jerk my shoulders and try to shake my head at the same time, trying to fidget my way out of murder plans. Fawn cocks an eyebrow, her eyes laughing at me.

Willow also finds my aggravation funny and smirks at me. "Do you ever think that they're the same person?"

"No, because I haven't pissed off the karma gods that much in any of my lifetimes."

They both laugh at the surly tone.

My sisters suck.

"So which was it?" Willow asks.

"This morning? Both of them. But rounded out with the trifecta of being out of almond butter."

I nod and grab the coffee cup marked with an *M* and take a sip. The sweet taste of coffee hits my tastebuds, and it's not a Nutella and banana sandwich, but it goes a long way in cooling my ire with this morning.

"Why don't you block him?" Willow asks.

I rear back. "And let him think he won? No."

"Meadow. You don't actually know this guy. Who the hell cares if he thinks he won? The sooner you oust him from your morning, the better off you'll be. Mark my words."

"What'd Griff do?" Fawn asks with a familiarity I don't appreciate.

"Griff? Since when are we using his first name *and* shortening it?" I squawk.

"Come on. It's kinda funny. He's an ass because he knows it bothers you. If we were in elementary school, I'd say he liked you. Maybe this is his adult way of pulling your pigtails."

Ew. No.

"Willow. He doesn't like me. We can barely live in the same building without toppling it. Don't get me started on the stupid shit he asked me to pick him up from Costco this morning."

Both of them grab their coffees and settle in, eagerly awaiting the next episode in the saga of weird shit Gallagher makes me buy.

Willow asks, "Was it another bearskin rug?"

"Or a smart toilet?" Fawn jumps in.

"More condoms, despite buying him a hundred-pack last month, and then he asked for the jumbo bottle of lube apparently sold there."

I didn't know lube came in that size, or that it was available to purchase anywhere outside of shady Internet sites where your whole identity is confidential.

"He did not. Costco sells that?"

I'm nodding before Fawn finishes her question. If I had to be traumatized by my neurotic neighbor, I'm sharing that experience with the both of them.

"They sure do, and based on the reviews, it puts all the other lubes to shame in the back-door-assistance department."

Willow's smirk morphs into a grimace of disgust and she stands, grabbing her coffee before saying, "Well, I'm off to meet with a client. Dinner at Fawn's tonight?"

Fawn nods and says, "Yep! We're having lasagna."

"Damn it, Fawn. I didn't sweat through a sixty-minute climb ride this morning to eat both pasta and cheese this evening."

"Sorry, not sorry! See you at six. Loves." She grabs her coffee and heads upstairs to her office.

"Loves," I respond.

Dad sticks his head around the corner of the kitchen and asks, "Who are we killing this morning, Sweet Pea?"

I'm surprised to see him this early. He's been toying with the idea of retiring—again—and usually comes in later. He's been mentioning retirement every six months or so for a couple of years now, but nothing ever comes from it. Especially considering we all get our competitive spirit from him. He's just lying in wait to take the top spot on the firm's case board. But we keep him on his toes.

Fawn, Willie, and I have a pool going on his actual retirement. Whoever gets within a month of the date of his last case gets all the moola. Routinely, we add ten dollars here and there, and it's up to a nice chunk of change after the number of times he's claimed he's going to start "scaling back."

"Nobody, Dad. Just bitching. What are you doing here so early?"

"Uh. Wanted to talk to you about something."

"Sure, what's up?"

Dad opens his mouth to say something and my phone buzzes in my pocket. My best friend's name flashes across the screen.

I hold up my finger to Dad and say, "One second."

I swipe to accept the call. "Hey, Jenn."

"Meadow." My scalp prickles and gooseflesh runs down my arms because she sounds terrified.

Please don't let this be what I think it is. Please.

"What happened?"

"I just got a breather call. A bench warrant was issued for him this morning."

Fuck. Fuck. Fuck.

I take a deep breath. Nothing good comes from an investigator losing her shit and panicking. Sweat beads on my hairline, and my heart thumps painfully against my sternum.

"Lock your doors. I'm on my way. I'll be there in ten minutes. Do not open the door for anyone, and I mean anyone."

I hang up the phone and Dad says, "Bobby called. One of your perps skipped bail. Martin—"

"Martin Hernandez. Jenn's ex," I interrupt.

"Shit."

I grab my car keys off the table and shove my phone in my pocket. "Yep. The idiot had court this morning and didn't show. Why did they let him out on bail in the first place?"

"I don't know, Sweet Pea. You want me to call Bobby and say you're taking the trace?"

I head toward the front door, Dad keeping pace with me. "I don't know, probably. But he'll run fast and far if he sees me."

"That's why we chase him down."

"Jennifer's safety comes first here. I think he called her this morning. I'll be back later and we can figure it out, but I have to go get her now."

I let the door slam behind me and run for my car.

Jennifer's house is in Glendale, a suburb west of Phoenix. After breaking a few land-speed records, I pull into the driveway and park. There's an older model Ford parked along the street, but otherwise no other cars. Dense black security screens cover her windows, and if you look closely enough, you can make out the security lights on the front corners of the roof with the cameras attached to them.

I know all about her security system. I helped her install it after all.

The flagstone path mostly muffles my footsteps as I walk up. Just as I cross into the shadowed cover of the porch, the door opens.

I pull Jenn in for a hug. Hard. We dealt with Martin being granted bail, knowing that he would eventually have to pay for his assault. Her security system wasn't the first part of us planning for him getting out of jail. Since he was arrested, she's moved from Phoenix to Glendale and not shared her new address with many people.

I'm grateful she's in a new place that he knows nothing about.

"Hey. It's okay. We'll figure it out. Let's go inside," I say, while rubbing her back.

We break apart and head inside. I kick off my shoes and set them in the little tray she has beside the door.

"I'm making some tea. You want?"

"Sure." I follow her into the kitchen.

Her movements are jerky as she fills the kettle. I hate feeling like this. My shoulders twitch with the need to get out there and look for him. To investigate and track this bastard down.

The slight tremor in Jenn's hand as she scoops out loose tea leaves is enough to get me moving. I step around the island and bump her hip with mine. "Here, let me. Tell me about the call."

The fear in her blue eyes pisses me off and weighs my shoulders down with guilt.

If I had seen the signs sooner, maybe we wouldn't be here.

No. I can't think like that. I'm better off focusing on what I can do.

There's nothing in the world that I wouldn't do for my family. And Jenn is definitely family at this point.

She sucks in a lungful of air and starts. "I was just getting logged into work for the day. I'd planned to work from home for the first part of the day since I have therapy this morning. My phone rang and it was an unknown number, but I answered it anyway. No one said anything, but then heavy breathing came through the line. I think I said something sarcastic like 'real mature, asshole' and I was about to hang up when there was a muffled pop in the background. It wasn't loud, but it startled me, so I hung up.

"Okay, what happened after you hung up?"

"The more that I sat there thinking about it, the more my gut started pinging. So I looked and saw the bench warrant was issued, then I called you."

After another breath I say, "We don't know a lot at this point, but Bobby called Dad—"

"Are you going to trace him?"

"Yes, even though if he saw me looking for him, he'd run far in the other direction. I still have to talk to Dad about the logistics, but"—I make eye contact and hold it—"you're going to be covered every single step of the way. You got me?"

Jenn's chin wobbles and a single tear escapes and runs down her cheek. "I got you."

Fucking abusers.

She's my best friend. The next thing to family and I couldn't protect her from one asshole.

"I think that you should come stay with me or my parents for a little bit. If that was Martin who called, then he managed to get his hands on your new number, and it's a safe bet that he might know where you live now. Let's operate with caution in regard to your personal information. Plus, there's safety in numbers. If you're not at Dad's, then you're at the office with us. If you can't get into the office, you can still work remotely, right?"

A small curl to her lips accompanies her reply. "I don't know—what do you think Andrew will say?"

I smile at that. Jenn had been a fraud analyst for a large bank, but after everything with Martin, Dad offered her a job at Phoenician as our office manager.

"I think there's not really a safer place for you than work right now and Dad would agree."

And there's not. Between Fawn, Willow, Dad, and me, there's almost always someone in the office. The security system is top of the line, something that Fawn—the overprotective one of us—designed.

I have a spare room and a pullout sofa. It's not much, but we can make it work if she decides to stay with me at night instead of my parents.

This might seem over the top. An abusive boyfriend getting out of jail is one thing, but after failing my friend the last time, I won't let her down again.

"Okay, I'll stay with you."

I bump my shoulder next to hers and say, "It'll be like college all over again."

Jenn smiles lightly. "Hopefully much cleaner this time."

I smile and pull my phone out to send a family group message.

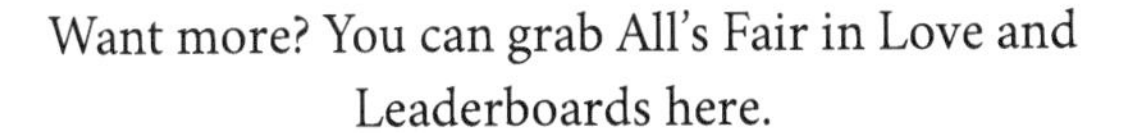

I silence my phone and tuck it in my pocket. I can answer their questions later, but for right now I'm going to shove the worry down and help my friend pack.

~

Want more? You can grab All's Fair in Love and Leaderboards here.

WANT ALL THE NEWS?

Sign up for my newsletter to stay up to date on the latest book news, receive exclusive content and be entered for giveaways.

Not a fan of newsletters?

Join my reader group! The Happily Ever After Addicts on Facebook has all the teasers, excerpts, random pickup lines my husband hits me with and bookish news you'll need from me!

ALSO BY ALINA LANE

The HeartFelt Series

Reclaimed Love

Love Reimagined

Uncovered Love

Phoenician Heat

All's Fair in Love and Leaderboards

Bridegroom and the Boardroom

ACKNOWLEDGMENTS

Dear Reader - Thank YOU for reading. I hope you enjoyed Felt, Idaho as much as I enjoyed writing it.

Nick - Thanks for tolerating my level of crazy and loving me everyday.

Sax, Jenn, Mel, Kan - You ladies are the literal best and your support means the world to me.

B & C - Do I really need to gush about all the ways that I love you? Thank you for being my bb's, thank you for being in my corner. I couldn't do this without you.

Jess, Dayna and the Ann's - Thank you for your keen eyes. Thank you for helping me polish and shine this story into the best version of itself.

Kate - You gave my book baby another perfect cover and I can't thank you enough.

Readers Writing Romance and The HEA Club - Thank you for being the best places on the internet for romance authors to hang out. Y'all rock!

If I forgot anyone — Thank you for everything! I'm gratefully absentminded.

ABOUT THE AUTHOR

A pocket-sized powerhouse, Alina lives with her personal Hunky Hero and two children in Arizona. Slathering on sunscreen and living life to its fullest she enjoys hiking, camping, fishing and rock climbing in her desert backyard.

When not hard at work on your next literary escape, you can find Alina embracing her bad-assery on Call of Duty, binge reading or shopping for nail dip sets to compliment her book covers.

Sign up for her newsletter to stay up to date on the latest Alina news.

You can follow Alina on:

Website: AlinaLane.com

Facebook: AlinaLaneAuthor

Instagram: AlinaLaneAuthor

Readers Group: Happily Ever After Addicts

Made in the USA
Middletown, DE
01 October 2023